House of
the Judas Goat

Douglas Kruger

CLARET PRESS

Copyright ©Douglas Kruger, 2025
The moral right of the author has been asserted.

Cover and Interior Design by Petya Tsankova

ISBN paperback: 978-1-910461-84-6
ISBN ebook: 978-1-910461-85-3

All rights reserved. No part of this publication may be reproduced, stored in or introduced into a retrieval system, transmitted, in any form, or by any means (electronic, mechanical, photocopying, recording or otherwise) without the prior written consent of the publisher. Any person who does any unauthorised act in relation to this publication may be liable to criminal prosecution and civil claims for damages.

A CIP catalogue record for this book is available from the British Library.

www.claretpress.com

The Polish girl was a high-value item. They would risk no damage during transit. That was why she woke up in a dog cage.

The last she thing remembered she had been in the house. The great house, way up on the hill. Now, she was moving. An engine rumbled beneath her, and now and then, centrifugal force from a sharp turn pushed her aching head against one side of the cage or the other.

She pulled the curtain of her own platinum-blonde hair out of her face and tried to look around.

The van was windowless, dark. The only weak light seeped in around the joints of what had to be the back doors.

Stupidly, she called out to her friends. She called out to the South African girl, who she liked and trusted. But no one answered. She was alone in here. The van shuddered over a bump.

How had this happened?

For one valuable second, her adrenaline had spiked at the discovery of her incarceration, but whatever she'd been dosed with was stronger than anything her adrenal glands could overpower, and her eyes closed again. Her head sagged.

Stay awake!

She forced herself to look. And she tried to remember. *What was the last thing, the last thing that happened before this?*

It hurt to think.

The boy. He had called her. Called her away from the others, to speak with him.

And then?

Some sort of struggling. Something had been done to her. Had he attacked her? *No. It wasn't him.*

The memory was so short, so fragmented. He'd called her down there, started to talk – *so charming* – then someone had done something that overwhelmed her, very, very swiftly, and then the memory went dark. But it wasn't the boy.

On the other hand, had he tried to help?

No.

In another twenty minutes, she was transferred from the van to a deserted airport hangar. She screamed. She shook at her cage, but no one answered. Then she was carried from the hangar to a cargo hold, screaming all the way. The plane took off, and in twenty-one hours she was in North Africa, in a country she could not identify, among people who could not speak her language, or would not if they could.

Still in her cage, she was delivered directly to the smiling buyer. The first thing he did was stroke her platinum hair between his fat fingers.

Waist-length platinum-blonde hair, unblemished skin. They had risked no damage, and no damage had occurred during transit.

BAIT

The difference was a single keystroke. The legitimate exchange program could be found at www.exchangeprogram.com, and thousands of school-aged children visited it each year without incident.

The lure was a misspelling. It included an additional 'e' on the word 'programe.' Both the English spelling and the American looked close enough for it to be dismissed as a simple typo. Or ignored. It raised no eyebrows. It never flagged up red. Parents dismissed it. Kids never clocked it in the first place.

It was that simple. That was how they caught them.

Their intended target was sixteen to seventeen year olds, with special preference for those who looked younger than their ages, a package that fetched handsome returns in the great houses of Saudi, the elite clubs of Russia, the fleshpots of Asia – and everywhere in between. They were also the easiest to get. Parents were less hesitant to send teens on a trip abroad. Or perhaps they were just happy to have a break from them.

The simple ruse paid off. In the short time it was live, they received ninety-three unique applications.

Of those, some lost interest. Some had the interest, but not the money. Others never got around to following through. And finally, there was a vetting process to weed out the most overt physical flaws. The attrition ultimately left thirty-two teenagers of disparate origins, all of whom were old enough to be on the cusp of independence, yet by a twist of genetics for which the organisers filtered, didn't look it. They packed their bags, bade farewell to their friends, and kissed their parents as they departed their countries, visas in hand and hope in their eyes, trusting implicitly in the organisation with the extra 'e'.

Getting the kids to America was only the first part of the ruse.

THE SUN GOES ROUND THE EARTH

He'd nearly frozen last night. But they hadn't caught him. And now he had the gun.

His head throbbed as he raised himself from the newspapers in the sharp morning light. It wasn't just the drink or the aftermath of the dagga. It was the gunshots. A noise like mosquitoes still rang in both ears. And every limb ached.

The sunlight of a spring morning in Johannesburg warmed the old army coat he wore. There was the sour-sweat stench on it, as usual. But now also the copper of new blood stains. Not his, the girl's. Some on his chest, some spattered over the brown epaulets. That was a pity. He'd have to scrub it. The coat from the South African Military surplus store had cost a week's wages.

He rubbed at his face and looked about. The plan had seemed perfect. These things always worked better when you had a traitor on the inside; the girl. For three months, she'd been working behind the counter at the jewellery store, and now they trusted her. She told them when the mall guards changed shift, she told them which items cost the most, she told them where the keys were kept. It was all perfect – *perfect* – like the ancestors were giving them a gift.

Pity about her. He'd thought they'd maybe hand her around after the heist, but now she was dead and he was wearing her blood. They were all dead. He was pretty sure of that. Now it was just him and the ancestors, if they were still watching. And the gun.

She'd been first to die in the big shoot-out with the police, who got there faster than anyone thought, and she danced backward like a fish when the shots caught her.

How had they been so fast? He wondered whether the police too had a traitor on the inside, but only for a moment. A swig from his bottle of Three Ships pushed the question down in a swirl of throat fire. There were other girls, other gangs, other opportunities. And now he had something he'd never had before.

Barely breathing, he checked beneath the newspaper. It was still there. No one had stolen it in the night.

A quick scan around the loading area behind the stores, squinting against that offensive Johannesburg sunlight. There were men about, here and there. A few day workers in overalls. They loaded and unloaded from trucks in no great hurry. But no one nearby. No one paying any mind to the likes of him; just another homeless drunk emerging into the highveld morning from his cocoon of yesterday's news.

He inspected the gleaming piece, turned it around in his fingerless wool gloves, careful to keep it beneath the rustling paper. Beautiful. Perfect black. Smooth, like an expensive thing. Wonderfully cold.

People who knew these kinds of things could say what kind of gun it was. He knew just one thing: *he* now made the rules.

They'd given it to him yesterday, told him it came from a housebreaking. Then they'd smoked dagga together for courage, piled into the bakkie, and made for the mall. That was before the whole thing went to hell – for the others. He was still here. And one gun richer. Maybe the ancestors were smiling after all.

These things were a crap shoot anyway. Half the time, men got away with it. Other times, half got shot. So even then, your chance of living was half. Good odds.

The distant truck doors slammed shut with a clatter of iron, and one of the workers banged the side panel. The truck went into reverse, beeping.

What a fight it had been. They'd had the take in their hands, fistfuls of watches, jewellery, leather, even the money from the till, which their girl had opened for them, pretending to be surprised.

Then the loudest explosions he'd ever heard. Even through the wool of the full-mask balaclava, so loud it made your thinking stop. Glass shattering, men falling, shooting both ways, loud, loud, loud. The girl wobbled backward, dropping to the tiles with two holes in her head, and she still looked surprised down on the floor beside him.

Had to have been a traitor. No way they could have gotten there so fast otherwise. Maybe she was it, getting paid by both sides. Or maybe it was love. She had a gangsta boyfriend and whispered it to him one night late to make him love her more. Didn't matter. She was dead now.

They'd fought their way out, shooting all the time, down big corridors, past shoppers and trolleys, running the length of an escalator, and pushing people out of the way. Others pulling their families clear before them, while the guards and the police followed them without letting up. They shot backward as the police shot forward, and people screamed and died everywhere, and it was loud, loud, loud.

But he was smart. Smarter than the rest. He fingered the gun as he remembered how clever he'd been.

The men kept fighting when they got to the great glass exit doors, making it clear who they were, shooting back at the police like that was the only thing to do. They even hit two or three, who crumpled to the tiles in their uniforms. But there was no way they were going to win.

He knew that much. So he stopped fighting. Right there at the door.

He went sideways along the outer wall, away from the few remaining men of his gang, and then he vaulted a wall. Through the back alleys where the trash was kept, where the heat from the air conditioners emptied hot garlicy smells into small alleys, pulling off his balaclava as he scraped past bins and pipes, and stumbled over trash.

When he came out the other side, he stopped running. Just stopped. It was quiet on that side. Peaceful.

Far away, sirens were coming. More police.

The whole world would be looking for a tsotsi. No one was looking for a man who wasn't running, a regular gent, not a gangsta. So that was who he became. He didn't even leave. Just put the gun in his jacket, gathered some newspaper from the garbage, and lay himself down on the stone paving beside the gravel of the loading area. He covered himself with newspapers like he was sleeping, then let the hours go by. He spent the night on the stone, like any vagrant.

All night he'd dreamed of the next thing, now within his grasp. A car. A beautiful car.

And the dead girl. Her face kept coming into his dreams. But also, a beautiful car. With a gun, you could have any car you wanted.

But he was clever. The ancestors had made him clever – or God – and that was why he was still alive. *So be clever again. Keep it simple.*

Don't go for the expensive one, the BMW, the Mercedes, the car with the rich man in it or the woman wearing expensive clothes. Those people can make thunder rain down on you. They can chase you and crush you from all sides. They have so many things: money, power, security, police, judges. Even if you kill them, the family keeps coming.

No. Find someone small. The smart wolf goes for the undefended lamb.

He took another swig of the fiery Three Ships. Stretched his lips while the whiskey burned his throat. Enjoyed the warming sunlight.

Around the corner, a small red Hyundai rolled slowly into view, pulling carefully into the loading area, almost like it was looking for something. It stopped. Right there in the middle, not even in a parking spot, and not near any of the loading bays.

The driver got out. Young woman, white and thin. That yellow hair they had.

The passenger door opened a moment later. An even younger woman got out that side – yellow hair too – switched places with the other. The older one was smiling and talking, but the younger one looked nervous as she took over the driver's seat. She looked young for it, but it was clear what this was.

Driving lesson.

He fingered the gun. Then he scanned the parking lot. Lot of distance between them and the nearest men. Long way for anyone to come running, if they tried to help.

And if they did, so what? He had something he'd never had before. A gift from the ancestors. Or from God.

It didn't matter.

He was God now.

⚔

"Get your tits in order. Stall this thing one more time, lunch is on you."

The younger girl smeared her face with both hands.

"This is too hard."

"Twaddle. You wanna be able to drive by the time you get to the States?"

"No?"

"Yes, you do! Come on, brain in gear. Car too. Put us back in first."

Kendall Mayor took a deep breath and blew it out, then ran through the mental dance one more time, speaking her thought process out loud. "Mirror, mirror, blind spot." What her older sister kept referring to as 'mechanical sympathy' was proving illusory. "You do it by feel, and that means there's no other way but practice."

The little Hyundai waited on her next attempt.

"Focus. Clutch in. Get us started again. Build the revs higher this time. You're too shy on the power."

Kendall thumbed away a bead of hairline sweat. She performed one final mirror check, ran her tongue nervously over her braces, then turned the ignition key. The clatter from the tiny engine sent a pigeon fluttering. The only other movement was three men in sweat-stained overalls, unloading boxes from a truck in the distant loading dock, stopping to pass a Coke bottle around and fanning themselves. Heat rose in quavering lines from the white tarmac behind the mall.

Kendall stared hard at the needle. She traced its arc as it rose past three thousand rpm, then four. The old hatchback shuddered and whined as it crested five thousand.

"That's more than enough. And nice concentration-face. You look like a constipated pug. You know there was an armed robbery here yesterday?"

"Seriously?"

"Keep the revs! Yip. Jewellery store. Big shoot-out. Okay, hold that, okay? Now start to think about your other leg."

Kendall bit her lip, transferred the full focus of her mind from the needle to the action of her left foot.

"Gently now, it's all in the clutch. Ease it out, but don't dump it. Feel the engine start to bite. What you wanna do is–"

The sudden rapping on the glass sounded male. Both young women started, neither having seen him approach. Kendall froze in the driver's seat, her gaze became fixed before her, as if denying the gun in her peripheral vision might make it go away.

"Kendall. Baby. Stay calm." Her older sister's voice was almost inaudible over the still revving engine. "Switch off, no sudden movements, do what he says."

More rapping, a second time, much harder. Right beside her face. It made her jaw clench tight.

No carjacking ever came at a good time. But this was only Kendall's second driving lesson.

Still, the tarmac was wide open ahead of her. The revs were holding steady. Her fingers tensed on the wheel. All she had to do ...

"No, don't!"

A final bashing on the window, this time hard enough to smash the glass. Beside her, Addie's sharp intake of breath sounded like terror made audible. People died this way every day.

For a split second, Kendall saw the flash of an image: two girls, dead and slumped together, bleeding into the cheap fabric of an old hatchback.

This would either work or it wouldn't.

She stomped the accelerator flat.

*

THE VALUE OF A THING

"Plenty of bites already. Should be a good harvest. We'll let it run to a thousand. Then we stop taking applications."

"Fine." The Organizer hated it when facilitators used words like 'harvest'. *"Tell me when you're there. But keep the site up. And give me a two-to-one ratio. Two females to every male. As broad a split of nationalities as possible. Something for everyone. Winnow it down, then we'll talk timelines."*

"Done."

"Use this line. This line only."

"Good."

The Organizer ended the call, then turned and looked at the client list. It was tacked to the wall in a mosaic. No names anywhere. No photos. No identification of any kind appeared on any of the notes. The secrecy served buyer and seller alike.

Each little sheet bore a neat digital contact key. Just a string of numbers, printed on plain white paper. But each string of numbers represented an entire channel for movement of the product. These were clients who valued discretion above all things. For all its simplicity, the Organizer saw an entire landscape. A wealth of hungry shoppers in a network that wrapped itself around the globe. The powerful. The mighty. The rich-be-yond-imagining. Untouchables in every land.

The Organizer ran a finger over the strings of code, one by one, caressing them in their faraway dens. Those tiny strings of numbers were worth hundreds of millions in the aggregate. If properly enticed.

The Organizer had something special for them this year. So simple, but so clever.

Kids in cages was a stupid marketing move. Every high-end brand knew you had to display the stock in its most flattering setting. Better framing increased the market value. *What's enticing about a kid cowering in a cage, shitting itself?*

No, that was for amateurs in the trade. The proceeds were chump change, a couple mil at best, even for multiple items.

For the real paydays, you needed the stock brimming with life. Vital. Juicy.

You needed them *playing*. You needed them *laughing*. Get them to flirt with one another, cry, form trusting friendships. You needed them to be tantalisingly naive, seductive in their innocent freedom. That was how you elevated detritus to Prada.

After all, what was the value of a child? It was completely subjective. As a lump of meat, not much. But as a specific person, who you've studied with interest, whose laugh you've lusted over as they gambolled in the wild? That was entirely different.

Raise the perceived value and you raise the payday, by orders of magnitude.

The art was in facilitating an uninhibited state. That's what any smart marketer would do. It was a simple matter of reframing. Don't sell cattle, one cow indistinguishable from the next. Let them choose their own version of an angel. You're not selling meat; you're selling a princess. Or a little prince. Tastes varied.

The Organizer got the idea by studying how a previous cell had worked. They'd used a house and the goat, but on a smaller scale, without the cameras. The whole principle had been different, and they'd missed a trick. Not this time. This would be special.

Sheets and sheets of discreet little numbers stared back at the Organizer. Mountains and mountains of money.

All that had to be done was reel in the buyers with delightful vignettes of youngsters at play. Ramp up the piquancy. Make these little darlings so absolutely, well, darling, that they'd be watched with quivering lips and hearts aglow.

That would open wallets.

And how best to do that? Make sure the kids have fun. Enough fun to let go. Starting with their location. They were going to *love* the house!

✶

The family huddled together like survivors of war.

The SABC News jingle faded into a car commercial, and Kendall's father repeated his ritual complaint, "Don't know why we bother to pay our TV license!" Their narrow escape hadn't even made the evening news.

Three bullet holes, right through the side of Addie's old Hyundai. A TV news crew had arrived outside the Mayor house in a suburb of Johannesburg to document the incident. They had nosed around the vehicle, spoken with the police inspector, filmed panning shots of the car from different angles, then posed the sisters embracing like they were glad to be alive, for extra B-roll. A cub reporter took a few quotes on a pad.

It hadn't been spectacular enough, and the reporter had warned them as much. "We covered a housebreaking last week. Three murdered with a panga. It got chucked for an ANC rally in Limpopo, but you never know, sometimes there's nothing else going."

Politicians were fond of saying that crime in the province of Gauteng had 'stabilized'. Kendall's Dad would sneer at the small TV on the old cabinet like it was his personal nemesis, "So it's the worst it's ever been, and hurrah, now it's staying that way? Thank you for that!"

All three Mayor women now sat in a huddled pile on a couch-seat, Addie and Kendall curled up half atop their mother. Her father sat alone, staring daggers at the TV like the attack had been its fault, but keeping one stray hand among the women. That hand had been there all evening. All three women held it back.

Addie would head back to campus soon. For now, her wounded Hyundai licked its wounds in her parents' driveway outside. Two shots had shattered the back window and ripped through the rear seat when Kendall pulled away in a cloud of tire smoke. The third and closest shot had drilled a hole in the B-pillar, inches from her head. The forensics inspector had found the slug embedded in the headrest and pulled it out with tweezers. The broken glass was now covered by cellophane from the kitchen drawer.

With his free hand, Kendall's father turned off the TV, then chucked the remote on the coffee table. It landed atop the pile of forms for the trip and the library book on California.

Kendall's father turned on the couch and looked at her as though he'd never seen her before. In the soft lamplight, the creases beside his eyes looked deeper than ever.

"Why did you do it?"

"Daddy ... You already asked me that."

"Dear, she's had that lecture from the police."

With the TV off, the silence in the tiny lounge was unbearable. The kitchen clock ticked. A cricket shrilled somewhere in a darkened corner of the house. A dog gave two half-hearted barks somewhere down the street, and Dobby pawed to be let out.

"You could have died, girl. Both of you."

Kendall's mother tried to stroke his leg, but he stopped her with one hand. His fingers went to his scalp, pulling at hair as though he could tug out the tension.

"You know we could have lost you both today. Help me understand. Why that? Why was *that* your reaction? Why not just get out, let him take it? That was such a risk."

"Dear, she's had enough for one day."

"Answer the question!"

Addie and Kendall's mother were both rubbing her back through the linen pyjamas. It had been reassuring at first, now it was kind of painful. She pulled her knees up and hugged them. "It was just instinct."

"Your instinct could have gotten you both killed. Both my girls."

Kendall heard Addie whisper, "Her instinct was right."

Before that comment started a fight, Kendall said, "I was facing forward like this. So, I had this sense that if I turned and looked at him, I'd have to do what he said. Like, once I did, then I'd be under his control. While I was still looking forward, it was as if I could decide. It was just for a second, but it felt like long. And I thought if I made the decision quick and went with it, just went, I'd get away. I just had to trust myself and go."

"What if you'd stalled? Think what could have happened. You're too young for all this nonsense anyway. You can't get a license until you're seventeen."

"That's only in three months."

"Oh, big girl!"

"Dear."

"Three shots! The guy took three shots, right at you. Point blank."

"Darling, that's enough."

"They could be dead. Both of them."

"You're going to have them in tears again. Stop it now." Kendall's mother scooped her daughters in tighter.

The next few silent seconds held like an impasse. Then her father let out a long sigh. Kendall wondered if this was what it felt like when war ended, before the last whisps of cannon smoke blew away.

The springs in the old couch creaked as her father rose. He picked up the form that had fallen to the floor, regarding it like a death threat. Dobby whined and pawed again at the door.

Kendall was still mulling it over. Why had she done it? For a brief moment, she had held her own life in her hands. Addie's too. Why *had* she done that?

18

Yes, instinct. Yes, she'd trusted herself to do it. But there was more.

Because it was right. It was the right thing to do. I knew it was. I could tell, so I did it.

Kendall held her hand up before her own eyes and discovered that the tremble that had plagued her since the shooting, the reason her Dad and sister and Mom had been holding her hand all evening on the couch, had subsided.

She discovered that she was proud of herself.

Kendall looked from her father to the form in his hand. In a careful voice, she said, "I still want to go."

He didn't move, but somehow it looked like he'd been punched. He set the form back on the table, looked at the bundle of women piled together on the couch.

"Not on your life."

Then he walked out into the driveway to smoke and look at the stars.

✗

There was no way she would sleep tonight. The house was too small. Her entire world was too small, and constricting further with every confiscated freedom. No more driving. No more trip.

Her Mom had dosed her with cough syrup as the only relaxant they had for a better night's sleep, and Addie had hugged her for a full minute before departing, following the longest lecture ever on not stopping completely at red lights and letting her parents know immediately when she got there. But still there was no peace in Kendall's heart. She could hear her parents' every tense whisper and agitated shift from their bedroom one door down.

Addie must have arrived safely at the dorms. Kendall heard her mom's phone buzz in the darkness and the ugly whispering let up for a moment.

Three thoughts ran in a loop through Kendall's mind. The first was that almighty noise. Shots loud enough to rock the world had echoed off the distant walls of the strip mall, even the hills beyond, and left her ears ringing for hours.

The second was the strange notion that her would-be hijacker had no face. She kept revisiting that moment in the car, imaging herself turning her head instead of driving away, but each time she tried to look, his identity remained a blur. It was weirdly frightening. Even in her imagination, she couldn't quite look at him, not straight on. He remained a faceless menace.

And the third, mixed together for no reason at all, and making the whole ordeal of bedtime feel like a cloudy delirium, was a philosophy term she'd gleaned from Addie a couple of weeks ago. It kept popping up, unbidden.

'Copernican Revolution.'

The tiny cell of her bedroom became a swirling vortex of uneasy memories: the shattering bangs, the struggle to see the face, the desperation to remember that illusive term, all grinding through her mind in a loop.

Copernican Revolution. The term was oddly satisfying. She hoarded the words, savoured them, forgot and then desperately tried to remember them again, whispering their lyricism under her breath as her eyes adjusted to the dark, and the man with the gun evaded her every attempt at a glimpse.

The wonky skylight with the bad latch admitted the silver of a clear Johannesburg night. It made her room cold, and sometimes you could smell the bougainvillea on a night breeze, for the latch never properly sealed. It was spring in the southern hemisphere, balmy during the days but freezing at night, though several layers of blankets from the charity store solved the problem. And she slept better in a snuggly chill.

Co-pernican Re-vo-lution.

Then the thunderous bang. Then two more, in quick succession.

No face. No matter how you turn. No matter how you try. Still, he's right there ...

Normally at around this time, her Dad would yell, "Lights out, girl!" from down the hallway, and she would respond, "They arrre, Daddd!"

Then he would yell, "You need the bathroom?", and she would say, "Nooo Daddd. It's all yours."

Tonight had been different. She'd cuddled up in bed with her parents for a while, and Addie had joined them too, until she had to leave. Eventually her Dad had carried her to bed, like he'd done when she was a little girl, and she would have sworn there was the slightest whimpering in his breath when he stroked her forehead, then walked out.

Dobby piled onto her bed a moment later. Turned around several times at the foot of her bed, circling the landing spot like an airplane in holding pattern, before settling down. Later, as the night became colder, he'd scrunch up to her, his snoring in the crook of her leg always reassuring.

Now, she heard her father's bare feet slap gracelessly over the linoleum flooring. The bathroom door opened and closed. Kendall tried hard not to hear more, despite the intimate proportions.

The words returned.

Her sister had held one balled fist aloft and showed an orbit around it as she spoke. "It's like, people in past ages thought the sun went round the earth, right? When Copernicus figured out the world is really going round the sun, they had to change the whole way they looked at things." She swapped her hands. "Ta da! The earth goes round the sun."

"We did that in geography."

"So that complete shift in thinking, that's called a Copernican Revolution. A total re-evaluation in how you see reality. You think it's one way; it's actually the other. You can use the term for anything, not just planets. Any moment when you realize something is the opposite of what you thought it was or that the whole thing works differently to the way you first believed. They do it in Scooby Doo a lot. The kindly old lady is actually the villain – rawhr!"

Kendall had chuckled. "I think I get it."

"Yeah? Really? So give me another example."

"Okay. So, it's like, imagine a family buys a kitten. It moves into the house with a big cat that was already living there. The original cat hisses at it all the time."

"Where are you going with this, squido?"

"Just listen! At first the kitten's scared. Eventually, it realizes the big cat is actually scared of *it*."

"Exactly. Role reversal."

"Ja exactly. And that's a ..."

"A Copernican Revolution. Don't say 'ja'. Say 'yes' or 'yeah'. In your example, it's like realising that a bully is really a coward. Once you have that epiphany, you see the whole situation differently. Everything changes."

Kendall had silently mouthed the word 'epiphany'.

The loo flushed. Her father's footfalls slapped back to bed.

She turned over fiercely, tugged at her bed spread where it was pinned beneath Dobby's weight, frowned into the claustrophobic dark, and concentrated. She had to keep the ugly gunshots at bay. She had to ignore the face that didn't want to be seen anyway. Dobby huffed at her.

She wondered if Addie would be able to sleep.

Addie had a Masters in Philosophy and Politics. She didn't have long to go on her doctorate. While studying politics struck Kendall as fantastically boring, she *did* find the idea of philosophy pretty cool. And being called a Doctor of Philosophy – that was outstanding.

Addie said, "It's not like anything from school, where they teach you what to think. It's more like ... *how* to think."

How to think. Awesome.

22

Another feather in Addie's cap was that she didn't treat Kendall like a kid. She spoke to her sister as an equal, passed on challenging books, like the edition of Hemmingway now beside her on the floor, marked with a pencil, with the full expectation that Kendall would read it. And Addie asked her opinion on things, then listened when she answered.

Okay, she also called her *gherkin breath, squid face, homunculus*. Always had. But Addie was real.

Kendall sat up in bed and rubbed Dobby behind his ears. Sleep was never going to happen. The Jack Russell made a gruff sound deep in the recesses of his impressive nose. He snuggled farther into the covers and returned to his doggie dreams.

She leaned over and parted the curtains, quietly – although Dad was back in bed, she still heard their murmuring.

In a perfectly black sky, she located the Southern Cross. It was crisp and clear tonight, wheeling above a South African nightscape. She released the curtain and sank back down into bed.

Her Dad was speaking fast, saying something about the world being more dangerous for girls. Kendall caught the phrase, "Eat her alive."

Somehow, they never conceived that their voices might carry through the house.

Her mom's voice was just above a whisper, but somehow it carried more. "So, we take this away from her. Then what?"

"Then she stays here. Safe."

"Not if this afternoon is anything to go by."

Kendall lost the rest. But she caught the word 'naive'.

His pitch rose. "She looks young, she acts young. And now you want to send her to the far side of the world."

"She took charge there. No, before you start, I'm not saying it was right, but that wasn't how a little girl acts. Besides, it's safer there. It's worse here."

"Safer? You're really calling America 'safer'?"

There was a second of silence. When her Mom spoke again, she seemed to be agreeing with him. "In some places, their crime is even worse than ours."

"Exactly."

"So, it's a no, then?" her Mom said.

Kendall held her breath. A line came to her from a movie. 'The walls of your bower closing in about you.' It was from *The Lord of the Rings*. The character was Grima Wormtongue, circling the beautiful Eowyn, who was young, pretty, blossoming, yet going to waste, close to tears while the evil man taunted her. 'The walls of your bower closing in about you.' The line had always haunted Kendall. Small house. Small life. Small world. Closing in and growing ever smaller.

"It's a no."

✷

THE STARS ALIGN

"The hosting is untraceable? You're sure?" The Organizer drummed anxious fingers on the table.

"It bounces around the globe. Continual relocation. Untraceable."

"And that doesn't create its own problem?"

"You mean if anyone returns to the site? No. It looks the same every time. Anyone goes back to check, it'll be there. But the contact mechanism is gone. Shut it down yesterday. It now says submissions are closed for the year. Email contact only from this point."

"What if they ask for a meeting?"

"Then we give it to them. AI. They speak to an avatar. We've done it five times now, it's utterly convincing. All of the parents who spoke to it subsequently booked their air tickets."

"Good. Good." The fingers stopped drumming. *"Arrival date for the cargo?"*

"Three months."

"Number of units?"

"Forty. Give or take. We'll winnow down further in the event of deformities, but the stock looks good. Then we have one week to display the items and move them. A week should do for the viewings. After that, we shut it all down."

The Organizer switched the phone from one ear to the other. *"A week is long. Too long. There's room for error, the units become ungovernable. Even with the Goat in the house."*

"What do you propose?"

The Organizer took a second to think, running an eye over the tacked digital codes on the wall, picturing each as a paying client with pockets as bottomless as their appetites, and trying to find a perfect ratio of risk to reward.

"Do this. Tell the buyers we're offering five days. Five days' viewing, no more. Day six and seven we close shop, clean up, lights out."

"Good."

"And the house?"

"All secured. We've gone with a hilltop residence. It's massive. Insular, private, plenty of rooms. Lot of entertainment for the units, but also no street access, no immediate neighbors, very high walls. The containment is perfect, or as perfect as you're ever going to get. I'll send you drone shots and interior photos."

"And schematics. Things we can't see."

"Good. On it."

"I want you to electrify the perimeter. Then scour it for surprises: old garage-door remotes, phone left in a box in the attic, WiFi from neighboring buildings, anything like that. Have someone spend a week there and watch for drone activity. No leaks, no surprises. And I have three more tasks for your team this week."

"Shoot."

"One. I want information on all units. Have them submit essays. What they like, what they hate, dreams, favourite celebrities, songs, food, fears, everything. That intel goes directly to the Goat. Use it for the winnowing too. Include a request for identifying marks: scars, burns, deformities, birthmarks."

"Why would they give that?"

"Pose it as a travel safety measure."

"Clever."

"Males are fine – buyers reject the blemished female items, so cull them."

"Done. Two?"

"Have them specify communications devices in advance of departure: phones, laptops, everything. Make and model, product ID. Absolutely no travel without that information."

"What if that changes? Kid gets a new phone."

"Mustn't happen. Tell them we provide a bespoke service on arrival. Based on their submitted devices and exact specifications, we'll have local sim cards, WiFi, and chargers ready for them. Make up something about insurance. They're all coming from another country, they don't know. Just so it sounds plausible. But we also scan the bags on arrival at the house. Set that up at the entrance to the house. Absolutely no surprises."

"Good. There will be signal blocking, but that's only meant as a redundancy."

"Will that affect my radio?"

"Good point. We'll test the frequency; make sure you can still communicate with the Goat. Three?"

"I want to meet him. The Goat. How good is he?"

A second's silence elapsed. The Organizer felt a moment of uncharacteristic panic, wondering if the line had gone dead, then wondering if the line was compromised.

"The Goat is fucking outstanding! Oscar worthy. We used him in Arlington, then the next year down in Guadalajara. Smaller operations than this. This is on a new level. But he's the best we've worked with. I wish we had ten of him."

"Isn't he getting too old, then?"

"Heading that way, but no, he looks young. I'd say this is maybe his last rodeo. Maybe one more. It's a pity. He's good. Real good. Final question: do we need to plan for unsold items?"

"Yes. We've never done a big house in one go. This many units, the whole world will be searching for them."

"Fucking risky."

"Fucking big pay day, and don't speak that way. Point is, they must never be found. Everything goes."

"Good. Done. I'll see to that too. We'll do stocktake on day six. … and on the seventh day, they shall rest."

"Don't do that, it's crass. And bring me the Goat."

*

PEACE OF MIND

The apartment in Warsaw was perfectly insulated. It was located in Stare Miasto, Old Town, and its triple glazed bay windows held the advancing Polish winter at bay, keeping the family cosy.

They were on the third floor. An unseasonably early snowfall held them hostage, making it difficult to get to school and work, but their attention was not on the drifts of snow scouring the cobbled street outside. All eyes were on the computer.

Agnieszka sat in front. She'd put on her prettiest dress. Her mom and dad leaned over her shoulders from behind.

The voice from the computer was warm. Grandmotherly.

"You're Agnieszka? Oh gosh, you're so very pretty. Just look at your hair!" The accent was American Deep South, honeyed and warm.

The girl blushed. "Thank you. Is a pleasure to be meeting you."

"You remind me of my granddaughter. And you folks must be Mom and Dad?"

The parents waved. "Thank you for your time. Agnieszka's very excited about all this."

"Oh, it's no trouble at all! We love getting to know our kids. Welcome to the program. I'm Sheila. Sheila O'Reilly. Head of international logistics. Fancy way of saying I make sure everyone's taken care of and all your questions are answered. You excited, Agnieszka? Looking forward to it?"

Agnieszka straightened the collar of her dress. "So excited. But a bit of nervous. I can't wait to be meet you of … all of … Sorry, my English!"

"Oh, honey that's no bother!" The woman on the screen wore square-rimmed glasses. Her chestnut hair was blow dried into soft waves. Framed by large windows looking out on a rural scene with a US flag on the patio, she sipped a cup of tea from a china cup with roses on it. "Your English is just great! You'll fit right in! We have kids your age coming from all over the world. Couple of months in California, you'll be yapping like a native."

"Thanks you."

"I'm in the beautiful state of Georgia right now. But I'll be joining you in California myself for Orientation Week. See, I like to take a hands-on approach, make sure everyone settles in just fine. So folks. How are preparations going? Anything you need to know?"

Agnieszka's parents took over. Would she be met at the airport? Must she bring transfer papers from school? How did they vet the family she would be staying with?

The grand dame fielded every question, peppering her responses with 'honeys' and 'dears'.

Reassured, the family ended the Zoom call.

"Bye bye, honey. See you soon!"

In California, 'Sheila O'Reilly' leaned back in his chair.

✗

Kendall retrieved the ladder from the corner. If the walls of her bower were going to close in, she could damn well climb above them.

She knew how to slide the ladder quietly over her carpet, and she knew just how far you could open its wooden legs before the hinge creaked.

She climbed it cautiously, barefoot, careful not to snag her pyjama pants, until she reached the skylight above. The glass sometimes fogged over on rare nights when it was so cold that she was permitted to keep her heater on. Tonight, the glass was clear. She opened the small skylight, hauled herself up through it and out into the chill night air.

The coarse roof tiles scratched against the softer texture of her pyjamas, so she tried not to move too much as she sat. She adjusted her weight carefully on the pitched roof.

Her parents were still at each other down below. Their voices, hissed and half-shouted, made her stomach clench.

She closed the skylight to block out the sound.

Their yard was strewn with the bric-a-brac of her father's projects. Overgrown mulberry and impenetrable bougainvillaea bushes and what may once have been neatly designated flowerbeds completed the effect. She gazed up and beyond the familiar mess to the moonlit rooftops of the neighboring homes and rubbed her palms, then her cheeks, against the cold.

Co-pernican Re-vo-lution. Your whole world changes in one go. Sure. As though she wouldn't be stuck here forever.

A thought occurred to her that brought a flush of guilt. She'd come awfully close to not being here at all. And Addie too.

Five minutes later, Kendall sat up with a jolt. She had dozed, nearly fallen asleep right out here on the roof. The Southern Cross had shifted in the night sky, pivoting like a wheel, and the owls had ceased hooting.

Escape the hijacker, then fall off the roof! Better get back down.

She was on her haunches, about to open the skylight, when someone pushed at it from the other side.

Her nerves still taut, Kendall started. Her foot slipped on a tile and the tile slid from the roof, shattering on the ground below.

With no tile, the foot sought purchase but found nothing, and Kendall began to slide on the pitched roof. She gasped as her stomach felt the beginnings of a drop.

An arm grabbed hers, fingers digging into her skin.

Kendall looked up. Her father's face, sticking out of the skylight, reflected her own shocked expression.

A whisper, face to face. She heard, "Fuck." It was so intimate that Kendall fought a badly timed smile.

"I was just ..."

"Come in," her father said, slowly releasing her arm so she could slither to the ladder. "We need to talk to you."

"Dad, I already know."

He'd already disappeared back down into her room.

Heart still pounding, Kendall trailed her father into the main bedroom. The lights were on, stinging her eyes. Her mother was tucked in bed, evaluating her strangely.

"Mom?"

Her father handed her a small sheet of paper. The permission slip that had fallen to the floor in the lounge.

Signed.

Her mother chuckled at her shocked delight. "Happy Birthday, Merry Christmas, and Happy Hanukkah."

"Seriously?!"

Her father said, "Don't ask for anything for the next ten years," and Kendall hit him like a torpedo.

"I'm going to America!"

"You're going to America," her mother said.

"This is the best thing that's ever happened to me."

"Okay, slow your roll," her father said. "There are some conditions we need to discuss."

✗

They sat on the hood of the wounded Hyundai. Parked at Lover's Leap atop the Witwatersrand ridge, they stared over the undulating suburbs to the gentle slopes of the distant Magaliesburg range, purple and rendered strangely lovely with the woodfire smog drifting over from the township of Soweto. Kendall lay back against the glass, using one hand to shade her eyes.

"Got a new term for you."

"I'm still getting the hang of Copernican Revolution."

"Tough nuggie. Learn or burn, butt face."

"Fine. Whatch'a got?"

"Gather round, kids," her sister said. "Today's term is ..." she ran an illustrative finger down the glass of the windscreen, *"Slippery Slope."*

"I love how you always make this like an episode of *Sesame Street*. So what's a slippery slope when it's at home? It's not something rude, is it?"

"No. But I like the way your mind works. See if you can guess."

"Brother!"

"Nope, I lack some defining equipment. I'll be your sister, and I'll be here all week; try the clam, as it very much were. So, go on, see if you can guess. Try to work it out."

The afternoon storm had never materialized. Nevertheless, the temperature was finally dropping as the sun began to dip, and the evening smog painted pretty purple streams through the sky. The hood of the car remained pleasantly warm beneath them.

Kendall gathered her wits and considered the elements available to her. *A slippery slope. If a slope is slippery, what happens? Stuff goes down it in a hurry, or in a way that's out of control. The key is 'downhill and going'. But this isn't an actual thing, right? It's an idea. It's got something to do with ways of thinking. So what the heck is a slippery slope, when it comes to ways of thinking?*

"It means ..." she ventured, "it means ..." she repeated, "when things go downhill and you can't stop them. Right? They have momentum."

Addie took her sunglasses from their perch on top of her blonde hair and pulled them down over her eyes, then aimed a smile at her younger sister.

"Not bad. You're actually most of the way there already. What I didn't give you was *context*."

"Okay, so what's the context for a slippery slope?"

"It usually has to do with a debate or argument. Someone is putting forward an idea. Arguing that their idea should be the new way things are done. A slippery slope situation can occur *after* that, if they get their way. See what you can make of it from that."

"Okay, let me think." Kendall pinched the bridge of her nose. "So, let's say two people are arguing … I'm going to give myself more 'context' by saying they're arguing over whether or not the legal age for driving in South Africa should be lowered to fifteen."

Addie chuckled. "Nice."

"It's not just because of our lessons. It's one of the topics our debating team really had to do at school."

"Cool, so roll with it."

"So, one side says that younger people *should* be able to drive. The other says they shouldn't. A slippery slope is when the whole idea starts going downhill and … oh, wait! I think I've got it!"

"Yes?"

Kendall's voice lifted an octave. "Say we argue that younger people *should* be able to drive. And we win our argument. Then someone comes along and says, 'Well, if younger people can drive, why can't they shoot guns?' Then another person says, 'If they can shoot guns, why can't they, like, be the president and start wars?' Slippery slope."

"Kendall?"

"Yes?"

"You freakin' little genius, you!"

"I got it? That's a slippery slope?"

"It is. You make an argument based on a fact that is wholly relevant."

"I knew I'd get it!"

"No you didn't. You thought you wouldn't. But I pushed you and then you did."

"Fine. But I'm still psyched I got it."

"That's because you're my little sister. And if I can possibly help it, you're going to be a thinker. Any twit with tits can be popular. And there's nothing wrong with that. But you can be a helluva lot more, and it only requires making the decision to be a thinker, not just a bimbo."

"No worries there. I can do the twit part if I want. But that's about it."

"Oh really? Then what do you call those?" Addie said, pointing.

"Tea cup saucers at the moment."

This set both girls laughing.

"I know it's shallow, but I still hope nature hands me a bicycle pump someday soon. Look at yours!"

"I guess *thanks*, babe. I wouldn't stress too much. You're developing just fine, *here*," Addie tapped Kendall on the forehead, "and, you know, there," she said, motioning at her chest with a mock grimace.

"Maybe I'll just have a boob job and get Double D's. Be popular and dumb. Then other people can do clutches and drive me round while I live on Instagram money," Kendall said, cupping her small breasts.

"Double D's? Aim high, naartjie nose! Why settle for anything less than actual watermelons?" Addie cupped her own slightly larger boobs and pouted her lips aggressively. "Yo Rambo, check out dese bazookas!"

Both girls were cupping and snarling when a hiker and his Spaniel crested the hill. They dropped their hands to their sides like small children caught stealing.

The man shook his head and walked off smiling.

They degenerated into giggles.

"We both did identical deer-in-headlights," Addie said.

"I'm glad no one was filming that."

When they regained their composure, Addie asked, "How you holding up?"

"Tired. I didn't sleep last night. But otherwise, I'm actually okay. You?"

"Yeah, rattled but fine. I just keep hearing that noise."

"It was so loud," Kendall said. "I'm thinking more about the trip than the … you know …"

"Near-death dramatic car chase."

Kendall didn't respond. She idly rubbed the bonnet beneath her.

"So, what do you need to organize for your trip?"

"Ah, there's tons. A visa. Booking the plane tickets, getting gifts for the host family. Stuff like that."

"And the group that runs the whole thing? Do they have some sort of screening process? See whether or not you're a radical terrorist with Mad Cow Disease?"

"No."

"No?"

"The site says you can just sign up and go."

"Really? Huh. Well, I suppose if you're paying your own way, and if you qualify for the visa, then maybe that makes sense."

"Ja."

"Don't say 'ja'. Say 'yes', or 'yeah'."

"Actually, they sponsor quite a lot of the living expenses. Basically we pay half, they pay half."

Addie paused, frowning. "But they haven't asked you for a meeting yet? Not even online?"

"No, not yet."

"And they've accepted you?"

"Ja. I mean, yeah."

"Oh … okay."

"What's wrong with that?"

"Nothing."

"They do send lots of emails. Mom's been answering them. In the last one they said they want me to write an essay about myself; things I like and hate, favourite books, songs, you know, stuff like that. And I've got to send a few photos of myself."

"Huh. Okay. Well, I guess that should do it. I wonder why they'd want to know your favourite song ..."

"There's an orientation week when we get there. It's probably for like, a welcome party or something."

A MEANS OF MANAGING THE STOCK

"You're the one they call The Goat?"

"I am indeed."

"You speak like an adult. You sound like one."

The boy stood in the antechamber, lit by a single beam from above, as though God had reached down to commune with him.

There was no furniture. There was nothing on the walls. The entire room was painted pure white. Moments prior, one of the facilitators had finally taken off his eye mask, then retreated before turning on the lights. There were no windows. Only a camera, and the speakers that relayed the voice of the Organizer.

"I speak like a kid when I need to. And I'm older than I look."

"How old are you?"

He turned a full three sixty, evaluating the white nothingness all around him.

"Why am I here? Normally I get my brief from the onsite team."

"There's nothing normal about this. Nothing on this scale has ever been attempted before. I wanted to meet you."

"Meet me? This is meeting me?"

"Your past record managing stock has been … exemplary. You know what exemplary means?"

"It means you should pay me more. Why can't I see your face?"

"I'm intrigued by your skillset. It's subtle. What's the key? What makes it work?"

"It isn't complicated. You make them like you." He looked into the camera. The directness of it, the way he squinted his eyes,

the Organizer had the uncanny sensation that he could see through the wiring. It was creepy. *"It's not about any one thing,"* he said. *"It's a thousand small things. And it's about how you manage … how confident people think you are. How certain."*

"And you? It never becomes real for you?"

"Real isn't a thing."

"It isn't?"

"Nothing's real." He reached out, touched the camera, his questing hand filling up the screen. It looked as though he might be unscrewing the lens. The Organizer got the sense of a fox in the pre-dawn light, constantly sniffing for advantage.

"Nothing? What's your conception of them, the stock? Are they real?"

"No. I'm real. Everything outside of me is bullshit. It's piles of crap on toast."

"Vivid. I assume your sentence constructions are less ambitious when you integrate with the stock?"

"Do you need anything else?"

"Just to give you the essays. From those 'piles of crap on toast'. We've placed them in your satchel. It will be in the vehicle when we return you."

"The eye mask again."

"I apologize for the discourtesy. An Organizer will be with you soon to reaffix it. I look forward to seeing your work."

"Will you be watching?"

"Yes. And so will the clientele, at all times. Does it matter if we do?"

"No."

✳

The pieces fell into place. Kendall's trip was set for late December, just a few months off. Winter in the USA. Apparently Californian weather was a lot like South African, so the winters weren't too bad.

She would fly via LAX. There, she'd meet the coordinators of the exchange program, who would collect her at the airport for 'orientation week'. She hoped whoever picked her up would be wearing a baseball cap. Then they would take her to stay with the host family. She would go to school with the host family's kid and be there right up until the American summer holidays, which were almost three months long, much longer than South Africa's more frequent but shorter holidays. They also called them 'vacation'.

She began planning the things she had to do before then: turn seventeen, get a job as a waitress or something. Grow boobs.

She wondered whether she might experience a white Christmas. A quick search on the internet revealed that California was technically classified as desert country. Even though the Highveld of Johannesburg was similarly dry, the phrase 'desert country' struck Kendall as wonderfully romantic.

It was also the home of Disneyland, Universal Studios, and famous beaches like that one with the theme park right out on the pier, with the colourful lights that glittered on the water. It all made her hug herself with glee.

*

THE TICKET

On the eve of Ticket Day, Kendall's mother showed uncharacteristic indulgence, suggesting they splash out on dinner to commemorate the moment.

"Nothing swanky. And nothing expensive off the menu! Specials for everyone. Just a small night out to celebrate." She disappeared into the bathroom to shower and told Kendall to be ready to go next, before the hot water ran out.

*

"We've had an issue with the site."

The Organizer's voice went cold. *"What kind of issue?"*

"Nothing important. Looked like a hacker was trying to get in."

"Law?"

"No, civilian. Incidental, not purposive. The kind aimed at any site, not specifically ours. So we crashed it. We're scouring the other servers. Once we're sure they're untapped, we'll put it back up. But it's not enforcement. Some kid somewhere."

"So it's dark right now?"

"Yeah, but we'll get it back up. And no one's even tried to log on for over three weeks now, so no one's missing it."

"You're sure?"

"We can tell. They all seem confident with email comms. We'll get the site back up anyway, in case. But it's not a problem."

"Fine. Let's talk about the house. The signal damping works?"

"Everywhere. We tested it from the corners of the property to the roof."

"But my radio will operate?"

"Just don't change the frequency. Or the privacy codes."

"Cameras?"

"Hundreds of them. Everywhere. Every mirror, every room. Most of the corridors. They're flush, so effectively invisible. Also the showers. Several angles around the pools."

The Organizer felt a cautious relief. This would work. The most ambitious marketing project she'd ever conceived. It was going to work.

"No further attrition?"

"None. The ratio's perfect. Two female units to every male. We delisted three girls with birthmarks. There's a question mark over a fat kid. Well, chubby. But that usually doesn't matter. Otherwise, it's a good batch."

"Chubby's fine. For a boy. Someone will have a preference for that. Race?"

"Black. London accent, family from West Africa."

"Graduate him through and let's begin transportation dry runs."

"Same as last time?"

"Same. All that changes is the scale. I perform initial contact and collection at the airport. Have your team ensure I can change the plates en route."

"Easy. We fit your vehicle with flippers, front and back. Press of a button, it rotates. You can change it twice en route. Do it under a bridge, something like that."

"Good. Thereafter, I deliver items to the house. Over the viewing period, I extract items and deliver to the buyers. Ideally, we want buyers to acquire two or more at a time. Single unit purchases slow the process, so we offer incentives for bulk. Highest incentive rates apply for sets of two girls and a boy."

"Why?"

"It keeps the remaining stock proportions balanced in the house," the Organizer explained. *"We sell more in total."*

"Does it matter? The margins are so high."

"It matters. Dubai already enquired about that. I'll inform the buyers, prep them to think that way."

She hung up, thinking about how every decent marketer offers a package deal. It would be sloppy to miss the chance to upsell.

✗

Stuffed with carvery, they ambled out of the restaurant. Kendall's parents walked ahead, unusually affectionate, with her mother's head resting against her father's shoulder. Addie leaned against Kendall, and her breath had pleasant notes of red wine. "It's been three weeks since your last driving lesson, Spitball! With gaps like that, there's not much point. You need to practice or don't bother."

"Okay. Pick me up from school tomorrow?"

It had rained while they'd eaten. The wet tarmac reflected the lights from the mall's signage, and the whole place smelled of ozone. Nevertheless, the rain had done little to cool the night air, which remained steamy and cloying.

"Deal. Bring the calmest version of your nerves. We shall attempt the mortal horror that is parallel parking." Addie was about to walk off to her own car, but stopped, turning on her heel. "Oh, I wanted to ask you something!"

"Yes?"

"See? There you go. You *can* say 'yes'."

"I've been practicing."

"Stellar."

Addie struggled to withdraw her phone from tight jeans pockets. Eventually it slipped out and she showed the screen to Kendall.

"That link you sent me for the exchange program. I just went to it again. Look at this."

The glowing white screen bore a sad-looking square face, floating over the words, 'This site can't be reached'.

42

"That's weird. Oh, look, it's the spelling," Kendall said, pointing at the link. "That's wrong."

"Yeah, I figured. And when I corrected it, another site came up. But it wasn't the same one as yours, it was a whole different bunch."

Kendall wondered where Addie was going with this. "My exchange program's site's just down temporarily. What's your point?"

Addie peered at the phone's screen a moment longer, her expression troubled. Then she pocketed the device again, got into her long-suffering Hyundai and shouted goodbye with, "All right, squid face. We have a date! See you after school."

When they pulled up outside their own gate, Kendall's Dad turned off the engine to conserve fuel and she hopped out to do gate duty. Sometimes he wouldn't turn the engine on again; just roll silently down the driveway in neutral.

She edged past the car, wishing for the hundredth time that they might upgrade to automatic gates.

In the night silence, she put her hand on the latch, as she'd done a hundred times before, then stopped. The gates fell inward, opening at her slightest touch. That had never happened before.

She stood still in the night silence for a moment. Then she leaned a little closer in and took a long hard look. The latch was broken. She looked down the driveway and saw that the outside light was off. Not just off, but missing. Pieces of shattered glass lay strewn on the ground beneath it, reflecting moonlight.

And where was Dobby?!

"Dad?" she turned. "Something's wrong."

"Get back in the car."

As she dashed back into her seat and shut the door, her Mom said, "Kendall, do you have that new phone with you?"

"Yes, Mom."

She handed it to her mother, who dialled the five-tone tune taught to every school child.

Her father removed a lug wrench from the boot of the car, slammed it shut, and the whole vehicle shook. He jogged quickly to the neighbor's house, rang the bell, saw the lights come on and the front door open. He waved urgently but didn't wait to talk to their neighbor. Instead, he slipped through the front gate, then disappeared around the side of the house, the lug wrench gripped in both hands like a bat. His usual slouch was gone. He seemed pulled taut.

Even the kitchen light was out, their familiar, welcoming little home transformed into a knot of menacing shadows.

The neighbor shuffled up beside Kendall's mother's side of the car, who opened her window but showed him one finger as she spoke into the phone. "Yes, someone's broken into our house. No, we don't know yet ..."

The neighbor, unarmed, wearing only slippers on his feet and boxers, looked from the car to the dark driveway.

Kendall quietly began to pray as she heard the address being given. The neighbor seemed uncertain about his role in all this. *Should he venture onto the property?* But Kendall's father was already returning up the drive. The tension in his stance had dissipated. His shoulders hung down.

"There's no one here," he said. "Looks like they smashed through the back window. Opened the rear door from the inside and carried everything out that way."

"Geez, we were here the whole time," the neighbor said, looking guilty. "I didn't hear a thing!"

"Dobby! Where's Dobby?" Kendall rushed from the car.

Her father brought her to a halt with a hand squarely on her chest. She lost her breath as she collided with it.

"Kendall, listen. I can't see Dobby. I want you to be ready. Dobby might be dead." His voice was calm. "I want you to let *me* find him, okay? Give me a minute. Stay here with Mom."

"I ..."

"Stay here!"

44

This time the neighbor joined her father. They spoke quickly but quietly as they headed back onto the property, the neighbor's sandals making slapping noises as they went.

Kendall sank back into the car, crumpling into the back seat. She began to sob. Her mother reached back and put a hand on her knee.

When the police arrived – three blazing cars skidding to a halt – the two men had still not found Dobby.

Kendall hovered like a lost spirit nearby, while the lights from the police cars changed their faces every three seconds.

"Dad, can I look for Dobby?"

The policeman and her father both regarded Kendall.

"Don't touch anything." And the briefest of nods.

The night had come alive. The flashing lights from the three cars, still rotating brightly where they stood, lit up the street in colourful strobes, probing every secret. Neighbors ventured out into the night to ask questions. In various groupings, half-dressed civilians and formally clad policemen gravitated to their drive, some making knowing noises as they inspected the broken gate latch. It was the saddest street party ever thrown on their block.

"Dobby!" Kendall called, cupping her hands, as she and her Mom circled the property.

The window facing the backyard, a large single frame, was completely smashed in. It looked like a gaping wound on the side of their home. Most of the glass had fallen inward, but there were still a few shards on the grass. They crunched under Kendall's sneakers.

"Careful," her mother said, taking her arm as they circled right back to the driveway, and to the flashing blue-and-white lights.

The lights were on inside the house, and Kendall's Dad was touring the small space with the officer, listing missing items, trying not to touch anything. Kendall heard it all through what felt like a fog. "The TV, there. The microwave. The computer our daughter did homework on, through there."

The old computer was next to worthless. But its contents were irreplaceable. All her private stuff: diary, music, messages from her friends, everything.

Her half-sized ladder in the passage had been knocked over. It lay sideways across the floor. Kendall's father stepped past it, directing the policeman to the main bedroom. "Geez, look at that, they even got my old telescope."

"Dobbyyy!" Kendall called into the house.

The officer pointed at the open hatch in the ceiling, "And that?"

"I store things up there. Woodworking stuff."

Kendall looked up, considering the dark hole in the ceiling. It was a ghastly missing tooth against the clean, white plaster. She lifted the ladder back up and dragged it into place beneath the hole, then started to climb.

"Kendall!"

She was already staring into the hole, her head out of sight of the others.

A few seconds went by in silence.

She waved a hand below the level of the ceiling. "Daddy, he's in there! Dobby's in there."

"Up *there*?"

Her head came down out of the roof. "No. Daddy, I think ...", she gulped and her voice changed, "I think he's dead."

"Come down off the ladder, my girl. I'll get him for you." To the officer and also to no one in particular, he said, "Why would they ... why would anyone ...?"

Kendall interrupted, "Daddy, *I* can. I *want* to. Please, he's my doggie. Let me get him."

"I ... okay. Kendall, just be ready, all right? This might be bad, it might be upsetting. We don't know what they did to him."

"I know."

Kendall pulled her weight up onto the first beam and immediately coughed at the dust. It smelled like old boxes and sour oil rags up here.

"You need a torch up there, honey?" Kendall could hear her mother's voice coming up through the floor.

"No, Mom, there's enough light."

There wasn't, but she assumed her eyes would adjust. The skylight Kendall used to climb onto the roof was part of a different section. This area was a long triangular prism running the length of the hallway. A haze of light leaked through from the house below, and a few streaks of silver starlight entered through gaps in the tiles above.

She began to crawl into the small space, making slow but steady progress through the weird network of wooden crossbeams and pipes and shadows. A pile of wood was slightly scattered, as though the planks had been shuffled. They'd definitely been up here, searching for hidden treasure.

There, at the far corner near the geyser, lay a small pile of fur, unmoving, unbreathing. Kendall's eyes fought to adjust to the dark.

She knew he was dead. But that was her dog, and *she* was going to retrieve him – no one else.

She heard the voices of the adults below, speculating. Her mother said, "They must have … what? Killed the dog to stop the barking?"

"And then? Threw the body into the ceiling? Why?" Her father was sceptical.

"Get it out the way, maybe." Then louder, her mother said, "You okay, baby? Don't step on the plaster, you'll come right through. Only the beams, okay?"

"Okay, Mom."

She was nearly there.

The heat increased substantially as she neared the geyser. Dobby's body was right beside it, lying between the beams, disturbing the dust on an expanse of plaster, his weight insufficient to damage the ceiling.

She squatted on the beam and leaned right up close to see. Still no good. She tried to lean over to lift him, but the angle was awkward. He was down below her. She adjusted one leg, stretching it out over a beam, so that she could counterbalance her weight while reaching down.

"Acck!" she exclaimed.

Kendall found herself staring into the open mouth of a dead rat, inches before her face. She started with fright, jumping back.

"Ow!"

"What?!" both parents shouted in unison from below. Their nerves were hyper extended.

"The geyser. Touched it. It's not Dobby, it's a rat, a big rat!" The pain lancing through her made her grimace and bite her lip to stop herself from crying out more. Her parents had enough stress in their lives. They didn't need to panic over her burning her leg.

The confusing tableau resolved itself into sense before her. The rat lay half over a curled rag. The rag had conned Kendall into thinking of a larger form: the rat's neck and head were the size and furriness of Dobby's nose. There the resemblance ended.

Kendall felt the dinner in her stomach rise up. She leaned away, trying not to see the gaping mouth, the lolling tongue and dirty teeth, the frozen rictus of a dead scream as the rat had turned on its side and reached for nothing. The dust and heat were gelling inside her nose. She breathed through her mouth. Shallowly. And inched her way back.

From the front door, there was a double knock and a voice asking, "Is this the dog?" The officer carried a small bundle of fur into the house.

Kendall rushed up to take delivery of the bundle. The officer held it away. "No!"

A second officer followed, holding a smaller load, wrapped in a towel.

Kendall stopped in horror.

The second officer held it up, wincing. "The rest."

"I'm sorry. I … they used a shovel. They … decapitated the head."

On top of the death of her dog, Kendall suffered the second indignity of not being able to accept the body. The pieces of the body.

"Please, will you take that outside," her father said. "I'll … come deal with it now."

A quick nod, and both officers turned back.

Kendall clung to her mother, still as stone. Her father sighed deeply and joined them. They hugged her from both sides while she trembled.

"I'm so sorry, baby," he said, and that was enough. Kendall broke down.

She sobbed as they rubbed her hair and clasped her shoulders. The policemen outside stood at a respectful distance.

The problem was, she had dared to hope. Now, so many things had just changed. Dobby was no longer a part of their family, their everyday life, their every arrival back home. He'd never dance playfully around their feet again and they'd never hear his voice as he chased off hadedas or guys slipping pamphlets through their front gate. *How much had they hurt him? Or had it been quick?*

He must have been brave. He must have gone after them. Fought them. If only he hadn't been. If only he'd run off and hidden somewhere.

Their house had been emptied of the few valuable items they owned. They were worse off now. They were going to have to rebuild their lives, and every cent would count, more than ever.

The trip was definitely off.

The Copernican Revolution was unwinding, reverse engineering itself, reverting to the old order. Gravitational norms eventually pulled all things back into their old orbits. The sun really did go around the world, as the ancients insisted. If you tried to toy with those weathered truths, the dragons fought back, restoring their olden ways.

Nothing ever changed. Nothing got better. Not for them.

THE SUN GOES ROUND THE EARTH

'The walls of your bower ...'

Kendall woke up several times that night. Each time with a start.

'The walls of your bower, closing in about you.'

It wasn't just the cocktail of shock and loss. There was also the searing physical pain.

Her mother had been surprised at the extent of the burn on Kendall's leg, and wanted to take her to the hospital. It was on her upper thigh, just below the hip, a truly ugly sear.

Kendall assured her it didn't hurt that badly, the pain of the burn paling beside what she felt in her heart. So they applied a cold-cream compress, gave her sweet tea and Aspirin, and said a prayer over the burn.

Each time Kendall awakened in bed, she lived out the same cycle. First the jolt of pain from the burn, then the adrenaline rush as memory overwhelmed her, then the tears when she looked down the length of her bedspread and didn't see Dobby. Then anger and rage reached incandescent levels as she warred with the world in the dark. Then the unclenching, the hopeless tears.

'The walls of your bower ... walls of your bower ...'

She'd drift off to an uneasy sleep, then repeat the cycle a half hour later.

Next morning, she had deep bags under her eyes. She didn't notice with her leg throbbing like a beacon of light.

One of the neighbors took a look, then whistled at what he saw. He was a paramedic and just one of several people who dropped by that morning with meals and kind words. He applied an apothecary's mix of antiseptics and salves, then covered it up again with a fresh bandage. He gave her a couple of anti-inflammatories and told her only to take them with food. "Or they'll burn your stomach lining."

They buried Dobby in the back yard, wrapping the small body with the head in a cloth, then lowering him down into the ground near the shade of a willow tree. Kendall tried to sing 'Amazing Grace', but only made it through two lines.

Back in the house afterwards, they sat together in a lounge that felt conspicuously empty without the TV on one side, the decorative plates that had been mounted atop a bookshelf on the other.

The topic got gently broached. "Kendall-pie, we need to talk about your trip ..."

'The walls of your bower closing in about you.'

"I know, Dad. It's off. It's okay."

"I'm so sorry, angel. I wish there was some way."

Her mother said, "We just can't afford it now. Maybe we can think about it or something else in two or three years."

"I know, Mom."

She stared at the discoloured blank mark on the living room wall where the TV used to be, and her unfocused eyes watched the stolen state of California recede into dreams.

Three days later, the mark on her thigh still stung, perhaps worse than before. The splotch of skin was red and angry, bubbled and stretched, like it might burst. Pus seeped out around the edges in tiny yellow rivulets.

Addie had picked her up from school in the red Hyundai.

Kendall glanced from the road to her big sister, then frowned. "What? Why are you smiling like that?"

Addie flicked her indicator, changed lanes. "Smiling? Moi?"

"You were. Like some weird cartoon criminal. What were you thinking about?"

"Nothing. Can't remember. Boy at varsity or something. Hey, pick a lane, Toyota face! Fifty five in an eighty zone. Get a life."

Kendall smelled a subject change.

When they arrived home, she saw a note hanging outside on the gate, fluttering slightly against the tape that held it to one of the bars.

"Now I wonder what that could be?" Addie said, pulling up the handbrake.

"Okayyy?" Kendall climbed from the car.

The latch had been repaired. Taped to it was a note the size of a postcard. Kendall pulled it free. It read: *K: Go to the rosebush.*

She turned to Addie, who was still in the car. Addie shrugged. Then showed a scooting motion. "You must be K. So, go!"

Kendall trotted to the bottom of the yard, near the patch of loose grass and mounded earth where Dobby lay. The grass was already starting to sprout over the freshly piled earth. There she found a second note. She pocketed the first in her school blazer and snatched the second from the thorn bush on which it was spiked. *Go to the loose brick.*

She knew the spot. It was on the other side of the yard, where they sometimes left a house key for each other. She knelled by the wall, pried the dusty brick loose – the scraping sound and dry concrete on her fingertips always made her shiver – and found note number three beneath it, along with the house key. *Go to the spoon drawer.*

"Oh brother!" She rolled her eyes, though she was smiling.

Inside the house, she pulled open the kitchen drawer. It had been neatly re-packed; mere days ago they'd found the contents strewn across the floor. It hadn't looked this neat in years. In the spoon division, she found: *Go to your pillow.*

How many more? And to what end?

As she headed for her room, she noticed Addie coming in the front door, still smiling conspiratorially.

On the pillow was an envelope with a red ribbon tied in a pretty, curled bow.

Addie was at her door, filming her.

Kendall teased the ribbon apart, opened the envelope and pulled out a folded pile of pages. The first was an A4 letter, with very little on it.

Bring me back George Clooney.
Brad will do in a pinch.
Happy belated birthday.
Love from the future earnings of Addie Mayor
via today's student loans

Behind were two pages of printed itinerary, and behind that, an air ticket with Kendall's name on it.

Kendall looked at Addie. Addie looked down at her phone, then simultaneously winced and smiled as Kendall's shriek tested the limits of sound distortion on the recording.

"Oh my freak! I'm going to America!!!"

Addie said, "You sure are, buttercup!"

Kendall panted for a second, then asked Addie, "Really? This is for real?"

"Real as it comes."

"How?"

"You remember that scholarship I got to do my PhD? I might have forgotten–" Addie coughed delicately into her fist "–to mention it to the student loans assessor and got next year's loan in full. Potentially."

"You're absolutely magic. You're the best and I love you."

"Awwww, thanks. I'm just your fairy godmother down on a little cloud to make all your dreams come true."

"Let's talk handover."

"Right."

"Our top priority: No traceable connection between me and any buyer. We've never done a house this big. The scale is massive, so it must be fluid from end to end."

"Play it out for me."

"It goes like this: on confirmation of payment, I extract from the house. I hand over to the courier, the courier hands over to the buyer. No buyer ever sees my face."

"Good."

"Purchases made in pairs or more is good. The fewer the handovers, the lower the risk."

"Right."

"I want you to secure two locations for each delivery: from me to the courier, from the courier to the buyer. I must never be in the same location as the buyer."

"You want soundproofing in the courier's van?"

"Yes. Soundproofing, sedation, physical restraints. Most of the time the cargo still trust me, right up to handover. But after a few days at the house, who knows? Might be strained. When they do bother to fight, it's usually at handover, so scout for remote locations. Extremely quiet. Abandoned buildings ... different one each time ... and back-up locations for each one as well."

"Good."

"Then the final locations: courier to buyer."

"We offering three options again?"

"Yes. Port, private airfield, or overland, if they want to manage their own final extraction from the US. But they choose from our venue options. Non-negotiable. Some ask for delivery to their premises. We do not do this, ever. No exceptions. They agree to our location or the sale is off, at the threat of revealing their proclivities to state authorities."

"Seriously?"

"Yes. And I want all those locations finalized in advance."

"You don't trust them for shit."

"That's why we're still in business. And we've never done it at this scale. No leaks."

"Got it."

"So, connect those dots. Then start running the couriers through dry runs. Make them load and unload empty boxes at each place to test it out. No shortcuts – that part matters. They need to experience the location in real-time, packing and unpacking, learn who watches, see what times are best, get a sense for whether there are cameras or eyes or law enforcement within a mile radius. I want them to develop total situational awareness in those places, a depth of local knowledge. Even an old woman watching from a window is enough to collapse the whole thing."

"I'll get the team on that today."

"I want this running smooth. So smooth that we have the house shut down, the whole stock shipped, and the team dispersed before anyone even asks where the items are. This will be massive. Global news. Eyes of the world."

"By the time anyone's paying attention, we'll be ghosts."

THE HOUSE AND THE GOAT

When the intercom binged for the inflight announcements, Kendall jumped for the hundredth time. The older woman in the seat beside her chuckled good-naturedly. A smooth disembodied voice announced, "Ladies and gentlemen, we are beginning our final descent for Los Angeles International Airport," and a rustling filled the cabin. Shivers passed down Kendall's spine. "Please ensure your tray tables and footrests are tucked away and your seatback is in the upright position."

After the screeching bump of touchdown came a world of pushing crowds. There were stairs, then queues, then counters, then more pushing crowds, more stairs, more counters. But there were also American flags everywhere. The TV screens even showed bald eagles as they welcomed you, which was beyond awesome. At the customs queue, the video on the giant screens was especially good, complete with cowboys, canyons, jets streaking overhead.

Each time she made it to the front of a line, she had to dig for a different set of papers and some of it made her panic. Each time, she just *knew* that the page she needed would somehow have disappeared from her folder.

Kendall was already starting to form a tentative impression of Americans. They talked so ... *uncarefully*. They were chucking about their words and thoughts like empty candy wrappers, barely caring who overheard them.

It was a little scary how no one seemed to mind pushing past her. This seemed to be a place without caution. *It wasn't exactly unfriendly*, she thought. That wasn't it. Just *informal*, as though maybe there was little division in seniority between grown-ups and kids. *Everyone a teenager*. Whenever she addressed a grown-up politely, saying 'sir' or 'ma'am', they seemed to smile in amusement, as though she were overdoing it.

With the 'whump' of a stamped passport still in her ears, Kendall stacked her bags from the luggage carousel on a trolley. Kendall held her trolley and scanned slowly over the throngs of people behind the barrier huddled together watching for their particular arrivals. So many faces. Some wore uniforms and hats, and calmly held placards at their chests, like in the movies. Others waved wildly as balloons bobbed from their hands. Plenty of signs. Plenty of names. But she didn't see hers.

She inched her way slowly down the causeway between the two lines of people. Then, worried that she might miss the sign for her, she stopped. Still nothing. There was just too much to see.

Just as she started to grow anxious, a boy made eye contact with her. It was direct, in a way that South Africans would have found challenging, even aggressive. But he was smiling openly. Kendall looked away twice, deeply confused. But each time she looked back, he was looking right at her, not even trying to hide it. On the third return, he waved.

"Kendall? You are, right? You're Kendall Mayor?"

"Oh. Yes, hi."

"Heya, Kendall. Super awesome to meet you. I'm Ricardo. *Ricky*." He stuck out his hand, grinning endearingly. Kendall met the handshake.

"I'm one of the other exchange students. Our lift is just outside. It's that way." He pointed easily over his shoulder, like a basketball player who tosses a hoop without looking. His every move seemed very free, very cavalier.

"The lady picking us up has the car ready at the curb, so our chariot awaits. C'mon, follow me!" With a confidence that Kendall wished she possessed, he took hold of her trolley and started to turn it. He wasn't rude, he wasn't a thief, he wasn't being aggressive. Kendall struggled to understand what he was. He was ... sure of himself.

Kendall walked away with the boy.

✗

Ricardo – Ricky – chatted up a storm as he manoeuvred Kendall's trolley through the crowds toward the exit, which was a pity, because Kendall dearly wanted her mind to herself for a moment to take it all in.

He was saying something about meeting the other kids, and how cool orientation week would be, and how he hoped there was a pool, and something about the wobbly wheel on her cart – *not trolley but 'cart'* – as she gawped at the high ceilings of the airport and the light pouring in through windows and skylights. Ahead was a big glass exit, and beyond it, *America*. Really, really America, for the very first time.

"Hey, I love your accent," he said. "Are you, what, like, British or Australian?"

Score one for Addie, who'd said that would happen.

"Oh cool! Damn, my next guess was gonna be New Zealand. That woulda been wrong too. I've lived in a bunch of places. Most people think my accent sounds Mexican. Well, either American or Mexican, but it's really kinda both. You know? Hey, you want a bite of my Snickers? I haven't had any yet, so it's not, like, gross or anything."

He really was an extraordinarily good-looking boy. Kendall would have liked to study his face a little more closely. Perhaps some time when he couldn't see her looking. For now, all she registered was the slightly-too-long black hair, and how rebellious strands of it fell around his eyes and he didn't seem to care. He held out the candy bar.

"Thanks, but I ate on the plane."

"Oh, cool."

The final glass doors were right before them.

"I can't believe I'm really here," she half whispered.

"It's awesome, right? Wait, this is the good bit."

The doors slid open and they pushed the cart out onto the concourse, out into California, out into the United States, out into the real, actual America.

"Feel that?" he said.

The wind hit her face with a chill winter mix of crisp desert air, fresh and sweet, even with gas fumes streaked through it. And the *sounds*. Joyful cacophony. It was all honking horns, revving engines, happy chatter, people calling out for taxis, doors opening and shutting, music from car radios, even the distant thrum of the huge planes taking off and landing somewhere beyond. And massive vehicles.

It was all … *wonderful!*

The boy seemed to be saying something again.

"Hey, you're going right past! It's this one."

"Oh, right. Sorry."

He held open the sliding door to a white van.

"I'll do your bags. You go ahead. Jump on in."

"Hey wait, where are you taking them?" Kendall called, as he wheeled her bags away. *South Africans are not as trusting as Americans,* she thought. Another difference she loved.

"Oh, they brought two vehicles. You and me are in the van. Dianne told me the bags go in the trunk in that one, behind. That's Dianne," he flicked his hair slightly as he pointed to a shadow in the driver's seat.

Trunk, Kendall thought. He said *trunk* instead of boot. It's like *elevator* instead of lift. She smiled and slid into the kombi. Or as he'd said, *van*.

In the driver's seat, a woman whispered the final words of a conversation into her mobile phone. She said, "Confirmed," then hung up without saying goodbye. The first thing Kendall noticed was her posture. For someone just sitting in a car, it was unusually good. Actually, it looked strange. It was kind of stiff, especially compared to the other Americans she'd seen.

The woman turned and slowly regarded Kendall. The look, slightly down the nose, reminded Kendall of times she'd forgotten to do her homework.

She may have been in her thirties. It was hard to tell. She peered from beneath the awning of a baseball cap, from behind oversized glasses, within a high-collared coat pulled up about her ears, despite the warmth of the day. *How long was it going to take her to smile?*

Kendall reminded herself that she'd hoped the person picking her up would be wearing a baseball cap.

From what began as a flat expression, the woman's face gradually emerged into the light of an extremely large smile. The teeth were perfect, almost too white.

"Hi," said Kendall. "I'm very pleased to meet you. I'm Kendall. Kendall Mayor."

The smile remained trained on her for a motionless second. Two seconds. Kendall almost spoke again. Then the woman's movements became animated, as though she suddenly started ticking at the correct speed. "Glad you're hear, babes, you're gonna love it." With that, the upright-postured woman turned and faced the front again. Kendall dropped the hand she had offered. Adjusting the rear-view mirror, looking for the boy, the woman said, "The trip go smoothly? No incidents?"

Like an army officer!

There was not an ounce of fat on her body. Addie had shown Kendall the difference between real boobs and fake boobs, and those ones stuck out a good deal further than nature ever intended. Kendall supposed that was a very American thing too, and reminded herself not to stare.

"Yes, very well, thank you! I should maybe have packed more socks in my onboard luggage, I think mine got a little wet. You know, sweaty, which is kind of gross. But that's okay, and everyone was very friendly, and even the food was quite good, and I'm looking forward to the orientation week. Thank you very much for this opportunity, it really means a lot to me. A lot."

"That's fine, babes, that's just fine."

Wow, Kendall thought, settling back. Somehow she felt taken to task. She wondered if she'd done something wrong.

Ricky arrived and hopped in the back row, scooting up along the bench seat. "Bueno! All packed. Anyone else to collect, or are *we* it?"

"You're it for this trip."

"Cool beans. Let's do this!"

Ricardo grabbed hold of the sliding-door handle. Instead of looking at what he was doing, he maintained smiling eye contact with Kendall, giving the door a theatrical shove beside him, like a circus shouter charming the crowd. The Mercedes was too well damped, and the door failed to slam as dramatically as he'd hoped. Dropping his head, pouting his lip with comical dejection at his own failure, the boy then eased the door all the way shut.

"Ta dah!" he said sardonically, and Kendall giggled into her hand. His smile came and went in an easy dance, and it was a little skew. Boyish and wonky, like Frodo in *The Lord of the Rings*.

Kendall squirmed a little in her seat. He was beautiful.

⚹

The scale of it all quickly became a sensory problem. Kendall filled up and began to suffer stimulus overload well before they arrived at their destination. More and more America kept pouring in through the window, as though scale didn't matter here.

She simultaneously wanted to soak it all up, but also to pull her hoodie over her head, cinch the toggles tight, and hide in a comforting cave of grey fabric in the speeding van.

Endless roadways in what seemed like every direction. And no one single business area. It just went on and on – homes and businesses, homes and businesses – occasionally broken up by a McDonald's or Dunkin' Doughnuts.

Ricky talked up a storm about orientation week, and how he was especially looking forward to International Songs Evening. He spoke to her, he spoke to the window, he spoke to the woman in front, holding court as though the world were his audience.

Eventually, Kendall checked out of the conversation and just stared out the window beside her. Ricardo's voice became a background hum.

Highway after highway, turn off after turn off, the immensity of it all merely grew beneath the clear blue Californian skies. The scenery, initially gorgeous and exciting, became a blur. She felt her brain shutting down.

So she tried to practice something Addie had taught her.

"Don't just look and see a place full of things. Of arbitrary stuff. Try to look and see human intelligence. Systems. Reasons. Specific functionality. Here, check out this photo on my laptop."

"I hope I can save enough for one like yours one day."

"You can have this one in a couple of years. Now look. This is a photo of a harbour. Quite a pretty one. Aesthetics are important. We are spiritual creatures. 'Aesthetics'?"

"Uh, it means, like, appreciation of beauty?"

"Good. Okay, now don't stop there. What human systems do you see? What decisions were made in this scene?"

"All right, let me think. There's a wall, a harbour wall, rather than just no wall, like on a beach. So that means someone built that wall, I suppose to stop the water – the tide – from rising past that point."

"Yes. That isn't incidental. People had to decide to do that, then work out the correct heights and so on. So you're right, that's not just a wall that happens to be there. That's a set of decisions by a

collection of minds, for a purpose. It implies community. Keep going."

"Oh. The boats! Look, they're in lines. They're not just bobbing around arbitrarily out there. That must mean there's some ... some system of rules at play. The boats are, like, parked."

"Yes, that's a system, and they're adhering to it. Don't say 'like'."

"Um ... the roofs of the houses. They're all shaped the same, with pointy tips."

"They are. Why?"

"To look the same?"

"Maybe."

"Or it could be something about the weather. Maybe it rains or snows a lot there, and you can't have flat roofs. Is that right?"

"Probably. Point is, you've got the idea. You went two steps beyond just saying, 'Oo, pretty boats!', which is where most people stop, especially girls, I hate to say it. So, look for underlying intelligence. Don't just flop down the road like a Kit Kat wrapper. Try to notice things around you: systems, decisions, intelligence. There are reasons behind everything, which means there are minds behind everything. The world makes more sense when you start zooming back and asking: What is this, in and of itself?"

Kendall tried to apply the technique to the world flying by outside the window. The trouble was, it was all so ... gigantic. Overwhelmingly huge, nothing like a contained harbour with pretty boats.

Okay, so it's big, she thought. *But that doesn't actually change anything. Give it a label, 'big', and let the label make it more manageable.*

Now start with the obvious. We're on a highway, a highway like I've never seen before in my life. How many, nine lanes? Nine lanes, just going in one direction! Nine the other way, eighteen total. So that means they were built knowing there would be a stupid huge amount of traffic. That's a decision, that's intelligence. Someone built massive highways because there are huge amounts of cars, which means

there's a lot of business and a lot of money. Okay, that's fairly sim-
ple. It's big. But it's simple.

The bustle seemed to shrink a little. Once comprehended, it was just surface shimmer. Just scale. *What else?*

"Check out that truck," Ric said, patting her shoulder. "You got any that big back home?"

Overtaking them, on the wrong side of the road for Kendall's South African sensibilities, was a Ford pickup on a scale that seemed comical. A young guy in a t-shirt drove it with a half-dressed woman beside him.

"That's an F350," Ric said knowingly. "And get this. You can even get a bigger one. It's shaped kinda like that, but it's like the size of a bus."

"Amazing."

The woman, Dianne, flicked an indicator and merged across three lanes – again the wrong way for Kendall. She took an off-ramp onto a smaller road. This one was two lanes wide, but it seemed to follow the base of a hillside, which at least made it more intimate. Instead of feeling like a tiny ant in a vast, open bustle, Kendall felt delightfully cradled by the sandy slopes and cossetting folds of golden shrub grass on one side. In fact, the semi-arid slopes and dry yellow brush looked a lot like Johannesburg in winter. Golden, pleasant. Big, open rolling land too, a bit like the Witwatersrand.

Four men on Harleys overtook them, clattering by like an old rock 'n roll song, weaving up the road ahead, their headscarves flapping. By contrast with their raucous liveliness, Dianne seemed like a mannequin, even as she steered.

A turn off. Another road, this time smaller, but still hugging the undulating hillside.

So read it, Kendall!

Well, if the roads are getting smaller, that means we've left main routes and we're heading into suburbs, right? Basically, the biggest roads come from the airport, and the smallest ones end right in your driveway. Surely something like that.

With a start, Kendall realized that the woman was addressing her.

"Pardon, I didn't quite hear that?"

"Your phone. You have it with you? I'll change the SIM card for you, get it all hooked up to the local networks. And your passport. That's very important. I'll lock that in the safe." She held one palm up over her shoulder.

"Oh, sure thing, thanks."

Kendall dug out her mobile and passport and placed them in the woman's hand.

"That the South African flag?" Ricardo asked, evaluating the pouch as it disappeared into the cubby hole.

"Yeah, it is. The new South African flag. Well, I guess it's like thirty years old now. But we still call it that."

"Very colourful. Muy asombroso."

"Any others?" the woman asked. "Laptop, tablet?"

"No, just that."

"Sure?"

"Uh, yeah."

"Ricardo, yours?"

"Promise not to check my browser history?"

Addie would have replied with something witty like, "You couldn't possibly pay me enough!" Dianne simply said, "Yes."

The boy handed his phone to Kendall, who admired the late model and the Ferrari wallpaper. She would have to make a point of asking him how many kilowatts a Ferrari had. She passed it forward to the icy woman.

They were on a steep ascent now, following switchbacks up a ridge.

As they climbed in height, visibility over the valley below expanded. Kendall yawned and her ears popped. Her throat felt a little sore, like she maybe had a bit of a cold from the flights. Nevertheless, light glinted off a hundred backyard pools down

66

there, mesmerising her, and palm trees marked the thorough-fares. Kendall wondered on which side the sea might be, and how far she was from that famous beach, Santa Monica.

The woman slowed, then turned onto a road that was all red brick. An enormous gate opened automatically before her. It bore Spanish words that split into two parts as they drove through. Kendall peered ahead. The road seemed to run up to some big hotel, set into the hillside. They must be collecting someone else here en route.

Unable to think of anything else to say, Kendall asked, "Is the house nice?", then instantly felt a little rude for phrasing it that way.

"It's gonna blow your mind, babes. Orientation week will be a blast."

Kendall didn't much like the woman's voice. It sounded like playing the wrong notes on a piano. Still, what she was saying sounded good.

They curved around a circular fountain where several stone cherubs blasted water straight into the air to land in a tinkling roar. The woman parked in the motor court and turned off the van's engine.

The suspension shifted as she stepped from the vehicle, Ric following boisterously from behind, while Kendall sat admiring the stonework and awnings on the grand hotel through her win-dow. The piercing California sun hurt her jetlagged eyes, but in exciting ways.

Outside, Ric and the woman stopped. They turned to Ken-dall.

"What's wrong?" Dianne asked.

"Nothing, why? I'll just wait in the van until we go to the house."

"This *is* the house."

Kendall's pupils dilated. "Oh! This isn't a hotel? I thought ... maybe ... we were collecting someone."

67

"No, we're here."

Recalibration. Kendall had been doing a lot of that since Addie taught her the word, and here it was again. This mountain, this monster, this beautiful, gigantic behemoth of stone and glass and wood and angles, was a *house! One single house. How much money did people have?*

Kendall stumbled from the van. She looked back the way they had come.

"So, that wasn't a road," she said.

Ricky laughed. "No, it was a driveway."

Holy cow! she said inwardly.

She turned and looked up, took a step back, tilted her head, then looked even further up.

"It's called El Castillo del Maestro," Dianne said.

"The Master's Castle," Ricardo translated. "Cool. I gotta confess, my house doesn't got a name."

Kendall agreed, "Mine's just number 823."

Ricardo chuckled and nudged her shoulder. It felt nice.

"Is that four stories?" Kendall asked.

"Five. It's recessed. Plus, a canopied entertainment area on the roof, so technically six. Seven if you count the wine cellars beneath. The turrets make it look even higher," Dianne said. She checked her watch, then added, "It's listed at sixty-nine bar."

"Bar?" Kendall said. "Doesn't bar mean ... *million*? Sixty-nine *million*?" If the woman was joking, it didn't show behind her dark glasses.

"That's right."

Ricardo whistled appreciatively as they both traced the building's outlines with admiring eyes. Then he asked, "And is it yours?"

"No, it's yours. For the next few days at least."

Kendall couldn't think of a response and tried not to gawp.

"Let's head in."

Horizons of manicured lawn away, down by the street, El

Castillo del Maestro opened its arms again. The second vehicle slid into the tall embrace of the gates and headed up the long drive toward them.

"They'll take it all straight to your room. Come along."

✳

The house. *This* was the house. Could you even use the word *house* on something that looked like this?

Dianne's heels made a tapping noise crossing the drive, dragging Kendall's attention away from the great monolith hulking against the hillside. Kendall wished she could walk quite that upright, though she wandered if her friends back home might laugh at her if she tried.

She turned her gaze back to the house and counted the garage doors. Six of them? They were bright red with curved arches, like a hobbit hole.

They approached the front entrance – a mangle of pillars, steps, and a recessed, angled door with overhangs. Kendall felt not the sense of getting closer to the building, but of its strange jutting parts growing larger to swallow her. The door itself was twice the height of a normal one, as though giants lived behind it. It was bordered all around by opaque glass, which made it look even grander.

Dianne mounted the steps, then entered a code into a touch-screen security panel. Air whooshed out as the door released.

Ric's tightened lips indicated that he was impressed. Then he showed Kendall 'ladies first' with a hand.

Kendall took a breath. She peered up at the oversized doorframe. She stepped across the threshold and into the house, watching her shadow advancing across the stone ahead of her.

Dianne pulled the tall door shut behind them.

The house pulled a curious trick. Kendall had expected it to open into a massive atrium, but it didn't. They found themselves in a tight passageway, like one of the walkways in an airport, metal and functional. It looked all wrong.

Dianne leaned right into the interior security panel and keyed in a code. Behind them, the cavernous door emitted a *'dzzit'* sound, followed by a convincing *'chunk'*. They were locked in. The thin woman led the way down the tight corridor.

It led to a ninety degree turn, and they followed the woman's clicking heels down the next passageway too. The space felt constricted. There was none of the breathing-out relief you felt at a welcoming home. Dianne said nothing, so neither did they.

Halfway down the tight corridor, a beeping noise began to emit from the walls.

Dianne stopped them. "Ricardo, take off your belt."

"Well, I mean I'm flattered ..."

"This is a metal detector," Dianne indicated upright metal beams against the wall, which Kendall had previously taken to be architecture.

"Huh, like at an airport," Ricardo said. He still had a rucksack with him. Kendall was beginning to feel antsy about not having any of her luggage.

"Take it off and step back through. With your bag."

"Definitely like an airport," Ricardo said. He drew his belt out through the loops of his jeans, accidentally hoisting his t-shirt with the motion, showing Kendall a quick glimpse of stomach muscles. She looked away quickly to spare him the embarrassment. Surely, he hadn't intended to expose himself that way.

He handed the belt to Dianne, took an oversized step backward. Then, glancing left and right at the apparatus, marched forward again with his rucksack. No beep. "Guess that was it," he said, and accepted his belt back.

"Kendall, will you do it too, please?"

"Okay."

Kendall took a few steps back, then re-joined the group. No beeping. Dianne seemed satisfied.

Ricardo was casually stuffing his belt back through his pants loops as they rounded the next corner. A sliver of his stomach was still showing, but he seemed not to notice.

A few strides later, the odd tunnel did, in fact, open into an atrium, and it was vast. Not only was it vast, but it was confusing to look at, with many layers and corridors, all jutting out at odd angles in a postmodernist visual cacophony, each element competing for dominance.

Kendall blinked. Her eyes couldn't find a blank wall or a simple space on which to rest.

Before she'd even tried to make sense of the architecture, untangling columns from balustrades, corridors from unevenly spaced and winding stairs, she noticed that the blinds were all drawn. The place was well lit within, though that fact was kind of weird too, in the middle of the day. And she couldn't actually *see* any of the lights – they were all tucked behind recesses and seemed to simply ... glow outward. The effect was beautiful. Yet false. It seemed unhealthy, even sickly, this early in the day.

It didn't seem to bother Ricky. "Wow! Damn, this place is bangin'! Check out the ... like ... waterfall thing! And dude, seriously! Is that an elevator? In a house?!"

"It is," Dianne responded.

"It's quite something," Kendall said politely. "Which way do we go?"

"That way leads to one of the main living areas. The other kids are there. But you should go up to the second floor first. Choose your rooms. Rooms for the young men are marked with a blue sticker on the door, the young women with pink. They'll bring your things up in a minute or so."

Pink again. Even at seventeen, there was no escaping pink.

The woman turned and headed back for the exit, and for a moment, neither Kendall nor Ricardo knew quite what to say.

"Excuse me, but, are you coming with us?" Kendall asked.

"No. Back to the airport," Dianne said over her shoulder, her voice echoing in the atrium. "Picking up the last three ... young people."

Standing in the echoing atrium, Kendall felt dumped. Scraped into a bin like bad food. Ricardo also seemed unsure of what to do.

The woman stopped and turned. "Ricardo, I know you just got here, but would you care to help me with the next airport collection too?"

"Oh," said Ricky, surprise in his eyes, before he glanced at Kendall, then back to Dianne. "Uh, sure. Hey Kendall, would you mind chucking my bag in one of the guys' rooms?"

"I ... okay." Kendall said. He pushed the heavy rucksack into her arms.

The woman was back on her phone, speaking at a whisper. Ricardo walked at a clip to catch up with her. The two disappeared from Kendall's sight.

Kendall remained planted, holding Ricardo's chunky rucksack. It had a musky guy smell.

She searched again for the mental peace of a single uncomplicated space. Everything was angles and outcrops, radial lines, poles and interplay. Her gaze moved from the plinth with the eagle to the plinth with the weeping angel. She looked at the elevators. Back toward the corridor. She tried to apply Addie's system for seeing intelligent decisions rather than just stuff, but there were *too many* decisions here, and none in any sort of harmony, as though disorder were the point, and she was too tired. The mental framework collapsed beneath her.

She felt hot tears coming.

She had reached the end of her trip, yet this felt all wrong. After long, meaningful hugs and tearful kisses at the airport, after being sent off by her parents like a conquering hero on a mission, then traveling halfway around the world and finally making it, she felt less like a brave explorer and more like a letter dropped through the slot of an absentee lodger, lying in the dust, waiting for no one.

For all this opulence, she felt uncared for.

Was that ungrateful? It probably was.

She hoisted Ricardo's bag with her left hand, touched instinctively at the small cross on her neck with the right.

Come on, Kendall!

She forced herself to move. Passing by the water feature, she now faintly detected the voices of other kids – perhaps lots of them – babbling somewhere down a corridor that honeycombed out to the right. She didn't have it in her to face hordes of newcomers just yet. A moment to herself in a quiet room might be nice; a second or two to gather her thoughts.

She padded toward the elevator, the awkward sound of her rubber sneaker soles squawking poorly on the rich stone floor, telling the world here came a beggar to the palace.

*

THE SONGS OF YOUR PEOPLE

"This is song from Poland. Where I come from. In English you say its name, 'In My Garden'."

The girl was Kendall's age, or thereabouts. She was pale with ruddy cheeks, as though she'd been freshly slapped, and her blue eyes looked like soft ice rather than deep water. She had dressed up for the International Songs Evening with what Kendall thought was an extremely pretty traditional dress. The white cotton appeared crisp and innocent, and somehow made Kendall feel good about life. It was tightly cinched in a corset, and the corset itself was an explosion of colour, bejewelled with glittering red and gold beads and twitching green tassels. The girl's hair was braided on either side with red ribbons at the ends, and she topped it off with an Alice band of flowers. Kendall could tell from her face that she felt radiant wearing it before them.

She was not the only one in costume. The freckled girl from Turkey wore a traditional outfit too.

None of the kids in the circle around the room poked fun. Kendall thought this very mature, very *cosmopolitan*, of her fellows. Clearly the sort of kids who went on exchange programs were just that bit more sophisticated.

They sat in the largest lounge they had located so far, on one of the mezzanine levels, empty pizza boxes piled on gleaming counters all around them, the lights pleasantly dimmed. This room, at least, was carpeted, even if it couldn't quite be described as homely. Their noise lent it a lively teenage feel, dispelling the cold modernity of the house.

Kendall took in the chattering, the singing, the lovely, messy *humanity* of it all. Yes, their presence really did transform this expensive heap of metal and marble back into the familiar and firelit cave of the tribe. Addie might have had something to say about how evenings like this were woven into the DNA of our species, right back through time.

The Polish girl's English was stilted, but she didn't let it slow her down. "The words to this song, it say, 'When I was young, I was like a berry in the forest, still growing. And that is when you found me ...'" the girl blushed slightly, "'my lover.'"

Tittering around the room. But just the right amount, not enough to earn Kendall's disappointment. They were a mature gathering after all, each here in representation of their country.

In the dimmed light, in the centre of the circle, the girl now began to sing, softly at first, then louder and faster. The song picked up and flowered into something enchanting – a quick-paced folkdance with a curiously attractive lilt. The group started to clap, and some of the girls in the circle swayed side to side where they sat with their legs crossed. The tempo of the song increased still further, sounding to Kendall like people in far-away northern lands spinning in circles in the snow. For a girl from sweaty Africa, that was more than a little exotic.

When the Polish girl finished and sat back down between a girl and a boy, there was a moment's silence. For a horrified instant, Kendall thought everyone was being rude. Then they snapped out of the trance and applauded uproariously. Kendall approved and joined in. *Very mature. Well done everyone.*

Next in line was a boy. Now that she thought about it, there seemed to be a lot more girls than boys, maybe about two to one.

"Hi all, I'm Tom. I'm from Athenry, in Ireland."

Kendall instantly adored the accent. Some of the kids said, "Hey," or "Hiya."

"That's A-T-H-E-N-R-Y, but I'm Irish, so we don't pronounce our TH's. They come out as T's. Atenry. Like, one, two, tree."

Laughter from the group.

"So, we hold the dubious record of getting the most rain in the rainiest place on earth."

He spoke for a minute about his home, ancient stone churches covered in moss, rocky beaches bathed in perpetual mist, and it took Kendall far away. Then he rolled up the sleeves of his jersey and did a decent job of a melancholic Irish number. It was about an old man who wished he was in some place called Carrickfergus, and it was fantastically sad. Kendall's favourite line was, 'For I'm drunk today, and I'm seldom sober.' It was such a strange thing to sing with such heartfelt yearning.

When the song ended, the boy said, "I'm looking forward to the week here wit you lot. Should be a right hoot!"

That earned another appropriate chuckle from the group. As he was sitting down, one of the girls Kendall might have described as a 'clunky, obvious type,' asked him what a hoot was, and the boy said, "You know, a riot." This didn't appear to clear things up for her.

The smell of pizza was strong, and now someone was handing around a three-litre bottle of Mountain Dew.

Soon it was Kendall's turn. Her heart thudded as she rose. She began to check that her uniform was tucked in, then caught herself. Old habits.

"Hi everyone. My name is Kendall Mayor. I'm from South Africa."

One of the girls beside her stifled a laugh. Kendall wasn't sure why. Maybe her accent? *Addie always said we sounded guttural to foreigners.* She tried not to let it throw her.

"Uh ... we have quite a lot of different traditional songs and cultures in my country. I can't sing in Zulu or anything, so my song is in Afrikaans. Afrikaans started from Dutch and Flemish, but it became its own language over a few hundred years in Africa, especially among the farming community. Our farmers are called 'boers'."

Some of the kids tried out the word.

"It's a bit of a sad song – sorry, I know the last one was too, so that's two in a row – but the way this one is sung, it sounds almost like a nursery rhyme. It's about drought on a farm in a dry part of South Africa, maybe somewhere like the Karoo desert, and a young girl watching her uncle struggle to survive."

There were no objections. No further comments. Just what looked like genuine interest.

"It's called Mannetjies Roux."

As Kendall began to sing, she worried that she should have chosen an upbeat number. What if the giggling girl just kept laughing at her?

But as the song progressed and she gained confidence, the sweet melancholy worked its magic and sounded good even to her own ear. Kendall was amazed to find she held the room rapt. By her own estimation, she was a decent singer, if not a brilliant one.

At the end of each verse, she paused to translate into English. "'And if, in the morning, you walk in the lands, you'll still hear his engine, with its clap, clap, clap. But my uncle's eyes are now forever closed. In his letter he sends greetings to Mannetjies Roux.' Thank you."

Kendall took her seat, gratified by what she thought was very generous applause. The Polish girl smiled and touched her shoulder. "Very sad song. Very pretty to me."

Kendall loved her accent. It was all harsh, male, marching noises, yet it was rendered elegant in the mouth of a girl. With an accent like that, she could play the femme fatale in a Bond movie one day.

Next it was Ricardo's turn, and the swarthy boy hammed it up from the start. He began his tour by waiting a second too long to rise. When everyone fell silent, looking at him expectantly, he pointed to his own chest and mouthed, "What, me?"

"*You*! Go!" the room erupted. The handsome boy stood up and bowed with a flourish. Around the room, pairs of girls whispered quickly to one another. Seated beside the Polish girl, Kendall shook her head and laughed at Ric's incorrigible performance. It already felt like they were old friends.

"All right, hey all, I'm Ricardo. Ricardo Alverez. I'm from a few places, really, so I guess I can just go ahead and pick. I'm gonna do a lounge-lizard classic. It's by this old guy called Billy Joel. This song is called 'Piano Man'."

Two or three approving voices whispered, "Yes!" The rest of the room looked blank. Kendall was proud that she was one of the few who knew the song, quite well actually. It was one of her Dad's favourites and occasionally played on a small CD player in his garage.

Ricardo whipped out a pair of dark glasses, slid them on to giggles from the girls, and began by imitating the playing of a piano mid air. Cool as ice and self-assured, he ran his finger over imaginary ivory and made the sounds. "Toodeloo-toodeloo-dooo." Then he crooned into a pretend handheld microphone, "It's niiine o'clock on a Saturday ..."

Kendall marvelled at the confidence it must take to do something that silly that smoothly. And in front of some thirty plus strangers. He was good, though. Not so much his singing voice, but his demeanour, his showmanship.

His imitation of a world-weary bar musician, talented but going nowhere and revelling gloriously in a failed, poetically tragic life, was bang on. It occurred to her that a lot of the songs this evening had featured a tragic melancholy. Everyone seemed to love it. It made the group happy, not sad.

With the sweep of his head, which he cast right back with his eyes closed, Ricardo even managed to look tipsy-but-not-yet-drunk.

Kendall dearly wished she could film this performance. She still didn't have her phone back and wondered if anyone else had theirs. Looking around the room, no one seemed to be texting or taking shots. It was so unusual among a bunch of teens that it looked strange. And another thing, there were no adults here. None. Dianne had dropped off pizzas along with the three final kids, but then it seemed she had just left.

Ricardo moved around the inside of the circle, flamboyantly recounting the travails of a real-estate novelist, and of Davy, still in the navy – and he even pointed directly at some of the girls as he sang, drawing more giggles and quick confidences behind cupped hands.

Kendall noticed that he kept working his way back to one place, a specific spot on the floor. Each time he did, he seemed to sink down into something like an Elvis position, ducking his head a little. Almost like he was trying to see something.

Kendall frowned. She followed his line of sight.

Oh.

On the far side, sitting cross-legged, were two girls. One wore jeans. The other, an attractive red-headed girl, also from Ireland, wore short-shorts. They'd ridden up. Though the girl apparently wasn't aware of it, the white of her inner thigh and her panties were showing. Worse, you could just make out the outer curve of her privates, framed by downy fluff. Ricardo was trying to peek, even as he sang.

Kendall flushed and looked down, embarrassed or cross, she wasn't sure which. She looked back at him, saw that he was still trying, even as he segued into the fourth stanza.

Had anyone else noticed? Kendall didn't want to draw attention; it might cause the red-head more embarrassment. *Thank goodness there were so many more girls than boys. And that everyone was fixated on Ric.*

Although, there *was* one boy ... he seemed to be aware. He wasn't looking at the Irish girl. He wasn't looking at Ricky either. He quietly observed Kendall, noticing her expression. A scrap of a blond in a soft blue sweater, he seemed to be the only one not rapt by the performance. He sat with his legs crossed and appeared to read Kendall. His hair was neatly combed, his gaze was gentle and contained, quite unlike Ricky's confrontational splash.

The blond boy did what Kendall had done with Ricardo, and followed her line of sight. His face opened a little with understanding as he spotted the girl with the wardrobe malfunction.

Kendall waited for the *boy-glee*. None came. Instead, he quietly stood. He passed around the back of the circle, took off his blue sweater, and, without a word, lowered it over the Irish girl's lap.

Barely anyone noticed. The girl started, confused. As realisation dawned, she tried not to look embarrassed. Her eyes darted about the room, seeking any who might be staring. Once she felt she was all clear, she smoothed the fabric out over her knees, then wiggled her butt around on the floor as she straightened the shorts.

Ricardo, now wrapping up the final chorus, simply turned and sang in the opposite direction, like he hadn't just been caught out. He was smooth, Kendall had to grant him that.

The blond boy made nothing of it. He returned to his spot, folded his hands in his lap, and showed nothing but cordial interest in the rest of the song. He never made eye contact with Kendall. Kendall smiled to herself.

There are *still true gentlemen in the world. Not everyone was a showman.*

She thought that she must make a point of befriending the conscientious boy with the lovely manners.

✗

Songs Evening morphed into Ghost Stories Evening. Despite the cold, it took place up on the roof terrace, where the outside air was nippy.

Addie loved ghost stories. Consequently, Kendall did too. And telling them way up on the roof of a Californian mansion in the winter night air struck her as beyond cool.

If you went close enough to the balcony, the view straight down induced vertigo. But looking out over the valley, Kendall discovered, what you saw defied belief. She wished her parents could see all this, the undulating sea of lights in the county below, the fast-moving streaks of night-time Cirrus way above. There were even occasional fly-bys from some large white birds; Kendall thought they might be seagulls, buzzing the balcony and scanning for snacks.

Some places, far off in the distant view, were disappearing beneath an approaching layer of coastal mist, though Kendall found she couldn't make out the ocean from here.

The gigantic house appeared to be made right into the side of a long chain of mountain. On one side, there was the driveway veering and stretching all the way down a steep hill to the front gate and then the switchback roads below. On the other side, almost sheer rockface.

The house was not really flush with the rock face; it just seemed that way from up here. If you gazed down the other side, there was actually a large backyard and sprawling pool tucked in the crook between house and rock. It seemed to be cordoned off on all sides by folds of rocky mountainside.

From here, she couldn't see any neighbors either way. Perhaps they were there, around the outcrop of the mountain ridge, tucked beyond view. Perhaps not.

Kendall was tired now – desperately tired – but the idea of listening to scary stories under the stars gave her a delicious thrill. She figured she would take in two or three, just enough to make her guts clench in that pleasant way that they do on a rollercoaster, then she would retreat to her bedroom. She wasn't especially worried about having nightmares tonight. She'd be too zonked for that.

Even up here on the roof, there was a pool: long, thin, oblong, lit from within. Not to be confused with the infinity pool below, shimmering with light on the next level down. This one was heated and gave off steam, along with a pleasant ozone smell. Nevertheless, it was currently unoccupied. No one was quite that brave yet.

The circle of kids was smaller now: some fourteen seated on an eclectic assortment of cushion-chairs the size of cars, and smaller, moveable box-seats that looked like Zulu drums. Two of the boys perched on the edge of a fire pit.

"Okay, here's one that happened to my sister, Yui," said a Japanese girl. Beneath her dark, hanging fringe, she looked mischievous and excited about the tale. "We live in Osaka, which is a big city. Not Tokyo-big, but big. And always very busy, day or night. One night my sister is coming home from work as a freeter."

"What's a freeter?" from one of the boys.

"That's almost like ... I guess, like an intern who's trying to find the kind of work they love. They work for free. Freeter."

"Cool."

"So, one night she gets off the train. Not really paying attention, she's mostly just on her phone. There are hundreds of people all around. My sister tells the story this way: she says you don't notice hundreds of people when they're all moving. But when one person is standing still in the middle of a hundred moving people, *that* person you see. So, she looks up from her phone and there's a woman, just one woman, standing there in the centre of the street. The woman is still, like she's frozen, and she's wearing a mask. The masked face is looking straight at my sister."

"Awesome," Kendall mumbled, already thinking of that throaty noise from her favourite Japanese horror movie and inspecting her arm for goosebumps.

"My sister's nervous, of course, so she pockets her phone

and speeds up a little. She turns the corner and ...?" The girl paused with a smile. Two or three kids volunteered, "There she was again."

A knowing nod. "There she was again! This lone woman. Just standing there. Middle of the crowd. Unmoving. Staring right at her through the mask. Now my sister's really terrified. She's wondering if maybe she's being chased. Or herded. So she starts to run. Down one street, through an alley, out into a public square – zig-zagging all over – and there are still lots of people everywhere. The way she's panicking, though, she eventually runs – bam! – straight into a complete stranger and falls to the ground, a little winded. The stranger leans down and takes my sister's hand to help her up. That's when my sister looks up to see who it is ..."

From beside Kendall, a black boy named Kweku leaned in and whispered, "Am I pretty?"

"Huh?" Kendall said.

"Watch this ..." (He had a British accent, and it sounded like 'wotch dis'). "The woman in the crowd. She's gonna say, 'Am I pretty?'"

Kweku was chubby, but carried his weight well. He wore a windbreaker for the cold, but his legs were in shorts.

"And that's when my sister realizes that the person holding her hand, now actually grabbing her arm tightly, digging into her skin and not letting go, is the woman in the mask. And the woman leans right up into her face. She asks, 'Am I pretty?'"

"Wot'd I tell you?" Kweku looked satisfied.

"My sister doesn't know what to say. So she says, 'Yes, you're pretty!' Then the woman takes off her mask and her mouth has been slit from ear to ear. Her lower face is just a mangled wound. She leans right into my sister's face and with blood on her breath, she asks, 'And *now*?'"

The girl leaned back and allowed the climax to take its effect.

A well-timed breeze flapped the fringes of a nearby canopy, and a couple of the kids jumped, then chuckled at one another.

Kendall leaned up against Kweku's shoulder. "You nailed it," she whispered, which made him smile.

Kweku offered her a fist bump. "It's, like, a Japanese urban legend. I heard it before in England, from one o' me mates."

"All right, I got one. True story." It was Ricky. He leaned forward, then brushed his hair back in one fluid movement.

"I got a little brother, right? He's five now, but he'd just turned four when this happened. Still small. So, my Mom and Dad take us to this resort town, right near the beach. This is in Colombia. *Stunning* place. And I meet this Colombian girl, right? Mariana. And she is mighty fine, like ba-boom!"

Yes, Kendall thought, *you had to add that.* The chill night breeze was starting to make the spots above her cheekbones numb. Her neck hurt a little too, both from trying to sleep on the flights, and from the cold mountain air.

"So, on the first day we're there, my folks go out to a restaurant. Special evening for them. I'm supposed to look after the squirt. *Whatever.* But I can have a visitor, so Mariana comes round, and there we are, we're like, deep in it on the couch, making out big time. Then my little bro walks in."

Kendall observed the smiles around the group again.

"He taps me and goes, 'A man was talking to me. He was very rude.' *Mood killer.* And first I think he's joking or confused or something, and I brush him off. Like, get out o' here, little dude! But he keeps standing there with these big eyes, and his arms are just hanging by his sides, like hanging limp. He's looking at us like some Stephen King kid, and Mariana says, 'It's creepy, tell him to go away.'

"So I ask my bro what he means. I just wanna get back down to business, but he says it again, and sometimes you can tell with little kids. It looks like he *really means* it. He says a man was talking with him, so he told the man, 'Hello, my name is

Jorge Alverez.' That's my brother's name. But then he says the man was rude to him. The man was rude, and went away.

"Now Mariana's getting scared. She goes, 'Like, aren't we alone here? Who was he talking to?' and then she says, 'Maybe you should go see what he means.' I ask my bro, 'Where was this?' And we nearly die when he goes: 'In my room.'"

The circle of kids on the roof smiled, leaned in.

"Total chills, right? So, the hotel we're in is nice, but there are some weird parts. Like there are these Alice-in-Wonderland doors in the bedrooms that lead into totally pointless spaces. Not a room, not a cupboard. Just like a hole, under a slope from the ceiling. And there are weird skylights with waving trees above, and our whole apartment is one long, twisting corridor. And now, not only is there some strange guy talking to my bro, but apparently, the guy is right there! In his room!"

The fringes on the canopy flapped again. The wind was picking up. Everyone huddled a little further into their jackets and blankets.

Kendall watched as one of the boys took out a cigarette, lit it, sucked in, and blew out smoke. She could smell it from here. He offered the packet to two of the girls nearby. One said no, the other accepted, and soon there were two red cherries floating in the night.

"I'm properly freaked out now. Mariana is too. Not to sound like a wimp or nothing, but I decide it might be best if we go check it out, like, *together*."

"Wiiimp!" one of the girls mock yelled.

"Yeah yeah! So we get up, Mariana straightens out her clothes ..."

And he had to add that detail too, Kendall thought.

Kweku whispered to her, "Bro, we get it. You's a luv stud." Kendall giggled. Kweku lay back on the tiles, his arms cupped behind his head.

"Our hearts are thumping! We walk down the corridor to

his little room, which is right at the far end. The door's half closed. I push it. My bro walks in. Inside, one of those weird Alice-in-Wonderland doors is wide open. I see it, and now I'm genuinely crapping myself! Like, am I going to have to climb in there, is someone gonna jump out at me?

"But my brother ignores it. He walks right past it and picks up the phone next to his bed and dials the hotel reception again. Then he hands me the receiver."

It took the group a moment. Then the laughter went on so long that the smoker had a slight coughing fit.

Inevitably, one of the out-to-lunch girls said, "I don't get it."

Eventually, with a cough here and there, the laughter died off and silence fell again. The smoker took a drag and blew out elaborately. Everyone looked around in expectation at who might go next.

Kweku rose up onto one elbow, gathering the attention of the group.

From beside Kendall, he said in his cockney accent, "Well, I can't top that for laughs. ('That' sounded like 'vat'.) But I fink I got one. A true one, from my ancestral home."

Kendall found it strange and delightful to hear a black kid sounding like a British TV show. And the term 'ancestral home' somehow added resonance. *Gravitas.*

"I grew up in London, yeah? But me family's from Ghana. That's West Africa. I can hardly remember it, but back when we lived there, we used to have a family farm. Sheep and goats, yeah? So, there's two types of goat farming in Ghana. There's the small-scale kind that tribes have been doing since forever, then the large-scale, organized kind. We had that. Sounds cringey to say it, but we were what you might call well off, least by Ghanaian standards. Which is … well, nuffing like …" He indicated the balcony and house around them.

"So, there's a reason you should have goats *and* sheep together, and the reason is, you can use one to fool the uva. See, goats are slippery sods. Like, properly evil when they want to be. There's a reason they's always linked with witchcraft and Satanism and suchlike. So, when it's slaughter time, what you do, you select one goat." He tapped the side of his head. "A clever one, see? He's got a special job. You use that goat to lead the sheep into the slaughter house. That one, he's called the Judas Goat."

"Seriously?"

"For real. His job, his only purpose in the universe, is to be a traitor. So, the Judas Goat leads the sheep right up the ramp to the slaughterhouse. And they follow him, right? Because he's confident, and they're scared. At the last second, the Judas Goat slips off down anuva ramp, a different one, just for him. But the farmer closes that gate to the sheep, and the sheep all go on, direct to their deaths."

"Cool!" said one of the boys down low.

"Harsh," said a girl, smiling with grim excitement.

"So one day – true story, yeah? It's nearly time for the slaughtering of the sheep, and our Judas Goat starts screaming in the middle of the night, but properly letting rip, right? Like someone's tearing off his limbs, or he's just seen Judgement Day coming or sumfing. All around it's chaos. Lights go on, people running, the whole compound can hear it, including the hired staff, and there's lots. At first, they can't find him. No one can. But eventually, they do."

"He was in the slaughter house?" the boy with the cigarette ventured.

"Oh no. He's in the sheep pen. He's inside this sort of shed, like a barn. How he got himself in there, no one can figure – if you seen how the farm's laid out, it's nothing short of impossible. But there he is. Or rather, what's left of 'im. He's been trampled to within an inch of his life. Even one of his eyes has come out, though it's still connected, by the nerve. Like, it's lying on the dirt and straw."

"Ew!"

"So, the goat makes these last gargling noises – if you heard one, they can sound eerily like a human. Then he dies in front of everyone, right there on the dust. Properly dead. Weird part was, there was no sheep. And now that everyone's attention is off the dying goat, they finally realize it. They go: 'What's happened to the sheep?' There's not one in the pen, nuffing in the shed, and when everyone panics and starts looking everywhere, no sheep in the entire farm. My parents call our neighbors and *their* neighbors. Bugger all! Just gone. The lot of them."

Kendall studied the faces around the rooftop. To a kid, they were riveted.

"So, me old man's properly gutted. And a year goes by. A whole year, yeah? My folks is just recovering from the financial loss. They've replaced all the sheep. They've even got a new Judas Goat. And the time comes around again. Slaughter time.

"Middle of the night, the goat starts screaming. New goat. Same screaming. Same time of the night – me mum even checked."

One of the kids smiled, "Holy shit."

"This time, though, everyone's on edge, ready for issues, see? The staff's been trained not to go straight to the goat. My old man told them: 'Anything funny happens, secure the perimeter first. We can't afford a second year of escaping sheep.' And the sheep *were* there, at the perimeter. They were trying to get out of the farm, bashing against railings, biting at fences, falling over each other, you should see these things, eyes wide, going properly batshit. But wif a fight, the guys manage to keep them in.

"So now the whole staff is occupied with the sheep. My dad gets this thought. *He* goes to check on the goat. Just him."

"Did he find it?"

"Oh, he finds it! Same place. Same *exact* place. My old man says he stands there watching as nothing, literally *nothing*, stamps the goat to death. Right there in front of his eyes. The goat is like, crumpling. Limbs forced in and down, neck broken, he's being pounded by something, but there's bugger all there. My dad tries to get to him, but that same something – that same *nothing* – pushes him back, and he falls flat on his ass. All he can do is watch. And whatever was in that barn taking vengeance on the goat just kept going, stomping, pounding, mauling it to death.

"No one else saw it. No one can prove anyfing. But my old man's temples turn properly grey that night, an' he's not an old man back then. Turned grey so quick and so complete that no one on the farm questioned his story. And that was the last time. The last time we ever used a Judas Goat."

A frozen silence ensued. One of the wide-eyed girls prompted, "What ... *was* it?"

Kweku smiled darkly at the moon and the stars. "Best we can figure?"

"Yeah."

"The ancestors can't abide a traitor."

*

All too soon, jetlag took its tremendous effect. Like a heavy parasite, it sucked thickly on Kendall's brain, demanding unconditional surrender.

She barely stumbled back down to her room, eyes swollen with weight but full of stars.

Two other girls shared the room – the one from Poland with the pretty dress, and a New Zealander. The arrangement wasn't so bad. There was plenty of space, an en suite bathroom the size of a swimming pool, and the beds were far apart, so it was nothing like camping or the horror of veldt-school.

Kendall undid her ponytail and ran her fingers over her scalp, massaging a fatigue headache.

The New Zealand girl stepped barefoot from the steamy

bathroom, towelling herself off and humming a traditional Hawaiian ballad from their Songs Evening, occasionally throwing in the words she could remember. Her name was Britney. She wrapped her hair in a smaller towel and said, "Anyone else fancy a shower? I moved all my kit out the way." *The Kiwi accent sounded a lot like the Australian one,* Kendall thought, *but a little flatter, more staccato.*

And it's nothing like ours!

The Polish girl said, "This house amazing. It taked me ten minute just to understand how to start shower."

"I know, right?" said Britney. "Like, what the heck are all those buttons?"

"In my home, is 'hot' or 'cold.'" The Polish girl showed two hands reaching straight out before her, turning taps.

"Yeah, mine too. This one's like some futuristic spaceship show."

Despite her fatigue, a shower did sound wonderful. Kendall was surprised to realize that she hadn't thought of it earlier.

Britney turned and dropped her towel to dress. Kendall wished she had that sort of confidence. Owning boobs as full as that must certainly help. Was *everyone* just bigger than her in that department?

"I shower in morning," the Polish girl said, falling dramatically back onto her pillow, feigning a swooning princess pose. "For now, I just dream about Ricky!"

The girls snickered. Britney said, "Honestly, I wouldn't even care if his little brother walked in on us!"

This brought a new energy to the room. The girls compared notes about Ricky, and it soon broadened out into a conversation about boys in general. Britney had gone the furthest with a boy, and therefore became the *de facto* conversation leader. Kendall enjoyed the connection with her fellow females, but she struggled mightily to keep her eyes open.

The Polish girl spotted the silver cross around Kendall's

neck. "I like you cross. My country in Poland very Christian too. Tell me what is like in South Africa?"

Kendall made a face that tried to express her ambivalence. "The parts God made are stunning. We say it would be perfect if it wasn't run by thieves."

"Ha! In Poland we know that too! Corruption! Though is much better now. *Much* better. My grandfather live in Communism before. He say is very scary."

"Hey, did you guys get your phones back?" Britney asked.

"No," said Kendall. "I was just thinking about that. For about the hundredth time."

"Me too no," said the Polish girl, sitting back up. Kendall still couldn't pronounce her name. It was something like *Agniska*.

"That's weird! I mean, they told me they've let my parents in Auckland know I arrived. Like, thanks, that's cool and all. But I want to talk to them on Skype. And I want to post photos of this crazy house on Instagram, and I want to get some shots of, like, all of us together, my roomies. I couldn't even film any of the Songs Evening."

"Yeah, me too."

"Me too."

"When *did* they say we'd get them back? I don't think that woman, that *Dianne* chick, even said. I thought we'd have them by now."

No one had an answer.

Kendall added, "And also, where *is* she? Where are any of the adults?"

Britney agreed, "I know, right?! Like, it's not just me. It is weird to leave a house full of teenagers alone. We *are* alone, aren't we? My parents would never allow this. They'd crap themselves."

"My parents too," the Polish girl said.

Kendall knew that by now her folks were probably anxious. No, that wasn't even close. Her family lived on the shoreline of constant crisis, always wondering which tsunami might take them out. The housebreaking, and the death of little Dobby, had only made things worse. They would be well beyond merely anxious by now, and it made Kendall feel terribly guilty.

Dobby ... The image of his little Jack Russell face rose in her mind and she tried not to entertain it. If she thought about him now, she would just cry.

But what to do about the phone? She could picture her Mom and Dad, the tense silence in the kitchen beneath that single yellow light, the way her father's fingers tapped the tabletop, then rubbed dryly together, then tapped, waiting to know if their youngest girl was safe. There was just nothing she could do about it. It made the pizza and Mountain Dew in her stomach lurch.

"Maybe I *will* have that shower," Kendall told the girls.

She pulled the larger of her two bags toward her and flipped open the latches. Then she paused.

Where was the lock? Had she removed it earlier?

Maybe. Okay, but then, where was it? She glanced around the nightstand, ran a finger over the bedspread. She bent down and examined the floor beneath her bed.

And the smaller bag?

Same story. No lock.

Were they on when I left the airport? She couldn't quite remember. *Maybe the airport security removed them to check for something? Did they do that? Were they allowed to?*

Concentration proved difficult. Black vortexes of slumber pulled at her mind. She lay back on the bed to ponder the mystery of the locks for a moment. Just for a moment. Then she would shower.

Three minutes later, the girl from New Zealand – last man standing – snickered quietly about the snoring. She did the rounds in the room, pulling a cover over the Polish girl, then another over Kendall, then went to turn off the lights.

✳

Screaming goats. Kendall's overtired, delirious mind went straight to screaming goats. She dreamed of living things being stomped to death by nothing, nothing at all. She also dreamed of slit-faced women, mean-voiced and intrusive, demanding to know: "Am I pretty?!"

Most of all, she dreamed of an Escher house with impossible staircases. Its corridors twisted back upon themselves, walkways led to nowhere, and shadowed archways started on the floor but ended on the ceiling, taking you anywhere you wanted, cunningly taking you nowhere at all. A house designed to be an endless trap.

From unseen corridors, the screaming of the goat.

MONDAY MORNING

The light pried at her eyelids, trying to rouse her. She resisted. She fought to remain beneath the surface.

Even as she did, her ankles sparked with flashes of intense pain. Kendall clenched her teeth and groaned into the plump duvet.

For a time, her jetlagged mind tried to incorporate the ache in her ankles into a hallucinatory storyline and she dreamed that Ricardo was gripping her there, gripping both ankles, clutching them spitefully tight, refusing to let go. He wanted to see her panties while she sang for him. He wanted to look at her privates, and a part of her sort of wanted him to, but also desperately didn't, not like that, not so embarrassing, not while he was smiling with such slit-mouthed malice.

Then the cloud of sleep dissolved. Yet the pain remained.

Kendall blinked twice, then raised the bedspread. She peered straight down the length of her own body under the covers. She discovered the source of the problem. She had passed out with her shoes on – was, in fact, still fully dressed – and the concrete weight of the sneakers held fast by the duvet dragged her ankles into awkward angles, cutting off circulation. The pain was remarkable. She must not have changed positions all night.

Her bladder ached too, come to think of it. So did her face, all around her nose and eyes. That was weird.

She blinked at the denim of her jeans beneath the sheet, trying to remember whether she had been wearing her jeans for two days now or three.

Gross. She might have to peel them off.

Then the blanket near her feet moved. A frisson of cold ran down her scalp as she realized someone was sitting on her bed. She thought instantly of slit-faced women behind masks: *Am I pretty?*

Kendall looked over the covers.

Perfect posture. Blank face. A mask of indifference. *Dianne.*

"You didn't shower last night," she said.

"Oh," Kendall attempted a goofy smile. "I guess I was so tired I just ... you know ... pfff!"

"You should have a shower. It's good after travel." She weighed Kendall up. "Have one now."

"Okay."

"Make sure you do it now."

Kendall felt like a little girl who'd been chastised for piddling her pants. She wanted to say, "Geez, all right!", but a lifetime of drilling in good manners restrained her. She also wanted to ask about her phone, but the strange awakening and the brusque command threw her, and by the time she thought of it, Dianne was leaving the room, stepping elegantly in that perfectly upright mannequin walk.

Kendall looked about her.

What's the big deal about showers? I mean, I get it. People have to keep clean, obviously – I'm not disgusting. But she made it sound all significant.

When she was seven, she'd spent a night at a friend's house, a friend she didn't really see anymore. Not on purpose, anyway. They had had a bath together. Behind the closed door, in the watery privacy, the other girl showed her a secret. If you filled an empty bottle with water, you could hold it beneath the surface and squeeze it out between your legs. The spurt of water ejecting from the bottle felt nice down there. Tickly and nice.

The experiment commenced with whispered excitement as they each tried it on themselves. Then the friend suggested they try it on each other. That felt nice too, in a funny way. But after a while, Kendall wanted it to stop, because it wasn't fun anymore. That was when her friend had changed, changed so completely that Kendall never forgot it.

"If you don't keep doing it, I'll tell everyone! I'll tell your Mom and I'll tell all your friends, and no one will ever talk to you anymore! No one will ever be your friend ever again!"

Kendall had said *Okay, okay,* and she went along with it for a few more minutes, bullied by the ugliness in the girl's eyes. But the whole thing had gone from exciting to yucky.

This felt similar. Insistent. Forceful. Ugly.

Kendall focused her eyes, returning to the present. The other girls must already be up and out. Scatterings of their clothes lay about the floor.

Huh. If Dianne was a clean freak, she hadn't seemed to mind those clothes everywhere.

Kendall rubbed absently at the burn mark on her upper thigh.

"Knock, knock! Ding-dong! Parp-parp! Hey there, Sleeping Beauty! Oops, can't go into a girls' room!"

"Hi Ric. Hi guys."

Even fully dressed, Kendall clung to the propriety of the blankets, lifting it to her chin. Ric leaned through the doorway, a posse of kids adding limbs around him, as though he were an Indian god, and glancing about his shoulders. He wore board-shorts with a towel draped over his shoulder. Bare chest. Those nice stomach muscles were showing again. Smooth skin too.

"C'mon, we're hitting the pool. The *indoor* pool and it's heated, to like, a gazillion degrees. Like soup. Be the soup, Kendall, be the soup!"

A boy behind him added, "There's even music under the water. I'm not kidding."

"Awesome," Kendall said, smiling. "Let me just have a quick shower and I'll be right down."

"A shower so you can swim?" one of the girls chimed in. "How lame is that?" It seemed like a cheap attempt to belittle her in front of Ricky. He was already a social focal point. And, apparently, a prize.

Ricardo waved a hand. "Nah, skip the shower. Just jump into your swim stuff. We'll wait. I'll guard the door, so these total perves don't spy on you."

I have significantly more concern about you, Kendall thought.

The door closed, but the noise of chatter beyond it remained.

Crap! Okay, you can do this, Kendall. It's just a swimsuit, and all the other girls will be in theirs too. Strength in mutual embarrassment.

Distrustful of potentially-peeping Ric as Guardian of the Door, she fished her swimsuit from the larger of her two bags and slipped quickly into the en suite bathroom. The extractor fan hummed a sonorous note. She didn't have one of those in her bathroom back home. You just opened a window for that.

Before anything else, she had to deal with each of her sore bits. *Start with the bladder. And feet.*

She pulled down her jeans, hauled off her top, sat on the toilet, leaned forward, and rubbed at the welts from her socks as she relieved herself. The surge of circulation through her swollen ankles stung, then felt wonderful, as did her relaxing bladder.

Two down, she thought, reaching for the toilet paper, which was amazingly thick. At home, they always bought one-ply.

As she leaned forward, there was another stab of that sharp pain on her face. *Sinuses.* That's what it was. She sniffed, but the action only increased the pressure. She tried to blow her nose into a wad of toilet paper, but it was so utterly blocked that it didn't work. Her eyes simply watered.

She flushed the toilet, stood, and caught site of the burn

mark on her thigh in one of several mirrors. She stretched her leg and did a turning pirouette. It had scarred a little, despite the bio-oil. The skin was pink and shaped a bit like Italy. It wasn't exactly a big blemish, but it was enough to undermine her confidence.

No way Ric's seeing that. Her eyes tracked upward over her bare skin. She also wished her boobs were bigger, even by a little. She studied the pink nipples. There was some boob, sure. Well, they were more there than not.

For a moment, she considered stuffing her swimsuit, then dismissed the idea as she considered how many things could go wrong with that plan.

Was it her imagination, or did the lights just brighten slightly?

She wondered what kind of boobs Ric liked. Some boys didn't prefer huge boobs. Maybe he was one of them.

Sure, Kendall. And some lions prefer porridge to a nice, meaty gazelle! You keep dreaming!

Still, he did keep talking to her. That couldn't be a bad sign. *And did you see how snotty that other girl got? She thinks I'm a threat.*

Kendall wrapped a sarong firmly about her waist, checked that it covered the welt mark, and took a deep breath.

All right, Kendall. Be the soup!

⚹

There really was music under the water. Ricardo joked that the whole thing was ingeniously designed to drown rich people.

Kendall wasn't brave enough to dive in, or to do a cannonball like some of the other kids. She took a last look over the fresco on the walls – an Italian hillside scene over tiles – and waded in from the curving steps with the golden metallic handrail, then sank under the surface, holding her nose.

Her sinus pain was extraordinary, but she stayed down for a moment and the music *was* amazingly clear down there. The floor of the pool was dark, but it was lit in a square all around the bottom corners.

"Awesome, right?!" Ric said, splashing his way over to her. His voice sounded echoey in here. Before she could answer, another boy dunked him under, and he came up coughing and pushing back his long hair.

"Pfff! Dude, you are so gonna pay for that!" And Ric was off.

Kids were summersaulting in, shrieking, splashing water in one another's faces – there were no adults present to issue the standard 'tut-tuts'. Some of the girls just sat on the edge, lapping their legs. A good proportion of the pool's content was sloshing about the surrounding stone tiles and up against carved marble pillars and poolside loungers.

The room itself was long and thin. The ceiling above was especially high, perhaps as much as three stories, increasing the perception of this space as a sort of underground cavern, with watery refractions playing off its mysterious heights. The decking surrounding the pool was the richest dark brown, with elements of flush metal in shining gold, and the fairy lights in the ceiling way above looked golden too. They were surrounded by a sort of shining box of illuminated ceiling. Kendall thought the colours looked nice, contrasting with the dark of the water.

She checked her sarong, tightening the knot under the water's surface. She inspected her imaginary boobs for the eleventh time and straightened her shoulder straps, using a backlit mirror that ran the length of one sidewall of the room. She looked around the long, churning pool and took stock of who was where.

She knew some of the girls in the deep end, though not really by name. Her two roommates were there too, chatting in the water as they clung to the ledge and let their legs float out behind them. Britney from New Zealand was trying to keep her hair dry, but the Polish girl allowed her whitish-yellow halo of fleece to float freely about her shoulders. Boys in and outside the pool were sneaking looks. If you knew what to look for, the girls were sneaking looks right back at them.

Kendall started wading over to her roommates, pulling at the water on either side of her, when something horrifying happened. Her skull seemed to liquify and pour straight out of her nose in a hot stream.

She slapped her hands to her face, but so much slimy content gushed out that it overflowed the cup of her fingers. She turned her head away from her friends and lowered it quickly toward the water, praying that no one had noticed. Ric and his new buddy were having a raucous water fight, which provided her with blessed cover. One of the boys was mock humping the statue of a mermaid on one rim, drawing eyes and laughter in that direction.

Kendall sneaked a glance down at her palms. The mucus was black, as though she had spent the past week inhaling deeply in the bowels of a coalmine.

She was far away from the edge, and so very far from her towel. Head low to the water, she waded urgently for the rim.

When she got there, an angel from heaven pushed her towel right into her face. She grabbed it and padded furiously, using the towel as both a tissue and a safe place to hide. She bundled the towel carefully as she drew it back from her face, making sure she wasn't connected to its woollen fibres by glistening ribbons from her nostrils.

"No one saw. Nothing to worry about. It's the air conditioning, from all that travel. It happened to me too, in the bath. Mine was inky black."

Kendall knew who owned that calm voice before she saw the face. The short blond kid. Rescuer of Irish girls, champion of propriety, and now, her very own poolside saviour. "My name's Timothy," he said.

"Kendall. Thank you *so* much. Er, I'm obviously not going to shake your hand."

The diminutive boy smiled where he squatted by the rim. "It comes like a river, though, doesn't it?"

"Like an ocean! I thought my head was melting or something. I could just die. Yuck, that's so embarrassing."

"But it feels better now? Your head? Your whole face?"

"Actually, yes."

Kendall padded at her upper cheeks with her fingertips. The relief was palpable.

"Just wait until you try an earbud. That's a sight. You'll lose a couple of pounds. Or kilograms. Whatever you measure in."

He spoke so nicely; didn't even try to sound nonchalant, as most boys her age unfailingly did. Some even tried to sound like angry rappers, which she found cringey and lame. But this boy, nothing but reasonable concern. Plus, he was right. Once you got past the mortifying social angst, her sinus pain was entirely gone. Waves lapped at her shoulders from where one of the girls had just dived in.

"No one's looking, if you want to blow your nose again. Into the towel. I'll go get you another one."

Kendall kept one arm with the bundled towel above the surface, looking like the Statue of Liberty as she ducked under the water. She felt her hair ballooning around her face, allowed the warmth of the water to fill her nostrils, then drove straight back up and used the towel to pretend to dry her face, being very careful not to make a noise as she blew.

True to his word, the boy returned with a second towel, his own.

"Are you sure you don't need it?"

"I'm sure, go ahead by all means."

She put her used towel in a bundle on the pool rim, accepted the second one from the boy. "Is it like a Spidey sense?"

"What's that?"

"You get tingles around damsels in distress?"

"Kids don't like to be embarrassed. Funny thing is they all

feel that way, and they all think it's only true for them."

"You sound like my sister."

The boy considered this statement. "Is she wise and prescient too?"

Prescient. Nice! It was right up there with *dichotomy*.

Beside them, wet feet slapped loudly on stone, the volume ascending as it came closer. There was a second's tense silence, then a gigantic 'plooosh!' Waves rocked in every direction, to shrieks from some of the girls. More of the pool emptied over the rim.

"You don't squeal," he observed. "Well done. Very mature."

Kendall's inner bells went '*ding*'. That had been the right thing to say. Pity he wasn't exactly sexy, like Ric. But still …

Ric appeared again at her side, wiping water from his face. "Hey!"

"Hey you," Kendall said. "Did you survive your waterboarding?"

"You should see the other guy."

She noticed that the blond boy – Timothy – didn't smile, as though Ric were intruding on something. *Very* interesting. This was genuine boy/girl jealousy stuff, which had never happened to her before. She tucked that away for later examination too.

Their small gathering quickly grew as Kendall's roommates washed ashore beside her. Kendall felt certain that she was the excuse, but Ric was the reason.

"Hey, no secret conversations. Sharing is caring," Britney said.

"Neat accent," Ricardo replied. "I got this wrong with Kendall, but *that* one's from Australia, right?"

"New Zealand."

"Damn!"

"You're 0 for 2, mate." Britney smiled anyway, tilted her chin a little. "And before you totally strike out, she's Polish, not Russian. I'm Britney. This is Agnieszka."

"I'm never getting that job as an accent detective. Hey girls. Ricardo."

The girls laughed, generously and a little too long.

Britney brushed wet strands of hair behind her ear and said, "Hey, has anyone seen the Irish kids? The boy and girl. I can't find them anywhere today."

"I saw them this morning, but not since. Maybe they're in their rooms," Ric suggested.

"Nah, I checked. I walked through the whole house, which took, like, half a year. And I asked everyone. It's like they just disappeared."

"I'm sure they're here somewhere. It's such a massive house, you might have been going one way while they passed the other way beneath you. Hey! Let's go grab some chow. There's a chef in the ... in that, like, breakfast-room area. Kendall, you haven't eaten yet, right?"

"I am quite hungry. I guess I'd better get dressed, though."

"No need, it's casual," Ric said. "Not the room, I mean. That's like a five-star restaurant in a hotel or something. But the mood. No one there but the chef and us. Just dry off with a towel and come like that. Why don't you all come?"

The girls eagerly agreed. Kendall turned aside to Timothy, who wasn't quite part of the group, "You wanna come too?"

"Thanks, I'd like that."

As Kendall began climbing the steps out of the pool, Ricardo grabbed playfully at the hem of her sarong. "What is up with hot girls hiding behind these things?" he said.

"Hey, no!" But her sarong came loose in his grip.

Immediately, one of the girls pointed. "What's that thing on your leg?"

Kendall tried to put a hand over it, but it was too late. Awkwardly, she let the hand fall loose.

Ricardo looked mortified. "I'm so sorry! I was only kidding around. Really, sorry. Here."

He handed her the sarong, looked as though he were trying to decide whether he should help put it back around her waist, stopped himself. "Dude, for real. I honestly didn't mean to ..."

"It's okay," Kendall said softly. "Not a big deal, it doesn't matter." She reaffixed it and pulled the knot tight.

Now he knew. They *all* knew. Maybe it wasn't as bad as Kendall had imagined. Really, the gushing nose thing had been far worse, and she was grateful to have gotten away with that. Of course, now they might ask about the burn. Especially one of those obvious girls. And then she would have to tell the story. And then they would all feel sorry for her, and she could think of nothing she wanted less.

... although, she might get a little sympathy from Ric.

Immediately her brain screamed at her: *At the cost of Dobby's life!* and a wave of guilt washed over her.

Oblivious of the storm in Kendall's head, the group dried themselves and the girls wrapped up in towels.

There was *one interesting thing, though*, Kendall thought. Ric genuinely looked like he was on the brink of tears at what he'd done. *File that under: Third Item for Later Consideration.*

⚔

The Head of Watch called the Organizer. *"One of the items is damaged."*

Dianne took off her glasses. Set them down. Rubbed her eyes. *"Male or female?"*

"Female. Looking at her right now."

"What kind of damage?"

"Scar."

"Shit."

"When I zoom, it looks like a burn. Maybe we should consider destroying the merchandise."

"That's big money. Might have to, though. Where is it? And how bad?"

"Upper thigh. It's small, but it's ugly. I'd say it's a disqualifier. Our customers pay for the vetting. Blemishes are dealbreakers, especially for the girls."

"Is it a decent item otherwise?"

'Good enough. White, blonde, thin. Looks pubescent. English speaking."

"I know the one." She turned her glasses on their side, balanced them on one frame, twirled them slowly around as she pondered.

"Would have fetched a good price," said the Head of Watch. "The youngest ones always do. Maybe our Colombian buyer – he snaps those up – but only in perfect condition.'

"It's a waste. Lowers our margins. Still. If it's necessary, have the Goat manoeuvre it to the exit. We'll pull it out. Although ... we might consider offering a discount."

"What, 'damaged item?' Maybe ... slash it down to half price, move it along quickly."

"Hurts our brand, but ..."

"But she's here, so it's too late. Okay, I'll make it a one-off. We get some more video of her in the pool, shower, toilets, then sell her on quickly."

✶

A contrite Ric offered to place their brunch order. Sitting at the counter in the breakfast area, he spoke to the chef in Spanish, rolling his Rs in a luxuriant way that suggested he was rebounding handily from the faux pas.

"What did you ask for?" Kendall said.

"I didn't. He just told me he can make three options: omelettes, flapjacks, or hash browns. Or a mix. Also, he's Bolivian. Name is Arsenio Flores. Nice man."

"You got *Bolivian* from just those few sentences? Isn't Bolivia also Spanish speaking? How can you tell the difference?"

"His accent, for starters. But mostly it's his '*ingos*' and '*angos*'. They're a dead giveaway. I haven't heard Spanish done like that in a while."

"You get round."

"So, guys, who's for what? Hands up for omelettes."

They sat at a curved breakfast counter in their towels, perched on bar-style chairs, their swinging legs lit by ambient lighting that leaked out from somewhere within marble folds.

To her amazement, Kendall discovered that she and Ricardo were the nucleus of the group. Everyone else radiated out from them, like they were some celebrity power couple. They fanned out along the counter in both directions. Kendall's two roommates were on one side, leaning in to try to scoop up their share of the conversation, along with two other tag-along girls with Ricky-dust in their eyes.

On the other side was the kid who'd dunked Ricardo in the pool – he had spikey brown hair and a very slight German accent – then another girl Kendall hadn't met, and, out on the widest orbit, the blond boy.

Some of the hands went up for omelettes, some for flapjacks.

Behind the counter, Bolivian Arsenio, clad in his pristine white smock, set about frying up their orders, chopping onion, and pouring sizzling puddles of golden liquid over a griddle. He repeated 'Bueno, bueno' over his moustache as he worked.

Kendall tried something. "Excuse me, sir?"

No reaction. Yet the man didn't appear to be ignoring her either.

"Mr Flores, señor?"

The chef looked up at his name. "Si, señorita?" He used what looked like a pool triangle to marshal mushrooms into order.

"Are you a permanent member of the household staff?"

With a theatrical shrug and a finger behind his ear, "Señorita?"

He didn't speak English ... which meant there was effectively no adult supervision here either.

Ricardo repeated the question to him. "¿Trabajas aquí permanentemente?"

"Ah! No, no. Solamente esta semana."

"He says just this week."

"Could you ask him when he got here, who hired him, that sort of thing?"

One of the Ricky fan-girls said, "That's culturally insensitive. In America, asking a Spanish-speaking person when they got here sounds like you're checking their legal status. People will think you're like a total Nazi or something."

Kendall was used to idiotic hyperbole, coming from South Africa under reconstruction. "That's your little ink-blot test, not mine."

"Huh?"

"Yeah, what *is* this third degree? Latinos under the lens?" Ric joshed. But he rattled off what sounded like a friendly patter of conversation, and the chef answered happily and at length.

Ric translated as he went. "He says no problem, he doesn't mind telling ... This was a dream job. He got here last week ... hired directly from home. He used to be a hotel chef in a high-end tourist joint in *Bolivia* – told you! He was hired through an online platform, through LinkedIn. Thought it was a joke at first, the pay was too good. Turned out to be real. What can he say? Here he is."

The chef chuckled and added something else, blowing into his fist and throwing imaginary dice.

"He says it came at a damn good time too. He'd run up a mountain of debt. I think he means gambling debt."

"Okay, just one last question."

Another Ricky-groupie said, "Wow, girl!" Ricardo himself gave Kendall a throaty sound of exasperation, but he waited for the question.

"Does he know any of the other adults working here?"

"That's a good question," little Timothy said.

Ricky asked. The chef held up a single finger that anyone, anywhere could tell meant, 'one moment'. He flipped three of the omelettes and dished two others onto the counter. The plates clinked and went sliding to the far ends. The chef dusted down his smock, leaned forward on the counter, and rattled off another long response, looking thoughtful this time.

Ricardo listened and prepared to translate. As he did, some distant warning bell of intuition caused Kendall to consider: *Ricardo could say anything.* No one in this group was capable of checking his translation.

But that was silly. The boy was a court jester. He was also a marginally sleezy crotch-watching Romeo, but what reason would he have for deceit? Kendall wondered why the thought had even flashed through her mind.

"Okay, so he says no. He hasn't met any of the other staff. His orders are strict, and they didn't even give him an access key. He says he arrives at the gate in the morning and rings. Someone opens without answering, he doesn't know who. Gate closes behind him. He goes around back to the kitchens – they're open – starts his work, and his shifts don't – *que es la palabra por coincidir?* – they don't *coincide* with anyone else's. No carpooling, nothing like that. Part of his contract is he has to leave at a certain time, and not – what's the word? – like, fraternize? He says it's *muy estranjo* – real weird – but who cares, because the pay's so good. Sometimes rich people are just strange. You put up with it. And then you buy a condo in Potosi on the Bolivian dollar – he says it's sitting at seven-to-one right now."

The chef tapped the counter with apparent satisfaction, then turned his back on them and started cleaning implements.

A silence settled as the consumption of steaming omelettes

and spongey flapjacks took centre stage. First to break the quiet was Kendall's Polish roommate. "I *still* not get my phone. You get it yours?"

A chorus of indignant *No's!* Everyone leaned in again.

They repeated last night's rant about wanting to call home and needing to post on social media, almost verbatim, although this time around the exchange was more passionate.

The Polish girl said, "Where is statue-woman, Dianne? She say she bring them back to us with SIM cards. I no see her today or anyone from in charge."

"Statue-woman! Crap, that's freakin' perfect!" said Ricky.

"I saw her this morning," Kendall said. "Statue-woman was sitting right on my bed when I woke up. Gave me one heck of a fright."

"What, up in our room?" Britney asked, leaning back to face her. "How come *we* didn't see her?"

"I don't know. I woke up and she was staring at me. Literally just sitting on my bed, staring at me. She said I had to have a shower, then she walked out. It was bizarre. Ricky, you guys came in just a moment or two later. You didn't see her?"

"Nope. Haven't seen her all day. Guess we just missed her too."

Britney slammed down her fork. "This is bullshit! I *want* my phone. Where the hell is my phone? Do you think it's here somewhere? Maybe we can just go search."

Ricky aimed that skew smile at her. "Chill, dude. It'll all work out. Let's have our eggs, then worry about that later."

"I don't want my eggs. I want my *phone*. I'm gonna walk to a neighbor and ask to use theirs, I don't care. It's been a whole day now. This is deeply uncool."

"I'll go with you," the little blond boy offered.

"Yeah?" Britney seemed to notice him for the first time. "Nice one, thanks, mate."

"First, let's take a walk around the house and see whether

we can find Dianne," he said. "Best if you can just get your own phone back. I'm sure she's here somewhere. Kendall saw her, so let's go take a look."

Britney accepted the proposal. To Kendall, she said, "Catch up with you later?"

"Sure thing."

Britney and the little blond boy left the breakfast counter.

Ricardo finished his eggs and held up his plate to the chef. "Tio? Poco mas, por favor?" He looked like some smiling Mexican Oliver. The chef set about preparing a second omelette for him, and another for the German kid.

There was no shortage of food. Quite aside from the omelettes, a third of the counter was taken up by buffet-style silver trays with deep pans full of rice, potatoes, sauces, and cuts of beef and lamb, just like in a hotel. Other stations around the area were laden with fruit and cereals.

Four girls still remained at the counter, an uneasy alliance. They turned to discussing the neat blond boy.

"His name's Timothy," Kendall offered. "I've seen him swoop to the rescue of two girls now. I was one of them."

"What kind of rescue?"

"Uh, just small things. Like, helping out."

"He's a perfect little gentleman," said the probably-Malaysian girl, thawing a little, now that Ricky was talking to another boy and momentarily not paying attention to Kendall. "Yesterday when I arrived, I told him I was feeling kinda homesick. He made me a cup of tea. Old-fashioned tea! He brought it right to my room. Then he said 'I hope you have a nice day,' like he was a porter or something, and he closed my door."

The other girl said, "Do you think that's his move? Seduce them with kindness?" They chuckled.

"Pity he isn't a little bigger and, like, more muscley," the first girl said. She stole a meaningful glance at Ric. "I like that." Ric continued eating.

Kendall said, "Fingers crossed they find Dianne, get our phones. I really want mine too."

This brought mumbles and nods from the group.

The conversation wandered for a moment.

"How do you make a rock counter glow like this?" one of the girls asked.

"I think it's marble," Ric said. "And I don't know. Maybe the light's beneath it. Looks cool though."

The Ricky fan-girls revisited Britney's threat to leave the premises. "It's a good idea. Walk down the road a little and find a house. Ring a neighbor's bell. What do you think, Ric?"

Ricardo pointed at his full mouth. He contributed nothing, but appeared to follow the conversation carefully.

✶

Later in their bedroom, Kendall lay on top of her plush bed-spread. She spoke at the ceiling, and Britney lay on her bed on the other side of the room, answering. The Polish girl was in the shower.

Kendall said, "When have you ever heard of thirty teenagers left alone in a house? Zero adult supervision."

"I know! Mate, it's weird!"

Kendall said, "This is how babies get made, among other bad decisions. And even just the safety aspect. What happens if, like, two boys punch each other senseless, or someone slips by the pool, or a kid starts throwing up, or, I don't know, an alien bursts out of the cook's chest in the cantina?"

"Totally," Britney answered. "I don't get it. Makes no sense. You'd think it'd be fun, but it isn't. Just kind of scary. Maybe scary's not the word."

"Unsettling," Kendall said.

"Yeah, exactly. And I *still* don't have my phone."

"Oh, hey. What happened on your walkabout with Timothy?"

The blond boy didn't seem like anything as casual or play-ful as a *Tim*. Somehow, he was a full-fledged *Timothy*. Even his manner of speaking was as neatly combed as his hair.

Britney gave a snide chuckle. "You know, I totally forgot! That funny little guy was so interesting, we ended up just strol-ling around and talking crap. I know it's weird, but I actually forgot I was on a mission."

"And then?"

"Well, I guess we talked for about an hour. We eventually stopped in the library."

"ooOOOoo!"

"No, not like that! I told him my whole life story, including the time I broke a leg hiking in Tongariro and had to get air-lifted out. I didn't mean to, I guess it just spilled out. Then Ric found us and called us to the movies room. That's when I saw you again. Isn't that funny? Ric just goes 'Hey! Come watch a movie!' and I forget all about how angry I am about the phone."

Funny? thought Kendall. *No, not really.*

"What? What are you thinking?" Britney asked.

Kendall rolled onto her side. Britney did too, facing her.

"Okay, hear me out. My sister has this thing, this *system*, where you look at the world and try to see intelligent decisions."

"Okay?"

"Well, this seems like the opposite. There are obvious de-cisions you make when you're in charge of a house full of peo-ple from around the world. Basic stuff. But all the obvious de-cisions are ... *missing* here. There are no adults. There's no one in charge, not even one of us. No bell to ring, no number to call, no emergency plan. We had an organized Songs Evening, which is the sort of thing you do, but even that only happened because Dianne told us it would, so *we* all got together and made it happen."

"True."

"And since then? I mean, when in your entire life have you

gone someplace where kids were given free reign of a seventy million dollar house? Or just free reign, full stop?"

"Bugger. It is super weird."

"What kind of orientation week is this?"

"Yeah."

"There's something wrong here," Kendall said. "Something *very* wrong. It's just hard to believe it, because – well, I don't know about you – but I've never been so pampered in my entire life."

"So, it's like, how could you possibly bitch in a five-star setting, hey?"

"Exactly!" said Kendall. "Where *is* Dianne? And where, exactly, are those two Irish kids? I'm telling you, they're missing. I know Ric said the house is huge so maybe we keep passing each other, but that's BS. No offense to Ric. But no one's seen them all day. Why would they leave orientation week on the first day? Without saying anything to anyone? Not even goodbye? How does that add up?"

The Kiwi had no answer. She chewed at a lip, shrugged almost imperceptibly.

Kendall's brain was fried after a full day listening to the growing warning of inner sirens. She sighed. "Think I'll go shower."

Britney smiled. "You said that last night, mate. Ya never made it."

"I know. Was it you who put the blanket over me? Thanks for that."

"No worries."

"Agnieszka's really taking her time in there."

Kendall was ninety percent certain she'd mastered the pronunciation. She had learned to mentally break it down into three parts – *Arg-neesh-kah*.

She rapped on the bathroom door. Nothing. So she knocked a little harder, called out, "Agnieszka?" Then she suffered a brief flashback to the housebreaking in Johannesburg as the door simply fell open before her hand.

She peaked through.

"She's not here."

"What?" Britney asked.

"Agnieszka. She's not in here."

"Mate, are you serious?"

"Look."

Kendall opened the door wide, stepped back, and waved a hand.

"What the *hell*?!" Britney said, rising and walking over. "I saw her leave that movie we were watching and head for bed. She told everyone she was tired and she left. *Alone*, not, like, with a boy or anything. And I know for damn sure she didn't come back down again."

"Maybe she's ..."

"Maybe she's *what*, girl? Wandering the halls like a ghost? Screwing Ricky's brains out in front of two other boys?" Britney's New Zealand accent thickened when she was cross. "I mean, for real?"

"No, you're right. That doesn't add up. And she was with us earlier, when we spoke about those Irish kids and how it didn't make sense that they'd left early. She thought that was strange too. No way she'd also leave without saying goodbye."

"Hey and her bags are gone!"

"Check the cupboards."

"Sure ... Nope, not there either."

Her bed was made, her bags were gone, there was no evidence their roommate had ever been there.

"So ... where is she?"

The two girls searched each other's faces for answers.

*

FOLLOW THE LEADER

Tuesday morning. Agnieszka was still a ghost. No one had seen her, and no one had seen her leave.

Kendall called an emergency meeting. She asked Ricardo to gather everyone.

"Like, *everyone*-everyone?" Ricardo asked.

"*Everyone*-everyone. We need to all be in the same room at the same time. Like a roll-call, to check who's here. No exceptions. Otherwise, it won't work."

"*Very* forceful! I like that in a dominatrix. All right, your wish is my gazpacho."

Ric rustled up two of his male friends, a Swede named Lukas and a Japanese boy, whose name Kendall didn't catch. Including Ricardo, they looked like a diversity poster. "Posse time. Let's roll."

When everyone was finally herded together, Kendall did a headcount.

"Twenty two, twenty three, twenty four," she announced. "There are twenty four of us. How many were there on Songs Evening?"

No one seemed quite sure.

"But we think more than this, right?"

They had gathered in the library, which seemed a sufficiently officious space for their purposes. Of all the rooms she'd seen so far, which was by no means even half of them, Kendall liked this one best. It wasn't just the comfort of being surrounded by books, which felt like precious calm and the background presence of wisdom. This room was also less complicated than the rest of the house: huge, yet a lot simpler.

115

Instead of the jutting angles and structurally confusing modernist design, this was a cavernous area, complete with an old-fashioned sliding book ladder. Its domed ceiling boasted a Renaissance painting heavy with clouds for mood. There was a great deal less polished marble here, and a lot more brown leather and dark wood. She even liked the smell of new varnish. One section of the wood panelling had recently been done. It looked wet and smelled nutty. Kendall wished she could teleport this room back to her house. And then move a bed into it and live there.

The general mood among the kids had changed. There were still a few jokers and elbow-nudgers – there always were in any group of kids – but the majority of faces looking back at her were scared.

There was something else too, and it surprised Kendall. They were looking to *her* to say or do something useful. For a second, her heart went up into her throat. Then she heard an inner voice instruct her: 'Get your tits in order!'

It sounded suspiciously like Addie. Kendall decided to get her tits in order.

"Okay, we don't have a clear number, but it was definitely more than this yesterday. Agreed? So, who's missing? We had the two Irish kids," she counted off fingers, "... boy and a girl. We had my roommate from Poland. Agnieszka. That's at least three."

Three hands went up. It was classroom behaviour, and they were treating Kendall like the teacher. She pointed at the first hand.

"Both of my roommates, two girls," said a Chinese girl with short hair and green-rimmed glasses.

"Okay, so four, five."

"My friend, Noah. He was from Denmark. Also, just gone."

"That's six. And you?" She pointed.

"Two girls from my room as well. Both British. Well, Welsh,

116

but I think that is British. I asked everyone, and I walked around everywhere. No one's seen them."

"So that's seven, eight. Any more? Anyone that no one's mentioned yet?"

The kids looked around, searching one another's faces.

Standing near Kendall, her sidekick Britney added, "So then, as far as we can tell, there were thirty two of us at Songs Evening. Two nights ago. Eight kids missing now and no one knows why. No goodbyes, no explanations."

A murmur of uncomfortable assent around the room. A cough, then silence.

Kendall asked, "Ric, you guys are absolutely sure you found everyone? There's no one camping out on the roof, or swimming? Maybe making out in a dark corner?"

"We checked the roof. We did find *these two* making out in a dark corner." Ric chucked his chin toward a boy and girl who were surreptitiously holding hands. They flushed but smiled. The joke went a ways to easing the tension in the library. "But yeah. Checked the pools, checked the gym, everywhere."

"Okay, so how about if we do this?" Kendall said. "Let's all go as a group and move through the whole house, literally from top to bottom and from one side to the other. We stay together so no one gets separated, and we search every room to make sure those kids really aren't still here."

"Fink we ought to take a look for phones while we're at it," said Kweku. "Be brilliant if we could just make a call." Kendall was glad to note he was still around.

"All right, phones and kids. Room by room. Then we assemble back here and talk again. Let's get going."

"Hang in there," Ricardo said. Everyone stopped. "If we split into two groups, we'd still be able to keep track of one another. Long as no one separates from their group. And we'd get it done twice as fast. Better still, five groups. One for each level of the house. Each group can walk a level, check each room for

117

a kid or a phone, and then be back here in no time. That way we'll be done in ten minutes."

There was assent from the group. Kendall didn't like it, though for no reason she could quite pinpoint. It just sounded like that moment in the horror movie when the band of stupid teens said, "Hey, let's split up!" You knew that was their cue to get picked off individually, then die grizzly, creative deaths. And did they ever have a surfeit of obvious girl-quips like, "Is somebody there?" Still, she couldn't quite find a flaw in the logic. And if they did stay with their groups, why not?

"All right, then. Make it four. Four groups of five kids and one smaller group from the leftovers. The top level of the house is the smallest, so *that* group can have four people. Who wants top level?"

It took a while, but the kids organized themselves and divvied up the search.

Kendall took the ground level. Her group included Britney, Ricardo, Kweku, and little Timothy.

Timothy said, "Let's start all the way on one side, and work our way across to the other."

"Cool. Then let's go."

Kendall cast an eye over the groups. They all seemed organized. Kids chatted quietly in their circles, and one by one, the groups headed out of the library.

There were several routes down to the ground floor. Kendall's group took the elevator, exiting into the large atrium that Kendall had seen when she'd first arrived at the great house.

"I'm not sure there really is one 'side' of this house. This *mansion*." Kendall speculated aloud. "It kind of radiates out in different directions."

"Yes, there is," said Ricardo. "That corridor there. That's the longest straight line. All these other directions here just kind of circle back on each other. I'm guessing if you had to see it from the sky, that side would be like a long stalk, this side would be

118

the flower. Maybe the head of a dandelion. And it's all sort of squashed up against the mountain."

"A *dandelion*?" said Kweku. "Bruva, hand in your man-card right this instant."

Kendall said, "All right, then let's head to the end of the long corridor, then work our way back."

It took them a minute just to walk the length of that stretch and find the end of the house. The last room at the terminal point was a sort of casual lounge, smaller than the one they had occupied for Songs Evening, yet it branched out both ways in a surprisingly long 'T' at the base of Ricardo's *dandelion*. It curved around a corner on one side to terminate just beyond a couple of steps and a baby grand piano tucked away in an intimate corner.

There were no phones there. Kendall didn't expect to find anything in the serving hatches or the draws that pulled out from beneath tables and stands, but she checked them one by one anyway.

They moved back down the corridor to the next room, a sort of scullery and kitchen for that terminal lounge. Stacks of washed dishes, drawers full of clean cutlery. Enough mops, brooms, and bottles of disinfectant in different colours, to halt an outbreak of medieval plague, should one ever reach wealthy California. Apparently, they sometimes did. No phones, though.

The next three rooms, working back, were formal lounges of differing sizes and smartness, the last of which was perhaps better described as an office or study. If any room logically should have a phone, it was this one.

No phones. No modems.

"Welsh *is* British."

"Huh?" Kendall said. It was Kweku, walking by her side. "Welsh people," he said. "They are British. I mean, technically."

"Right. Got it."

"Look at it," Kweku nodded toward the others. "You can actually *wotch* the life go out of them. It's depressing."

119

He was right. Kendall could see that the group already seemed dispirited. Arms hung at sides, and the way they searched showed they didn't believe they would find anything. Maybe the other kids were having better luck on one of the other levels.

It took a good deal longer than the ten minutes Ricardo had estimated, and that was just to work through their one long corridor. Back in the atrium, from which several smaller corridors radiated outwards, they had to decide which way to go next.

Ricardo said, "We've got the idea now. Why don't we each take one of the offshoots and work our way back around to here. One of us can stay in the atrium ... you know, in case one of our missing kids suddenly decides to streak through here laughing wildly."

"This is serious, Ricardo," said Kendall.

"I know, chica! I know."

"I don't much like splitting up."

"We're not. We're just each circling round and returning."

"That's splitting up."

"Okay, you got me. Let's split up."

"Timothy, would you stay here?" Kendall asked.

"Sure thing," said the blond boy.

"Okay ... Uh ... So there are four other directions, but technically, that one heads up a level, to a mezzanine. So, I guess we have three."

Kweku said, "Right, then. The two ugly boys can go off *there* and *there*. You fine ladies go down that one, yeah?"

"Good. See you back here."

As they circled the corridor that led by the movies room, a large restroom, and what Kendall assumed was some sort of coat closet, Britney took Kendall's arm and said, "I think that black kid fancies you."

"Kweku? I think so too. I like his accent."

"And I think Ricardo fancies you too."

"Really? If that's true, I'm doing well."

"And, last but not least, I think even little Timothy might have a crush on you, although if I'm being honest, I think he might have one on me too. In his own quiet little way, I reckon he's quite the ladies' man."

"That one's sweet. We'll have to arm-wrestle for him."

"I'll totally take you. Mate, I'm like Vin Diesel!" Britney flexed a bicep and pulled her best 'flexing' face. Many things the New Zealand accent may be, 'gangsta' was not one of them.

They rounded the corner and discovered an unusually small door; the entrance to the movie room's projection booth. Within, there was a short staircase leading up to a tight space that was no more than a tiny cubbyhole, but Kendall checked it out anyway, even moving papers and old DVD boxes aside on the small counter that looked through glass into the room. She was getting desperate now.

As she reached the bottom of the claustrophobic staircase and closed the small door again, a loud 'crash' reached them from the atrium. It was closely followed by a keen wail of pain.

"What the hell was that?" Britney asked.

"Come on. Let's get back."

✶

Timothy lay on the stone floor of the central atrium. He was twisted into an awkward position and lay clutching at his left ankle. He was halfway between the base of a staircase and a sheer drop from a chest-height mezzanine-level walkway. He wore an expression of abject shock, and as Kendall and Britney arrived, he looked up at Ricardo, who stood beside him, as though he thought the taller boy might bite off his head.

"What? What happened?" Kendall asked.

The boy couldn't answer. He just sucked in a breath and made a 'ffff' sound. He appeared to be striving valiantly not to cry in front of them. His face seemed paler than usual.

Ricardo had a hand on his shoulder, saying something to him. Leaning over Timothy, Ricardo looked twice his size. To Kendall, Ricardo said, "I think he fell down from that ledge." He kept his hand on Timothy's shoulder.

Britney said, "We'd better get him to ... I don't know, maybe one of the couches? Is there like a hospital area in this house? Or, what's less than a hospital? A sick room? Infirmary?"

Kendall said, "Just use that couch, around there."

Ricardo said, "I'll lift him," and Kendall caught a flash of horror in the smaller boy's eyes.

✳

There were no medicines in the house, but several of the kids had brought basic painkillers from home: Aspirin, Disprin, a few boxes of anti-inflammatories.

Timothy gladly accepted three extra-strength Tylenols with a glass of water. Kendall held up his head as he drank. She asked him to move his toes, which he was able to do, so nothing was broken. Yet the boy looked pale. He occasionally shivered. They put a blanket over his legs and told him to stay there on the couch.

The reconnaissance meeting in the library never took place. Britney had gone upstairs to let everyone else know what had happened, and now the kids drifted down to the ground level in small groups, reporting what they had found.

"We got nothing. No phones, and none of the missing kids. Not on our level anyway."

Each report was the same, and though some of the kids remained there, hanging around the couch where Timothy was laid up, most eventually wandered off. Kendall wanted them to stay, but she didn't have a next step, and there was Timothy to see to.

It was now mid-morning and Kendall had no idea what to do next.

She stood up beside the couch on which Timothy lay. Ricardo, Kweku, and Britney were still with them. She cast a suspicious look at Ricardo. *What exactly had happened back there?* Ricardo had stayed diligently by Timothy's side since the incident, giving Timothy no chance to talk without him present, and all Timothy would say was that he'd tripped and fallen; just a silly accident. That didn't fly at all. Nothing about it felt right to Kendall.

She said to the group, "Maybe we *should* try to get out of the property. Go find a neighbor."

Britney said, "Yeah, I think so too."

"Let's start with the obvious. Ric, would you and Kweku go check the front door?"

"I already did," Ric said. "It's locked."

"Would you humour me? Both of you, together?"

Ricardo shot her a questioning look. Kweku seemed to pick up on it too. He grabbed Ricardo's arm and said, "Come on, squire. The lady hath spoken."

Kendall was starting to like Kweku.

She watched them leave, then turned to Britney, "Would you mind checking if there's a way out to the front driveway through the back gardens?"

"If I didn't know better, I'd say you were trying to get rid of us."

Kendall held meaningful eye contact with her for a second.

"Yeah, all right, mate. Fine. You will update me later, though?"

Kendall nodded.

When Britney left, Kendall knelled back down beside Timothy and leaned in close. "So what really happened there?"

Timothy raised his head slightly and looked in the direction Ricardo and Kweku had taken. He looked genuinely scared. He shook his head, *no.*

"Come on, Timothy, I need to know. I won't, like, get you in trouble with anyone. I have no intention of starting a fight. You can tell me. Please?"

The boy hesitated a second longer. Then, "He *pushed* me." He said it in an appalled whisper, like a confession of vile sin. "Pushed me! Right off that ledge. I was sitting with my feet hanging over. He came up and started talking to me, as though everything was normal. Then he put his hand on my back. Like we were buddies. Then he shoved me. Hard!"

"Why did he do it?"

"I have no idea! Honestly, the fright I got was worse than the pain. And then he threatened me not to say anything. Leaning over me. Then you arrived."

Kendall searched his eyes. "That makes no sense. He's been super friendly to everyone else."

"Well ... maybe it's ..."

"It's what?"

The boy took a deep breath. He seemed reluctant to go on. "Maybe it's because he likes you. *Likes you,* likes you. And he doesn't ..."

"Doesn't what?"

"Doesn't like me talking to you."

Kendall screwed up her face. "You think?"

"Can you think of a better reason?"

Kendall couldn't. But would Ric really hurt another kid, and particularly a much smaller guy like Timothy, out of jealousy? He seemed too smooth for that. Too chill. Too unthreatened by the world and certain of his place in it. If he needed to win a fight, he could do it with wisecracks and a jaunty smile. *Could he really be capable of violence?*

There was something else too. The incident had altered their plans. They were all working together – the whole household of kids – with a simple but good plan to report back and then make the next decision. Could it be possible that Ricardo had thrown a spanner in the works to stop them from exploring every nook and cranny? *But why?*

It was hard to believe. He was *so* charming, and in such an

124

open and easy-going way. Okay, so he did have a panty-peeking problem. But most boys were pretty gross about sex stuff when you came right down to it.

No, it didn't add up.

So, what did that leave? He was a gigantic bully? That didn't seem to work either. Bullies were also show-offs. They made a point of doing their pushing and shoving *in front of* others. This was different, more strategic.

The word 'psychopath' flashed through Kendall's mind.

Oh, knock it off, she told herself. *Now you're being melodramatic, girl. No one's a real psychopath. Well ... someone must be a real psychopath, otherwise there wouldn't be such a word.*

'Precisely' – Addie's voice seemed to whisper.

"I keep thinking of him like my older brother, but he's nothing like him. Certainly not as smart."

Kendall said, "Oh, you have a brother?"

"I do. Very clever guy. He got a bursary to study, which was good. Our family's struggling a little. You know, financially."

"I have a sister like that!" Then Kendall lowered her voice, "And don't be embarrassed. My family too. A little."

"Yeah?" Timothy almost looked hopeful. "All the other kids here give the impression of being ... a bit ..."

"I know what you mean," Kendall said. "All of this," she looked at the house in general, "This is totally foreign to me."

"See these jeans?" Timothy said, almost proudly. "My brother's hand-me-downs, after they were our Dad's hand-me-downs."

Kendall put a finger through the belt loop of her own jeans and smiled ironically.

Timothy said, "Seriously? You too?"

"Seriously."

He beamed at her.

Then the smile drained away as he looked over her shoulder. Ricardo was back. He and Kweku reported that the front door was indeed locked, and that after three attempts at obvious codes – *1-2-3*, *3-2-1*, *0-0-0* – the keypad had locked them out entirely.

"We can try again in ten minutes," Ricardo said.

"Weird for an indoor keypad to do that," Kweku said. "Locks normally keep people *out*. What if there's a fire or something? Do we just turn to crispy toast while pressing buttons?"

Kendall looked back down at Timothy, whose face was now a mask. He said quietly to Kendall, "Could you give me a hand? Just to that bathroom over there?"

"Of course."

The boys offered to assist, but Kendall shooed them away. She could tell that Timothy just wanted a moment to himself. He still looked like he was trying not to cry in front of her.

She pushed open the door to one of the downstairs lavatories. Timothy went through and the door closed on a spring behind him. Ricardo watched, then said, "I'll go look for other exits."

On his own, Kendall noted.

As she watched Ricardo walk away, a purposefulness in his step, the word wouldn't leave her. It sat coldly in her gut. She turned it over and over, pondering whether it fit.

Psychopath.

⚹

"Talk to me."

"I don't have much time."

"We'll be quick. Don't let the stock hear the crackle. How are they?"

"Nervous. But holding together. Not yet in full rebellion. They made their first genuine attempt at a search today. Next they'll try to find a way out. They want to get to another house for a phone."

"How long until full rebellion?"

"Depends. The scale is different this time. In Guadalajara I kept them aiming in the wrong direction until day five. By then the

remainders were too terrified to keep trying. It happens, if we can draw it out. They fold into themselves. Collapse."

"Ring-leaders?"

"The South African girl."

"Her? Interesting. The damaged item, we're selling her cheap. No takers yet. Would you like us to remove her from the house?"

"I can handle her."

"Good. Then she stays. Until she sells."

"Can I go?"

"Any other threats we should know about?"

"Nothing unusual."

"Good. Go."

✗

Timothy was back on the couch. From their position by his side, the small group watched as two kids approached at a run, their footfalls echoing through the corridors, shouting, "Guys, we found a way out!"

"Seriously?" Kendall asked as they skidded to a halt, panting.

Ricardo trailed just behind them. He said, "Yeah, it's true. Come check it out."

Kendall turned to Timothy, "Will you be alright here? You want us to take you along?"

"No, it's not serious. I'm okay. The tablets are kicking in. Go ahead."

The group went together, following the flustered leaders, who ran ahead shouting, "Come on, this way!"

They discovered, though, that the victory was not as complete as advertised. What the other kids had found was not a way out of the property, just a way out of the house and into the back yard, an entirely self-contained area. Excited all the same, one of them shouted, "Here! It's through here. Check!"

All the glass doors out to the back were locked, with no obvious latches. The windows too. But not this serving hatch. It opened between one of the smaller kitchens and an outdoor patio. The hatch was large enough for kids to get through, if you first climbed up onto the inside counter, and if you didn't mind a bit of a squeeze.

Ricardo opened the hatch, allowing a block of sunshine to spread across the counter, then climbed up and went first, showing how it was done. Whether he was a psychopath or not, Kendall discovered that his bum looked pretty great as he wriggled his way through.

After that, Kendall, Kweku, and Britney, each climbed through in turn, with Ricardo helping them down on the other side.

Then it was Kendall's turn. As Ricardo took hold of her by the hips and lowered her gently to the ground in the sunlight outside, she thought, *He seems so kind, though. Effortlessly kind.* The feeling of his hands on her hips also wasn't entirely unwelcome. Still, she couldn't help wondering if she might be enjoying the intimate touch of an essentially bad person.

Kendall forgot her inner debate once the sunshine touched her face. Technically it had only been a couple of days since she'd been outside during daylight, but apparently you missed the outdoors and the feel of fresh air on your skin faster than you'd assume.

This was semi-desert mountain air in the Californian heights. Winter air, crisp, but warm enough to be pleasant. Kendall touched her cheek as though she could rub it in. It was delicious.

They took an amble around the grounds out back. Most of the space was taken up by a massive pool and surrounding gardens. Kendall looked up from the pool surface to the rock face of the cliff into which the property nestled, then looked around in all directions.

It's an amphitheatre.

The backyard was substantial, but completely contained by the cupped palm of the mountainside. The house was guarded on three sides by nearly sheer rock. Looking up at the rockface, Kendall was reminded of the day she'd arrived here and looked straight up the severe walls of the house itself – and again it made her take one dizzy step backward. Toward the top of the crags, there was palisade fencing built right into the rock; a certain barrier for anyone brave enough to scale that high.

So, no way out there. Even if you could climb that high.

Of the lawn space between rock and house, the Olympic-sized pool took up most of it. Kendall and her friends were on a slightly raised patio. From there, three separate walkways led down to the pool, with three separate staircases, each occupied by flanking sentries of alternating vases and marble fountains.

Though the small army of reclined deck chairs faced it expectantly, this pool was covered. Hibernating for winter.

The remaining space was a stylish assortment of brightly painted changing rooms in a variety of light colours, like those on tourist postcards of seaside utopias, as well as luxury pool decks and multiple bar areas, with palm trees casting shade here and there. The palm trees all had ground lighting, aimed upward like searchlights at their fronds, now turned off.

The kids tried door handles and discovered that everything was locked down tight. Some of them peered through the glass into one of the wooden bars.

After a while, the elation of freedom gave way to realisation. This was merely a larger contained area. There wasn't even a way around to the sides of the house.

The groups of kids split and dissolved and atomized into smaller and smaller groups. They wandered around singly or in pairs. There were some eighteen of them out here in total, slowly realising that the back area was merely an extension of the same bubble.

Still, it was warmer out here in the sun. And with high rock walls all around, there was little wind, so some of the kids started pulling off jackets and opening buttoned shirts. One of the girls was clearly proud of her belly button ring. She adjusted her skirt downward *just so* to make it visible.

"Hey, c'mere!" Ric said, taking Kendall by the hand, a mischievous energy in his voice. He pulled her out of sight of the others, whiplashing her around one of the colourful changing-room boxes.

"Check it out. This one's open." He flicked the latch.

Kendall was just starting to think *Okay, so what?*, when he pulled her inside, quietly closed the door behind them. The sun disappeared, the noise disappeared, and suddenly she found herself standing very close to Ricky, very close indeed. With the door shut and no one around, the sensation was intensely intimate.

Ricardo inched his body closer.

He smiled at her, all white teeth and dark lashes framing big brown eyes. His direct gaze was beyond disarming, especially up close like this. Ten urgent thoughts wrestled for dominance in her mind. She wanted time to work out what she thought of Ricardo, maybe to gather more evidence, but his hands were softly alighting on her hips, right there on the hips again, and it felt amazing through the denim. He clearly intended to kiss her.

His lips looked so nice, full and slightly parted. She dearly wanted him to do it. She also thought he might be some sort of monster and wanted him to stop. Added to all that, she was still embarrassed about the scar on her hip, and though she wore jeans, his hand was right on top of it, making her self-conscious.

So many thoughts at once.

She tried to yell at herself internally to do something, but found that she flat-out did not know what to do. And if she did nothing, by default, he would make the decision for her, was even now beginning to do so.

From right up close, Ricardo looked playfully down at her one hip, where his fingers moved over the fabric on top of her scar. He even rubbed the spot lightly. He said, "I like it. It's like a character mark. Makes you unique."

"Really?"

"Yeah. Uniquely Kendall. No one else."

Her stomach flip-flopped. His lips were so close to her own now, brushing her cheek as he emitted a soft breath.

Ricardo dipped easily down to his knees, then kissed her right over the scar. She gasped.

"Wait!" she said.

He moved his lips up to her stomach, let his fingers stray around her waist. He kissed over her bellybutton.

"Hold on, wait."

He was kissing his way straight back down, his lips moving over her jeans, over the curve of her panties.

"Uh, no! Stop," she put a hand on his forehead, flinched away with her hips before his mouth could make contact there.

Blood thundered through her ears. "Not here, okay?" It sounded lame, even to her own ears.

Ricardo smiled up at her. Very quickly, he kissed her right over the fly of her jeans. Then he rose slowly, kissed her twice on the cheek. She put her hands on his chest, not quite pushing him away.

Any of the other girls in the house would have given a right arm to trade places with her; might even have openly fought her for such a chance, would certainly have allowed him to do whatever he wanted down there with his mouth.

Not like this.

She needed to sort through her impressions of the boy, to figure out who and what he truly was. Tim was still back inside, lying on that couch, and Tim said that Ric had pushed him. And not one of those stupid *boys-being-dumb* play-pushes. A push intended to harm.

He'd nearly pushed *her*, in a whole different way.

And yet …

One of his hands, still on her back, softly stroked the skin. It nearly made her knees give in. The other hand gently cupped the back of her head, scrunched slightly at her hair. It made her feel so mature, so grown. This was surely the most exquisite discomfort of her life – she wanted to but she didn't – and it was made all the more intense by her certainty that someone would find them here at any moment. She almost laughed at her own agonising awkwardness; put a hand over her mouth.

No one's going to find you, though. There are no adults, remember?

And with the return of that constant ice-shower of a thought, the mood dissolved.

"Come on," she said, taking the hand that was stroking her hair, pulling it to her lips, and kissing the knuckles. "I want to know if there's a way out of this house."

"Si, señorita. Me too. But wow, I sure would like to kiss you."

Kendall's inner thermometer made screaming sounds. He was able to say it so openly.

Ricardo was the one to open the door. He held it for her, a slit of intruding sunlight touching his skew smile.

Outside, two boys stood at a distance. When Kendall and Ricardo emerged, the boys gave a questioning thumbs up. Ricardo waved them away.

Had that been a setup? Prove you can kiss the girl? See how far you can go with her?

Kendall wasn't sure. Kendall wasn't sure about a lot of things.

She turned to confront Ricardo, but the question was interrupted by sudden running. Hard running. There hadn't been any shouts or calls, but it was clear that *something* had happened – seven or eight kids were all rushing to the same place.

"Come on," Ricardo said, taking her hand again. She allowed him to, and then they were both running.

The kids were gathered at the base of the rocky slope, on the far side of the pool. At their feet, one of the boys lay on the ground, just the way Timothy had, only this boy was unconscious. A girl in a skirt kneeling next to him said, "I think he's still breathing."

Kendall's roommate pushed her way through the small crowd. "Stand clear, please," Britney said. "I've had first-aid training. Let me through."

Kendall watched as Britney gently took a pulse, checked his nostrils for air. The others around the perimeter stood transfixed. Some rubbed at their hands, or tugged at their clothing. Looking around them, Kendall had enough time to think, *We really are just a bunch of kids.*

"He is breathing," Britney said. "He's alive. But don't anyone move his neck. We have to keep it still."

The boy started to groan, coming around.

One of the other kids said, "Here's his hat-thing." And handed her a yamaka.

"That's not important now," Britney said, placing it beside them on the grass. She leaned across him so her shadow shielded him from the sun. She instructed him, "Lie still, we don't know if your neck is hurt." But the boy sat up on one elbow and looked about. He seemed to be okay, if somewhat dazed. He had a generous collection of brown and red scrapes, and one leg of his trousers was torn wide open.

"What happened?" Britney asked.

Another boy, wearing a backward yellow baseball cap, pointed upward and said, "He climbed those rocks. He got right up to the fence, way up there, I saw. I think he got shocked. He kind of jerked back, then fell ... all the way back down here."

"Like an electric shock?"

"Yeah, exactly."

Kendall considered how great a fall that had been. He must have tumbled down several rocky ledges on his way down, like a ragdoll. If he'd fallen straight down, he would be stone dead.

From the ground beside Kendall, the injured boy now wiped a hand over his eyes and said, "That thing shocked me like a chaser."

"A what?"

"Pig. My teeth bit together. Then I … like … tumbled the whole way down."

"Anything broken? Can you wiggle your toes?"

The boy could not, in fact, wiggle his toes – the left ones at least – which dispelled the last remnants of drowsiness. He was fully conscious now, sore and scared.

"Does this hurt?" Kendall squeezed his upper leg.

"Yow! Fuck! Ow, ow, ow!"

Ricardo mumbled to Kendall, "Let's call that a *yes*."

"Okay, it's not your back then. You can move the upper part of the leg? Try for me? That's good. Okay, easy! I think it's broken down here."

"It's throbbing. All down this side."

"All right," Britney said. "All the boys, help me carry him inside. Watch out for the scrapes and be especially careful with that leg."

"Back through that hatch?" Ricardo asked, looking doubtfully at the wall and the small, raised hole where they had climbed out.

"Back through that hatch. This is not going to be easy, but it has to be done."

Two injuries. Inside of twenty minutes. Plus, we're all right back where we started, inside the house. Kendall thought wryly, *We're not getting anywhere here.*

Timothy was on one couch – sitting up, but keeping his

weight off his sprained leg – and the second patient was on another, transforming the semi-formal lounge into a makeshift infirmary. *How long until the next patient arrived?*

Britney alternated between the two, playing nurse and applying ice packs, ordering kids around, and generally looking business-like.

Kendall stood back from the group. She leaned against a wall, arms folded, trying to gain perspective. Her mind was whipping between concern for the two on the couch, the disquieting pull of those sexual moments in the changing room, and the bizarre reality that even an attempt to get out had proven dangerous. She couldn't slow the spinning, as though her brain was in a tumble dryer.

There was no shortage of Disprin among the kids. And the girl with the anti-inflammatories had two small boxes and no hesitation about sharing. But they were still weak responses to the pain from a broken leg. And still, no one knew how to get the injured boy out of the house. No one knew how to call for help.

The boy with the broken leg – his name was Eli Solomon – was sweating around his brow. His yamaka was back on. Every few seconds, lines of muscle pulled taut on his neck. He breathed quickly and winced occasionally. He was starting to shiver.

Britney demanded of no one in particular, "Get him some really sweet tea. Loads of sugar."

The kids were all looking at one another to see who would go when a familiar approaching sound froze them in place.

None of the kids had soles that hard. Certainly, none of the girls in the house wore heels. No one walked that confidently. That distinctly formal and uniquely unfriendly '*click-clacking*' could only belong to one person.

Rounding the corner from the atrium, posture as perfect as ever, Dianne strode into the room.

As one, they fell silent. The icy woman wasn't alone. Two men walked beside and slightly behind her, each carrying heavily packed grocery bags suspended from surprisingly large hands. Dianne's expression was not especially friendly, nor did the men smile or show much reaction to what they saw.

"What happened here?" Dianne asked, removing her dark glasses and pocketing them. She looked down on the boy with the injured leg.

Incredible, Kendall thought. *We haven't seen her in a day and a half, she strolls in and scolds us like naughty kids. And we fall in line.*

"He's ... um ... he fell outside from that rock wall ..." Britney pointed vaguely.

"We think his leg's broken," someone else said.

As they spluttered to explain what had happened to the boy, Kendall noticed that there was an impulse to blame the kid, as though *he* had done something they were ashamed of, as though it were important to shift the blame for attempted escape.

Why are we *the ones doing the explaining?*

In fairness, one or two of the kids crowding around the scene *were* trying to ask about their phones, but the woman shushed them. "Yes, yes, I have your phones! But we'll deal with that later. First, I must get this boy to a hospital, you can see that!"

"Can't we get the phones before you go?" one of them asked.

Dianne ignored him, snapping, "Gentlemen, assist me here?" She addressed this not to the boys who had done the heavy lugging for Britney, but to the two men who now set down their grocery bags and approached. *Who were they?* They asked no questions, made no objections, said nothing. Both wore baseball caps, pulled low.

One of them lifted the injured boy as though he weighed nothing. The boy breathed sharply, trying not to cry, then held onto his yamaka so as not to lose it.

"What about *him*?" Kendall asked, pointing to Timothy on the other couch.

Dianne hesitated. She asked the boy, "What's your name?"

"Timothy."

"Anything broken, Timothy? You need to go to the hospital?"

Timothy looked terrified of her, and even more scared of the other large man, who now looked like he might approach. "No, thank you. I'm okay."

To the kids in general, Dianne waved a hand and said, "Take these supplies to the kitchen. The chef will be in momentarily. I'll return in an hour."

"Excuse me," said a girl from India. She had extraordinarily thick, bushy hair, and a tiny face framed in the middle of it. She'd worn full traditional dress on Songs Evening and still had faint traces of henna down her arms and hands, and told everyone she lived in Bangalore or as she called it, Bengaluru. Her nose was large, but long and swooped, and it made her look elegant.

"I just wondered if you knew where my roommate went? Where all the missing kids have gone?"

A chorus of *yeah*'s from the rest, but respectfully subdued.

The man carrying Eli shifted the boy's weight and once again Eli tried not to cry out. He turned to leave. The other walked beside them, like an honour guard. Or a bouncer. Already they were heading for the exit, the boy wincing and moaning as they went.

Dianne responded, "Not everyone's staying the full week. Some have already gone to their foster families." She turned and escorted the men toward the atrium.

No one responded. The kids looked crestfallen.

Is that it? Kendall thought. *We're going to give up that easily?*

It wasn't just the woman's portrayal of unassailable authority. It was also how fast it all happened. And the fact that the boy with the yamaka really did need to get to a hospital.

This felt surreal. *In fact*, thought Kendall, *it looked less like a chance arrival than a well-planned excursion into enemy territory.*

Could this all be … planned?

No, come on. How do you plan a broken leg?

Certainly, the timing was convenient. Kid breaks a leg. Instantly, Dianne arrives. With back up. *I mean, seriously, what are those two supposed to be? Bag boys? They're huge men. And they don't speak.*

Kendall watched as some of the kids obediently lifted parcels and dutifully began hauling them off to the kitchen. A smaller group trailed after Dianne's entourage, though with obvious trepidation. Kendall followed them.

Halfway across the atrium, Dianne's clacking heels halted again. She turned her full confrontational pose on the stragglers in her wake, and pointed to two of them.

"Cheryle, Adilah. You two come with us, please. The rest of you, head back now."

"Why?" Adilah asked. Cheryle came walking up as well. She said, "But we don't have our bags."

"Don't worry about that, it'll be taken care of. Just come, please. Both of you. The rest of you, head back. We'll talk soon. Back in one hour. Go on, now." When they hesitated, "*Now*, please."

Dianne's resolute stance brooked no argument. The rest of the kids, not sure quite what to do, idled for a moment longer, then dispersed, as though they were a trickling stream and Dianne a rock. The woman watched them go.

Incredible, Kendall thought. *This is a simple game of wills. There's no reason for us to walk away, other than her standing there telling us to, and making it uncomfortable if we don't. So, we do. Because we're young.*

Kendall, alone, remained where she was. Dianne regarded her as if from a judge's elevated bench.

It took all of Kendall's will to remain planted and not retreat to the shielding anonymity of the group. But some deep place inside her insisted that she must stand. So she stood.

Eventually, Dianne said, "This boy is in need of medical assistance."

Kendall replied, "I'm not stopping you."

The man carrying Eli shifted the kid's weight once again, this time harsher than was necessary. Eli couldn't help letting out a sharp cry.

Kendall said, "I'm not even standing between you and the door."

It was true. Why didn't she just go?

Kendall flushed as she spoke this way to an adult. But she said it, and she remained standing. She added, "What? Don't you want me to see you leaving?"

"Nonsense!" Dianne said. "Why would that matter to me?", and to Kendall's surprise, instead of heading for that strange passage to the front door, she turned and pressed the button on the elevator. The elevator opened with a metallic *'shuck'*, the men entered with the boy, Dianne ushered the two girls in as well, her hands firmly on both of their shoulders, and when they were in, she quickly pressed the 'close' button.

Kendall stared in confusion.

The car of the elevator dipped out of sight.

Down? But there is *no down!* And yet, there went the car, plunging out of sight.

A moment later, Kendall ran to the elevator and hit the outside button.

The car returned. There was a soft *'bing'*. The doors opened,

139

repeating that metallic sound. Kendall lurched in through the doors and pawed over the buttons. But they were just as she remembered them: Ground, 1 – 2 – 3 – 4. You had to take a small staircase to get to the fifth level. There *was* no basement. And there was no button for a basement either.

But I saw it! I watched it. That thing went down. *Now it's empty, so they went down and out … somehow.*

Dianne had mentioned a couple of wine cellars, but no one had found those yet. Kendall's own group should have found them when they searched the bottom level. If there were cellars, Kendall assumed they would nevertheless be locked, given the throng of teens in the house, and certainly they *had* found several locked doors.

Fighting incredulity, she assured herself, *But they did go down, I watched them!*

She stepped back out into the atrium. She inspected the doors from the outside, looked around their edges. Then stepped back into the elevator and checked the wall panel all over again. She even ran a finger over the featureless space where a basement button might have been, leaning right in to inspect the smooth surface, in case there might be a haptic screen of some sort. All she saw was her own frowning reflection and the pulse of her moist breath. Her searching fingers found nothing but their own smudge marks.

What the heck?!

With no answers presenting themselves, Kendall took two, slow, backward steps back out again.

A handful of straggling kids wandered back into the atrium. They stared worried question marks at Kendall.

And just like that, we're a house full of kids again. And once more, we're all alone. Only now, there are even fewer of us.

Kendall mentally revised their number down to twenty one.

✱

Minutes later, the smell of food emanated from the kitchen. It reached in seductive tendrils down the hallways.

Despite her anxiety, despite everything that had just happened, despite how badly she wanted to ignore the tug to service mundane needs like eating, and to find a place to *think* instead, the invitation was overpowering in its simplicity. It smelled like hot dogs. Saliva pooled in her mouth.

Kendall was famished and she wasn't alone. By the time she got there and heard the sizzle, it seemed the whole household was scattered all about what Ricardo had called the breakfast area. Some were already eating – it *was* hot dogs, gourmet ones – some of the kids were handing plates around, and some were quietly waiting for theirs, just as if no one had broken a leg searching for an escape route, just as if Dianne had never mysteriously appeared and then vanished again every bit as enigmatically.

Kendall sighed. She gave in to the idea of food. Maybe this whole thing would still resolve itself, and everything would turn out to be fine. Just an odd few days and a couple of silly misunderstandings. Off to her host family as planned. *Was that still possible?*

Anything is.

She wasn't winning the arguments in her own head.

The counter where they had eaten omelettes was occupied, but there were tables and booths available around the main floor. Ricardo, Kweku, and Britney, occupied one of the tables beneath a set of three lanterns that hung at uneven lengths from the ceiling above them. Timothy, leg extended, sat near enough to be a part of the group, even if still on a somewhat wider orbit.

Ricardo pushed out a chair with his leg. It slid easily against the highly polished wood. "Grub, chica. It's real good. Snatch it while it's pipin'."

Barely twenty minutes ago, he had tried to ... nuzzle her privates. Right now, Kendall couldn't have been less in the mood for his banter.

On the other hand, he did hand her a plate with a mountainous hot dog, stuffed to overflowing with so many piled and shredded ingredients that Kendall couldn't count them beneath the mess of coloured sauces. Even the bread looked wonderful. Its outer layer was as craggy and dust-covered as the rocky amphitheatre outside, and it crunched within Kendall's fingers as she lifted it and searched for an entry point for her mouth.

The group munched in silence.

"Same chef," Kendall observed. Her friends turned and glanced at the counter.

"Right. The *hear-no-evil* guy," Kweku said.

Kendall considered that statement. That was technically true. He spoke no English. The only Spanish speaker here seemed to be Ricardo.

Even as they ate, she could see the chef doing his shrugging 'I don't understand' gesture and smiling his polite smile to another of the girls at the counter.

Was that response real? Or did he actually understand?

The chatter around the space was subdued. At Kendall's table, there was none whatsoever.

Kendall finished another bite of her hot dog, glanced about, then did a double take.

Through full mouths, Britney, Kweku, and Ricardo, all asked, "What?" at the same moment, trying to see what she was looking at.

"The chef!"

"What?" said Britney, craning her neck. "I don't see him. Where is he?"

"Exactly!"

His station was empty.

"Come on!" Kendall said, abandoning half of her hot dog. "Let's follow him out."

The others merely remained seated.

"Aren't you coming?" Kendall asked them, surprised.

Britney said, "Well, I mean ... Dianne said she'd be back as soon as she took Eli to the hospital. And she says she'll have our phones for us. And ..."

Kweku concluded, "And we're all full of hot dog."

Kendall said, "Are you guys serious?"

"I'll come," Timothy said, and began wobbling to his feet.

"Sure?"

"Sure. I also want to see where he went. If you don't mind lending me an arm."

The boy seemed to be able to put some weight on his foot. His first few assisted steps were slow, *very slow*, but as they made their way around the tables, his gait gradually grew a little smoother.

"Just need to stretch it out," Timothy said. "That actually seems to help."

Behind the counter and the chef's area were white double-doors with circular windows. They led into the kitchen.

"What are you doing?" one of the girls at the counter asked as they made their way by.

Kendall began to respond, "Checking to see which way–" but just then the doors opened and the chef came back out, nearly running over them.

After a moment's mutual surprise, the chef held up a tray with fresh hot dog rolls. He asked, "Más para ti, chica?"

"Oh, sorry," Kendall said, suspecting it was pointless as she did so, but feeling the need to explain anyway. "I thought you'd left. Thought you'd gone! Never mind, sorry."

With that, she began escorting Timothy right back to the table, watched by most of the kids at the counter. The chef set about frying more hot dogs.

143

Timothy smiled. "Awkwaaard." Which made them all smile.

Kendall helped Timothy back into his chair, Ricardo once again pushed her seat out with a foot, and said in a dramatic movie-announcer voice, "Sometimes … they come back!"

"Doesn't all this bother you, Ricky?" Kendall asked. "We spent the whole morning looking for a way out. Now we're all eating hot dogs like nothing happened."

"Course it does," he said. "It's just, I'm hungry. We all are."

Bellies full, the others followed their conversation. Ricky wiped mustard off his lips. "And we're not giving up, sweet Kendall of South Africaland! I'm with you. It doesn't make sense that we're sealed tight in here. We're like bugs in a jar. We *gotta* find a way out, we can't spend a whole week like this. But we also gotta eat."

Kweku said through a full mouth, "And vis is bloomin' outstanding. Best hot dog I ever 'ad."

Kendall looked at Britney, who shrugged, then patted her mouth with a napkin.

"All right then," Kendall said. "We *do* have to eat. But I'm not letting that guy out of my sight. When he goes, I want to know how he does it, even if I have to ride on his back."

Around his hot dog, Ricardo mumbled something that sounded like, "Kinky!"

Kendall's table settled once again into a slow conversational patter. They talked about the boy who fell, about what they might try next, though with less conviction than Kendall might have liked, and Kendall tried to maintain her concentration on the chef, although her mind kept slipping away to the almost-kiss situation with Ricky. It didn't help that he occasionally stole glances and aimed naughty smiles at her. Each time she broke eye contact with him, she jerked herself out of it and tried to monitor the chef again. But her gaze kept sliding back to temptation. His face was like some irresistible magnet.

144

During a moment's lull in the noise, Kendall jolted out of her fugue with the realisation that she hadn't glanced at the chef in minutes.

Still there. But he was cleaning the counter, clearing away plates, gathering up. It would be soon now. *No more Ricky!* Kendall told herself. *The guy is about to go, and you'll miss it!*

From behind Kendall, there came a gulp, and then a glopping liquid sound. It was followed by loud and disgusted cries of revulsion from several of the girls in a radius around them, and then three or four chairs slid back fast in unison.

Timothy sat with his arms raised like a preacher. He had vomit all down his shirt, pooling in his pants and running onto the floor.

The whole room stared in shock. One of the girls at a nearby table peered at the hot dog glop spreading slowly across the floor, scrunched her face, and nearly threw up too.

Into the sudden quiet, Britney, who had appointed herself Florence Nightingale, rolled her eyes and said, "If it's not one thing, it's another. Mate! Someone gets some towels, please?! Quickly."

She rose from her chair, careful not to step in the sordid liquid, and squatted beside Timothy. "Any more or do you think that was it?"

Timothy shook his head. *No more.* He used the back of one hand to wipe at his mouth. He looked as though he longed for nothing more than to fall through a hole in the ground.

"I'm sorry. I think it's the painkillers," he said.

"Right, you. Come on, let's get you up to your room and into a nice warm shower. Kendall, give's a hand? Boy, mister, you're having a really crap day, aren't you!"

A girl's voice from the back of the room whispered, "That is so gross!" and Kendall too fought hard to suppress a gag reflex.

Kendall wasn't quite sure where to put her hands on Timothy. She found a dry patch on the boy's arm, and together the two girls helped him to his feet. The way cleared before them as before some leper shedding body parts.

As they rounded the last table, dripping somewhat and smelling like sour mustard, Kendall glanced back over her shoulder.

The chef was gone.

WHAT WOULD ADDIE DO?

The promised hour went by. Dianne did not return. She did not return that day.

The twenty-one remaining kids once again dissolved into dispirited groups. They sat around, loped around, haunted different parts of the mansion. In the evening, they picked at the food from the buffet counter in the dining area – there was more than enough and it had been kept warm – and they allowed the hours of the day to simply run out.

As evening gathered over the Californian hills, some of the kids tried to rally a little and put together another movies night in the cinema room, just to keep spirits up. Just for something to do. Just as a way to combat the gnawing uncertainty. The showing was *Night at the Museum*.

Kendall didn't feel like it.

Two of the other kids didn't feel like it either, but apparently for different reasons. It was the couple who had been found yesterday making out. Kendall had watched them slip out, giggling happily, into one of the bedrooms. *That was their business*, she supposed. She wondered how they could be in the mood, under the circumstances. Once the door had closed, there were no further sounds to be heard.

Everyone else, including her roommate, was stuffed into the cinema room down below.

Now Kendall was upstairs, alone, lying uneasily on her bed. She alternated between praying for guidance, trying to fathom what was going on here, and drifting in and out of semi-fantasies about Ricky: Ricky with the lips, Ricky with the skew smile,

Ricky with the very, very nice hands so firmly planted on her hips as he stood perilously close to her within the private little changing-room cabin with no one else watching. Ricky, who wanted to put his tongue there.

Why *hadn't* she gone along with it? Well, for starters, because they could have been caught. There were kids right outside. Also, she wasn't sure it would have ended there. She had the impression that if she had given Ricky an inch, he would have confidently led her to way more. *Morals. That's one reason.*

She liked him, but could he be trusted?

Timothy – poor little Timothy – said that Ric had pushed him right off that ledge, *hard*, and out of pure meanness. What about that *psychopath* thing?

Possible psychopath thing, Kendall corrected herself. *It was just a thought, and you* are *talking about a seventeen-year-old after all, maybe eighteen, not a mask-wearing freak in some slasher movie. Realistically, what are the odds?*

Yet Kendall was old enough to know that odds were only numbers after all, and psychopaths didn't present as monsters. Addie had told her that. Often, they came across as the nicest people. And that was because they intended to. They *knew* how to con you. They could do anything – or be anyone – to get what they wanted, but it was all an act. Addie said they were perfectly capable of understanding emotion, but they processed it strategically. They didn't *relate* to your emotions. Instead, they *read* them, looking for an advantage.

Did that sound right? For Ricky? Did it fit?

Hands firmly on her hips. Confident and terribly close, leaning right up against her. Nuzzling her neck. Placing a slow kiss right down there, so she could feel it through the fabric, making her gasp.

Yeesh, girl!

Kendall flipped over onto her stomach and tried once again to concentrate. Why was it so *hard*? Her unfocused eyes stared out across the empty room.

She really wasn't sure if the psychopath thing fit – even wondered what had caused her to entertain the thought in the first place. It was all gut instinct, and gut instincts were *not* trustworthy. It may do for tough, self-assured heroines to 'follow their hearts', but as Addie often told Kendall, "The heart is a perfect moron. Follow your *brain* instead, okay?"

What do I think of him? And why the hesitation? What's wrong here?

Another part of her mind said, *Everything is wrong here.*

Yes, she answered herself. *I know everything is wrong with the house. But I don't mean that. I mean about Ricky. Just Ricky. Do I like him? Do I trust him?*

She allowed that to percolate for a moment as she thrashed back over onto her back and peered at the ceiling, wishing for a skylight like the one in her tiny bedroom back home, wishing for Dobby on her blankets snoring up a storm, wishing she could just go back to South Africa, be with her family again.

She tried to think back to her first flash of mistrust toward the handsome boy, who seemed perfectly infatuated with her, against all odds. When had that been? The airport, when he took her trolley? The panty peak during Songs Evening?

No. It had been while Ricardo was talking to the chef. *Yes, that was it.* She had wondered whether his translation was trustworthy.

But why? Mistranslating a chef? As crimes against humanity go, you'll need to do better than that, Kendall.

Although, that was even before Timothy had said anything about him. The Timothy thing came after her first flash of concern about Ricky. So then, had that been some sort of intuitive insight?

She needed to think clearly. And she needed to think a whole lot less about Ricardo, and being so close in a cabin, and the thrill of his lips nuzzling right there, and a whole lot more about this strange and possibly dangerous situation they were all facing in this house, this enormous, luxurious, ridiculous house. And she had always done her best night-time thinking under starlight, up on the roof.

✗

The fresh night air seemed to re-invigorate her brain, as though there hadn't been quite enough oxygen in the rooms below. Kendall breathed in deeply. It was cold enough to sting, but the slight pain in her chest felt satisfying. When she let it out, her breath steamed just a little.

She surveyed the darkness of strange and still distant California way down below, and thought about the nature of Copernican Revolutions. Kendall was glad she had the rooftop to herself. As was her habit back home, she had brought a blanket along, and now sat mummified in it, just a head erupting out the top, as tiny lights miles away betrayed the movements of unconfined humans on far-off aptly named 'freeways'.

The view from her roof in South Africa was nothing like this. She pictured their messy little garden, bordered by neighbors all around, some of their security lights burning late into the night. She winced a little with homesickness. Even the sky here was unfamiliar. It was weird to look up and not see the ever-present Southern Cross. Whatever that spangle of dots was, she didn't recognize any of it.

Okay. Let's get a grip on all this.

The situation here was deeply wrong. It was time to think, *really think*, with no distractions and no more self-delusion. And certainly no side-tracking into Ricky-pie la-la-land. He just made her head swim and her groin tingle.

Kendall decided to attack the problem from the outside in. Addie had taught her a way to do that. She'd said, "It's a basic problem-solving technique. Sometimes you don't begin with the granular detail, a close-up of the problem itself. Instead, step right out of it so all you can see is the big picture. Tell yourself the story of the big picture. Find a way to circle it. Then work your way back in."

Right ...

She pondered what it took to re-conceptualise the whole world around you, and to see the earth spinning around the sun, when, for so long, you'd been invested in the opposite model. Maybe conceiving of a different model wasn't the hard part. The hard part was truly *believing* it, believing it so much that you ceased to see the optical illusion, like that picture of the young girl with the hat flipping into a picture of an old woman with a bonnet. Or the lady at her dresser transformed into the skull ... not a friendly woman, but a symbol of death. *Would you even see the second picture if you didn't know it was there? If you hadn't been told?* Perhaps the really hard part in seeing things differently was just believing the switch enough to act on it.

Truth be told, Kendall thought, *she was already most of the way there.*

Okay. So do it. Shove yourself. Push yourself over the hump. Say it out loud and get it done. That will help.

"This is not an exchange program," Kendall told the stars. "It just isn't. And it never was. This is a con."

Good. Good!

Okay ...

She breathed out very slowly, allowing her gaze to shift from the terrace to the railing, back up to the stars again.

That's done.

She hadn't always known it. The problem, in fact, was that it had been gradual. Addie would have said it was '*frog in the pot*'.

Then when did *it start falling apart? When did the curtain begin to fall away?*

Probably from the time she began noticing the lack of adult supervision. *Songs night?* Yep. That was the first time, though it wasn't so noticeable because there had been food and an organized event. *If they give you food, you don't seem to notice what they're doing to you. Probably some life lesson in that.*

The next morning, then. That was when it really started unravelling. No adult supervision around the *pool*. That was weird in anyone's language.

Yes, those had been the early warning signs, the eerie early creakings of a vast machinery beginning to reveal its basic underpinning.

But it was hard to believe it. It was surprisingly difficult to really accept that something was wrong, wrong enough to be dangerous.

Well, sure. But that's why we have the term 'Copernican Revolution'. It's unusual. Most people can't or won't believe that everything they ever thought was backward. We don't want to, it's not nice. It's also why we have the word 'con'.

What made it so difficult in this case?

Well, it all looks so good. And we're excited about it. We want it to be real. Everything here looks so amazing, so expensive, so incredible. Plus the food is awesome. When you see all that with your own eyes, it doesn't seem believable that the whole thing, the whole enormous thing, could all be a ...

Addie's voice prompting her, '*A what, Kendall? Say it.*'

... a trap. A gigantic trap! The house. The whole thing! But then, that's what the fly thinks, right? Wow, free food! Right before the Venus flytrap swallows it up.

Addie's voice again. '*Good. Now keep going.*'

Every trap is disguised, when you think about it. In fact, what would be truly weird would be a trap that looked like a trap, which would be no trap at all.

Once again, Kendall spoke the words out loud, "This is a trap. The whole house. It's a con. It isn't real."

And there was something else. There was a subtler trap than the locked doors, the sealed windows, the electrified fences, that insurmountable cliff face. The trap was an *idea*. It was what Addie might call 'social convention'.

We all think we have to behave, because we all think we have *to behave,* Kendall thought. *What we should really be doing is burning the whole damn house down!*

She banked that idea. It was a good one, though perhaps only as a last resort. After all, what if she were wrong? What if she were mistaken and she burned down a seventy-million-dollar luxury Californian mansion? How would she explain that? Would she go to jail? Imagine trying to talk her way out of that one.

And there it was. The power of social convention. *That was exactly how it worked, right? Why it worked.*

Every indication screamed to the even half-sane observer that *everything* here was off ... dangerously off ... but still. *What if? What if you're wrong?* It was incredibly hard to overcome that little voice of warning, of caution, of hesitation, that your parents had spent a lifetime instilling: You can't damage an expensive house! You're just a kid. What do you know?

Ludicrous. The odds were your very life versus being shouted at. No contest, right?

But was it a matter of life or death? Who knew? What the heck was the point of all this?

Over her blanket cocoon, Kendall's face reflected anger. *You bring kids in from all over the world. They pay to make their way to you, you put them in a house, and then ... what? You extract them one by one? Why? I don't get it. If this isn't a student exchange program, then why bring us together, give us this great week while peeling us off, one at a time? I mean, what, are they like ... selling children or something?*

Kendall went gooseflesh.

Oh, shit.

Yes.

Once she had said the words to herself, they fit. They made perfect sense. The fact that they were all exceptionally good-looking youngsters, even if Kendall was on the skinny side.

It made evil but perfect sense. And though she tried, no competing ideas could now dislodge that one in her mind.

But this looks nothing like a ... a child-selling thing!

Yes. Exactly.

Say it. Out loud, once again. Say it, so you believe it.

"They're selling us. They're *selling* us. One by one. That's what's going on here. That's the point."

A strange calm settled over her.

Saying it aloud changed something in her. It felt like permission to believe. The content of the belief was awful, sure, but accepting the belief provided solace of a kind. It was as though a terrible screaming red siren had finally been turned off. Admittedly, the siren was off because the disaster was here in full. But at least now the disaster could be faced. It was no longer a mounting fear, a clawing doubt, the ghastly suggestion of a cancerous possibility. It was plain truth. And now it was time to face that truth with open eyes.

Out loud again, she said to the cars far below, "It *is* a trap. And if we have to do extreme things to get out, then we should. We must. Before it's too late. Before we also disappear out of the house to ... who knows where?"

Where did they go? Where was Agnieszka, right now?

Kendall breathed in and out for a few moments, feeling the sting of the cold night air on her cheeks, not quite knowing where to go next with her thoughts.

A night bird of some kind flicked by in the dark. She watched it swoop down into the valley, grow smaller. Once again, there was a coastal mist creeping up toward them, shrouding parts of the land in night-time silver.

Some additional grain of discomfort still nagged at her. Her inner Addie was still nudging at her to keep thinking at this problem, still insisting there was more, and that working it out mattered.

Okay, so, what?

It had to do with the nature of the trap.

Even if you accepted the child-selling model, which she did, there was something that didn't make sense from *their* point of view. Kendall tried to formulate the thought. It came to her. *Why on earth would you leave kids you wanted to sell unattended?* It only made sense if the sellers felt guilty about what they were doing and wanted to give them a final holiday as a consolation prize. And somehow Kendall didn't think that was likely. *But why else this whole extraordinary experience?*

The words came into Kendall's mind in Addie's voice, spoken flat and plain. '*The instant that boy got hurt, Dianne walked in and removed him.*'

She knew!

Somehow, Dianne knew what had happened. Of course she did. The timing was too perfect. And there had been no other point to her incursion, she certainly wasn't returning their phones and she clearly had no intention of coming back later, even though she'd said she would.

Okay, the groceries. But still. She walked in, picked up the boy, and walked back out again. With big men to help with the carrying, which she couldn't have done alone. Then she never came back. The groceries were not the point. *The boy was.*

And that means, we are not being left uncontrolled, Kendall thought.

More pieces of the puzzle fell into place.

The kids had performed songs and swum and made out on couches. Then they started disappearing one by one.

We're merchandise being displayed. Different body types. Different ethnicities. Different personalities.

We aren't unattended. They're watching. We think there's no one in control, but we're wrong. The control is in here – with us.

155

✗

"No offense, but when I pictured myself in the sack with two foreign babes, you were never a part of my fantasy, Kweku. Nor you, Timothy."

"Relieved to hear it, mate."

"Ditto, I'm sure."

Kendall had invited the core group to her room, to her bed, and beneath her covers. They sat cross-legged like small children on a first sleepover, holding the duvet above all of their heads and conspiring in the gloom beneath. She'd even turned off the lights in the room, to probing questions from the group. All Kendall had said by way of explanation was, "Get under. I'll explain then."

Now the tented figures of Britney and Ricardo flanked her on the left, just about knee to knee. The bed was big enough for them to make a loose circle, with Timothy and Kweku to her right. The illuminated dials on three of their wristwatches provided an unexpected sickly green glow, which moved wildly if any of them gestured. Kendall made sure to separate Timothy from Ricardo, positioning Kweku between them as Switzerland.

"Why are we here?" little Timothy asked.

Kendall was glad to see that he had rebounded. His stomach seemed to be behaving. She was also glad to note that he had brushed his teeth, though she didn't mention it.

"I think they're watching us with cameras," Kendall said.

"Is that why we're all holed up in here, in our military-grade camouflage?" Kweku asked, poking at the duvet.

"Try to take this seriously," said Britney.

"There's nuffing more serious than me. I'm serious like a toofache."

Ricardo asked, "Why do you think that?"

"First, because after that kid broke his leg, Dianne walked

straight in, removed him, and then walked straight back out. It was like she knew. So *how* did she know? Second, because … okay, so this is a little embarrassing, but I guess we're past that now. The other day I got undressed in the bathroom; this one up here, in our room. I was looking at my … you remember, the *burn* on my leg … in the mirror. And the lights went up slightly. Just the bathroom lights, and just as I was standing in front of the glass."

There was a second of silence in the bed tent.

Ricardo said, "Is that it?"

Now that it was out of her mouth, it did sound lame.

Ricardo added, "I mean, we were *expecting* the Ice Queen to arrive, and she did. If she didn't come back, maybe it's because she's been at the hospital. And the lights in your bathroom flickered. Like … so?"

Her case was sounding flimsy.

But Britney added, "OMG, now you say it, I think that happened to me too, exactly the same! You just reminded me."

"*What* happened?"

"I got …" Britney glanced at the boys, dropped her voice tone a fraction, "… undressed for the shower. I stood looking in the mirror, and the lights went up. Just a bit, like you said, but they definitely did. And that's not all." She thought for a second, then screwed up her nose. "Oh gross!"

"What?"

Britney hesitated again. "When I … sat on the loo, I thought I heard this '*zzzt*'. I remember looking around to see what it was, but there was nothing. I hadn't thought about it 'til now. No, Kendall's right, guys! And the timing – both of us, *girls*, standing naked in front of the mirror and the lights go up? Come on, mate, that's not nothing."

"Do all girls stand naked posing in front of mirrors? If so, sign me up for mirror duty immediately."

"Ricardo!"

"Okay, okay! What exactly do you think it means?" he said.

Kendall paused for a moment. "I think there are cameras behind the mirrors. I think they're watching us. Maybe even filming or photographing us. That sound you heard, Britney, that was maybe like zooming in. Sorry! And that means there might be cameras throughout the rest of the house too."

The congress under the covers took a moment to ponder this.

"What would be the point?" Kweku asked. "It's pervy, but I don't get it."

"I had three thoughts about that," Kendall said. "One is it's, like, porn. They're getting photos and videos of us, maybe especially the girls. Two is it's for some sort of blackmail. They get bad photos of us, then bribe our families not to release them. But I don't know, that one seems the least likely, because how could you really bribe people with just naked photos? Sure, it's embarrassing, but they're not really doing anything wrong in the photos. And besides, too many of us are too–" here Kendall paused, searching for the right word, "–short on money to make it worth their while."

"And the third?" Timothy asked.

"The third option is the scariest. And I also think it's what's really going on here. I think the photos of us are like a kind of ... show."

"Like advertising?" Timothy said.

"Exactly. *Advertising*. They're advertising us."

"Why?"

"Because they're selling us. They're selling kids."

In the grey-green gloom, Britney's face looked horrified. "What do you mean, like ... as slaves?"

"Maybe as sex slaves or something. I don't know. But, yes."

"Are you freakin' serious?"

"Yes, I am. Very serious."

"Like a ... like a shopping site for total pervs?"

"Exactly. Men who buy kids."

Silence again, as the group digested the ideas. Kendall expected Ricardo to object first. But Ricardo conceded, "We *did* walk through that metal detector when we came in. It was like a whole corridor for it. That was a pretty weird thing to do in a house."

Britney said, "To make sure we didn't have phones, you think?"

Kweku said, "You know what we could do? We could just break a mirror."

"What?" Kendall asked.

"Break a mirror. Smash through the glass. Find out for sure. We're sitting here going around in circles. Why don't we just check, right now? Then we'd know."

Timothy said, "Are we ... certain? Certain enough to actually do that?"

"Why not?"

"This is a very expensive house," Timothy said. "I believe you, Kendall, and I'm all for finding out. I'll go along with the decision, but ..."

Ricardo picked up from there, "... but dude, this place is worth over sixty mil! Like, hello! He's right. Wouldn't that be ever so slightly – I don't know – totally freakin' insane? Like, what if we're wrong?"

Social convention. There it is. It didn't take long to find us, even in here, hiding under our little blanket.

Addie's voice in her head: *'It didn't find you. You brought it with you.'*

We are the social convention, aren't we?

Ricardo went on, "I don't like to use the phrase 'conspiracy theory', but ..."

"I'll take the rap for it," Kendall asserted. "If there's any trouble to face, I'll make up some excuse, like I slipped and hit it with a hair drier or something. I don't care. But I think we should do it. I want to know."

"Mate, I actually think we should, too," said Britney.

"Dude! Sixty million bucks! We're guests. And we're teenagers. You can't go smashing the mirrors in the homes of multi-gazillionaires. It's insane."

"Ricardo, if we decide to try it, will you stop us?"

"Well ... no." He rubbed at his chin in the gloom. "I just think it's ... what's that British word you used, Kweku? *Bonkers*?"

"Vat's the one. But it isn't, mate, not really. It's just a mirror, not the whole house. And it's a good way to be sure."

"Anyone else vote 'no'?" Kendall asked. "Okay, then. We agree, with one objection."

"You guys are nuts, but *fine*. Smash the stupid thing if you must."

Kendall said, "Next, we have got to find a way out of this house! Today we tried all the obvious stuff. None of it worked. Everything's locked or electrified, or ... I don't know ... *glued*. Tomorrow, we have to do better."

"Break more shit?"

"Yes, Ric. If necessary, we'll break more shit."

"Sassy girl!"

Timothy volunteered, "I was thinking. The only person who ever does get in and out of here seems to be that chef guy. Maybe we try a little harder to do what you wanted to do today, Kendall? Follow him?"

Oh yeah! Kendall had forgotten about her aborted attempt to tail the Bolivian. "That's right! He walks in. He walks out. We stick to him like glue."

"... and walk right out with him," Timothy said.

The duvet moved around as the whole group murmured their assent.

Kweku said, "So ... shall we get smashin'?"

Ricardo grumbled something.

Timothy said, "Maybe not right now."

"Why not?" Kendall asked.

160

"Think about it. If we do discover a camera, and someone is watching, then *they* will know that *we* know. Right?"

"Okay?"

"So maybe we shouldn't smash it tonight. We don't know how to get out yet."

Kweku said, "That definitely would tip off anyone watching."

"Oh. Geez. Good point," Kendall said. "Okay, so tomorrow morning we shadow the chef and figure out how to leave. Then, once we know we *can* get out, we smash the mirror to make sure we're doing the right thing. Then we go. That's about it, yes?"

"Yes," they all said at intervals.

"Good," Kendall said. "Then I believe we have a plan."

✗

"I need a favour. Two, actually."

"Go."

"The camera. In the South African girl's bathroom. I need it removed."

"Why?"

"They want to break the mirror tomorrow morning to check for them. They'll call me first. I need you to get rid of it right away when she leaves the room."

"I'll send someone in. Second thing?"

"No chef tomorrow. They want to try to follow him out."

"Noted. Nothing else?"

"Nothing else for now."

"Good work. The South African girl. Still the ringleader?"

"Yes."

"Want her removed yet?"

"Leave her in. Everyone's looking to her for what to do. If you extract her then the rest will panic and make the situation worse. So long as I manage her, *I can contain everyone."*

REBELLION

Wednesday. The great 'Mirror Smash' was scheduled for after breakfast, but the event hit several unwelcome snags.

For starters, they all slept longer than they should have. The winter mornings were dark, and the stress and jetlag from the time differences were taking their toll. No one had risen early, no one had awakened the others, and so they had simply lost a large swathe of the morning.

Kendall looked at her wristwatch. It was now 11:30. So late, and the chef still wasn't at his post behind the griddles. No one else had seen him earlier in the day. Nor was there any replacement. The steel surfaces gleamed unused after their last cleaning.

There was still plenty of food laid out, ranging from hot meals in the buffet-style sunken trays to a wealth of fruit and snacks like granola bars or packets of crisps on the counters.

Nevertheless, this reduction in the number of adults in the house, from one to zero, quelled appetites. Most of the kids just picked at snacks and looked worried. That heady sense of unchecked freedom from Day One was now utterly dead. The mood had completely transformed to one of fear. No one used the pools. No one proposed watching movies or gathering for songs.

The second unwelcome surprise was that five more kids were gone. Just like that. Simply gone.

It must have happened late last night, or early in the morning. Kendall's little group remained. Timothy, Kweku, Ricardo, and Britney. They were now down to sixteen kids in the house.

She sat lost in her own world of thought.

Maybe our next step should be to move into just one or two rooms, she thought. *Maybe cordon off certain areas. Make the house smaller.*

Kweku echoed the theme of her thinking. "How the hell do they do it? How do they keep getting kids out wifout our noticing?"

The friends grunted assent, but the conversation died again. Ricardo swirled the last of a Coke in the bottom of a glass, looked at it for a listless moment, then swigged it.

Britney volunteered, "You know, she probably just walks in, calls the nearest kids to go with her, tells them not to worry about their bags, and walks right back out with them. Simple as that."

Kendall thought, *Maybe we should post a sentry at the door.* And *at the elevator. And, if we can figure out which of the locked doors it is, the wine cellar. If there even is one.* There were several locked doors though. The idea would require too many sentries.

They allowed another two hours to tick by, waiting on the chef, talking, picking at snacks.

Kendall hated this meaningless inertia; this slow, ongoing nothingness. It was dulling. It made it too easy to give up and do nothing. They were coasting, allowing time to go by, and that seemed dangerous.

"Right! No more. Everybody up. Let's go break that mirror."

Britney said, "But we still don't know how to get out."

"I don't care," Kendall said. "I want to know. We already know, but I want to know for sure."

"Me too," Timothy said.

"Ah hell, why not?" Ricardo said.

The group appeared to rally. They pushed back their chairs simultaneously.

Good! Kendall thought. *We're in business again. We're doing something.*

"Nice!" Kweku pounded a fist into an open palm as he walked. "Let's go break some shit!"

*

"I guess … stand back?"

There'd been no need to say it. Kendall wielded one of the small wooden stools from beneath the dressing table, held it by one leg in two of her hands, and took up a stance, hoping she was strong enough for this. She hesitated for a moment, glanced at her friends.

"Kendall," Kweku said. "If you're waiting for our permission, then you're doing this wrong."

Fair enough.

"Here goes."

She swung the stool with everything she had.

Kendall had expected a crack, maybe even for a large part of the mirror to dislodge and fall to the floor. She'd been ready to scoot her feet out of the way.

The results were much more dramatic than that. The mirror surface burst like a pressurized balloon. The explosion sprayed a shock wave of tiny glass shards everywhere around the bathroom, even hitting the side walls, scratching and tinkling to a stop at the base of the bath.

None of the pieces were big, but the corona reached all the way to the door, where the group took a step backward on their toes.

Kendall opened one of her eyes, then the other. She took stock. She prodded a small piece of glass off her lips with her tongue.

No cuts? Nothing seemed to hurt. She was peppered with flakes and stones and powder-sized specks of white. As she lowered the chair and brushed them off her arms, her shirt, her jeans, and her hair, Britney said, "Wow!"

Ricardo added, "Dude!"

The friends waded into the room, using the sides of their shoes to scrape a clear path as they progressed.

The mirror had been backlit, LED bulbs creating ambient lighting around its edges. Other than those bulbs, there was only tiled wall. One of the tiles was slightly chipped where Kendall's swing had punched clear through the mirror. On another was a tiny hole, which may or may not have been drilled through the wall – it was hard to tell, even from up close. *But no camera.*

She heard the '*shiiink*' of glass being scraped aside as the group joined her, gathering to examine the empty wall. A moment ago, she had been terrified at the prospect of seeing some sort of lens back there. Now she was disappointed by its absence.

That had proved nothing.

Nobody said a word.

Kendall could feel them looking at her, looking at the vandalized wall, back at her.

"I was *so* sure ..." she said. She waited for an 'I told you so' from Ricardo.

Britney said, "Mate, I was too. I don't get it. I totally expected ..." She petered out. "I just don't get it. Then what's the point of all this? What's *really* going on?"

Timothy put in, "Do you think maybe we're all just being paranoid after all?"

Kweku, who had been silent up until now, pursed his lips for a second, said, "You know what? Sod it!" and picked up the stool where it lay on the floor. Brandishing it by one leg, he marched from the room, crunching over the glass.

"What? Where are you going?"

Kweku didn't answer, but his gait was determined, so they followed, back across the glass, less carefully this time.

He marched out of the girls' room, across the corridor, into one of the boys' rooms, through the bathroom door, and, without hesitation, swung the chair full tilt at another large mirror.

Before the group could say anything – before the exploding glass had even completed its long skittering slide across yet another set of bathroom tiles – they saw the tiny rubber casing mounted into the wall, shielding the cold, round glass eye of its all-seeing lens.

✳

"They know."

"Yes, we were watching. Can you still hold them?"

"I can," the Goat said. "But not for more than another day, day and a half. This changes things. They'll be desperate now."

The Operator and the Head of Watch glanced at one another.

"What do they do when they're desperate?" the Head of Watch asked.

"Depends. Maybe try to burn it down."

The Operator thought for a second. "If they want to, let them."

"Okay."

"But guide it. The place is rigged with sprinklers. The attempt will buy a little more time, and time is all we need. Take them to one of the smaller rooms so the damage is contained. Minimal."

"Good."

"We've confirmed sales of seven more units. I'll have them removed tonight. We're getting there. That brings it down to nine. Draw it out as long as you can – there's a lot of interest. We might still sell off the entire batch, and we're already in the black. All additional units are now pure profit. The longer you draw it out and the more we sell, the bigger your bonus."

"I know."

"The South African girl ..."

"Yes, she's still leading them."

"We don't have a buyer for her. But we can remove her, have her destroyed, if you need. We're all on site."

"I told you, I can handle her."

"Stick with her, then."

"That's what I'm doing."

✗

"Here, this room," Ricardo said, pushing open the panelled wooden door.

"Why this one?" Kendall asked.

"Because it's on *this* side of the house, facing the driveway. That's the way we want to go. And if we can break it, the window here is big enough to climb through."

It was the largest of the formal office-style rooms, down on the ground floor, off the longest corridor.

Kendall glanced at her wristwatch, then considered the sunlight outside. It was already 3pm. In mid-winter, that meant there wasn't much day left. They had accomplished frightfully little today.

Ricardo found a paperweight in the shape of a Shakespeare bust on one of the leather-clad writing desks.

"Weaponizing Shakespeare?" Kweku said. "That's sacrilege."

Ricardo hurled the bust at full tilt at the centre of the window.

It bounced straight off and hit him hard in the shoulder.

"Ow! Geez!" he exclaimed. Then he shook the fingers of that arm, as though the entire arm was numb.

Kweku said, "Give's a shot, yeah?" and once again walked out of the room.

They followed him into the next office along, where he reprised his role as chair swinger, using a straight-back wooden seat with cane cushioning. They all flinched and leaned back as he swung. This time, though, the chair simply bounced off the reinforced glass and smacked back into him.

Kweku bent over double, blowing on his fists. Kendall

thought that must really have hurt, because he closed his eyes, but made no sound.

From his crouched position, Kweku said, "My old man once told me what it felt like to get kicked by a donkey ..." and left it at that.

"All right then. We head back to that breakfast area," Kendall said. "Nobody leaves anybody else's sight, okay? We get some food – enough to keep us going – and we take it with us to the atrium, so we're right there by the elevator and the front door, and then we – uh, it's like a military word ..." Kendall made a huddling gesture as she searched for the term.

"Barricade ourselves in?" Britney suggested.

"Yes! We get ourselves a secure corner where we can see anyone coming or going. We stick together, *barricade* ourselves in. We don't let anyone get snatched."

Britney said, "We should invite the other kids to join us. Everyone should be there."

"I agree," said Kendall. "That also gives us some strength in numbers. Then if we have to rush Dianne, we can."

This bold new thought caused the group to pause.

⚹

Kendall murmured, mostly to herself, "How long does it take to get a pillow and a jacket and come back down?"

Fifteen kids bunched into one corner of the atrium at the entrance to the great house, minus the Indian girl, Aadab. She was still upstairs, gathering her things.

The group of fifteen positioned their encampment across the atrium floor from the elevators. At acute angles, they faced both the elevator doors and the corridor that led to the front door, so that whether an approaching threat came from left or right, they would see it. Their backs were to one wall, or the closest thing to a blank wall in this strange, multi-layered house.

Were their situation not so serious, Kendall might have laughed at their little barricade.

We look like a sleepover at my cousin's.

Britney was even having her hair braided by one of the other girls. The Teutonic effect suited her.

Kendall studied the inert elevator. She waited for the carriage to move, or for the digital '*bing*' to signal. *Something*. Without really looking, she accepted one of the biscuits from the packet doing the rounds and took a bite.

Now that just about everyone was gathered in one place, and no one was walking about the house, the corridors radiating out from the atrium seemed threatening in their emptiness. They were fully lit, just as ever. They were clean, opulent, sumptuous, every tile polished to a glow. Just as ever. But up until now, there had been kids scattered all about the place, making noise, and adding the patina of life and the bustle of animation. With everyone gathered into a timid nucleus, the corridors were quiet and seemed only to lead to threatening destinations. Or perhaps to nowhere at all. And night was falling. Plenty of places for ghosts and goblins and snatchers of children.

Still the elevator sat dormant. Kendall rubbed her fingers together, the way her father did when he was stressed.

They had to agree on what they would do if Dianne *did* arrive. If they weren't prepared, then they would do nothing again. Just remain a baffled group of youngsters, lamely enquiring about their phones.

The woman's strength lay in her unwavering self-confidence. And their weakness lay in their hesitation. Their sense of her role as the adult in charge. They had to be ready this time, ready to rush her if necessary. There were boundaries to cross, and that took mental preparation.

Of course, rushing her would be a lot harder if those two big men were with Dianne.

We still have some bigger boys here. Enough to maybe pin down a large man, maybe even two. But only if we do it like we really mean it. No hesitating.

And then what … ?

One step at a time. For now, it's time to address the troops.

Kendall wondered at how easily this newfound role was coming to her. A month ago, she'd have been mortified even to speak in front of her class at school. A few days ago, she'd have felt her heart thudding in her chest each time she met someone new.

There was a two-word phrase that caught something of the spirit of change within her: 'Needs must'.

This new Kendall didn't feel wrong. But it didn't feel entirely comfortable either.

Kendall couldn't wait to get home to Addie and her parents, to Johannesburg (which now looked ludicrously safe), to her school and friends. To the old her.

The other girl finished doing Britney's braids. Britney turned from side to side, showing off the results.

Kendall swallowed the last of her biscuit and was just beginning to rise to address the group, when Britney said, "I gotta go to the loo."

Kendall deflated somewhat, lowered herself back down.

She looked worriedly at the elevators.

"No, don't worry," Britney said. "I'm not heading up there. Although … do you think maybe I should? Should someone check on Aadab?"

Kendall thought about it. "No. If she's coming back down, she'll come back down. If she's not for some reason, like, if she's been taken somehow, then we might lose you too. We're still assuming kids are being taken out the elevator or the door. But we don't actually know. Not for certain."

Britney looked relieved. "Good. I'll just use these ones here, then. You coming too?"

"Nah, thanks. Don't need to."

"I'll come." It was the girl who had been making out with her new boyfriend in one of the rooms. She was European, though Kendall forgot which nation she was from – maybe Austria? – and she wore a droopy oversized sweater that flopped over her hands. She'd been sitting with her head on her boyfriend's shoulder. She now stood up in a sort of pirouette and stepped daintily over two other kids, then took Britney's arm, as though she couldn't bear not to be leaning on someone at all times. Some girls were like that. Touchy feely.

Kweku mused aloud, "Oldest tradition in the world. Girls going to the loo togevuh. Fancy going to the loo with me, Ric?"

"Store it in your accordion, Kweku."

"Hey, there you go, mate! Nailed it! Fist bump for dat!"

Kendall gave a half smile, then turned to watch the elevator again. *Seriously, where was Aadab? Should they maybe all go check on her as a group?*

A minute passed by, and Kendall listened to the idle chatter of the kids around her. She ate another biscuit. Two minutes expired. Five. Ten.

Kendall was feeling guilty about the Indian girl upstairs. She hadn't wanted to risk Britney disappearing after her, but what if they did all go together?

Fifteen minutes passed.

Twenty.

Ricardo leaned over and whispered, "I know girls like to do marathon restroom trips, but under the circumstances, don't you think maybe you should go check on those two?"

He was right. Kendall hadn't even been thinking about Britney and the other girl down here.

Yet somewhere in the caverns of her cautious soul, warning bells sounded. Everyone was thoroughly freaked out and determined to band together, and Britney knew it. Right? Yet she'd been gone for twenty minutes.

Could the danger be as close as the bathrooms? *Surely not.* The bathrooms were *right there.* If you walked a few steps that way, you could just about see the doors from where they were gathered in the atrium. Just about ...

Timothy, who missed nothing, sidled closer to Kendall and said, "You should go, but not alone. Take us all with you."

Ricardo said, "But then no one's watching the door or the elevator. Wasn't that the whole point of camping out here? So we can see if anyone comes in?"

"The way *I* see it," said Timothy, "the whole point was to stick together and not separate."

With Ricardo on one side and Timothy on the other, Kendall felt like the cartoon character torn between the whispered motivations of an angel and a devil. *Which one should she listen to?*

"Okay, everyone!" Kendall said to the entire group. "Listen, those two haven't come back from the bathroom yet. Let's all go check on them, but let's do it together. As a group. It's just round there. Then we all come straight back. Okay?"

One of the boys mumbled, "Okay," and everyone ambled to their feet, most dripping biscuit crumbs.

It took a minute to organize and mobilize the ramshackle commando, but everyone came along, leaving a nest of discarded items behind.

The nearest lavatories were designed hotel style, with multiple urinals and cubicles, in anticipation of large numbers of guests at the house, perhaps for social gatherings or business events. The door was just a few hundred feet down the corridor from the atrium, though not in a straight line. Nothing in this house followed straight lines.

There were two curving staircases, a waist-high water feature to walk around, then a small arched bridge over a faux river that dissected one of the corridors, such as might be found at the bottom of an English country garden.

At the doors, Ricardo said, "Guess we're all going into the ladies' room."

Kendall, in the lead, leaned against the heavily sprung door. It yielded to her shoulder.

The lavatory was opulent with swooping marble and tiled counters, well-lit mirrors around one wall. And it was empty.

"Britney? Britney!"

Over Kendall's shoulder, the boyfriend called, "Isabella!"

Kendall marched into the bathroom and along the stalls, slamming open all the doors. She knew it was pointless – the place was obviously vacant – but she did it anyway. She even checked for holes in the back walls.

Ricardo said, "What the freakin' heck?! How?!"

The other kids all looked shocked, not least the girl's boyfriend, who double-checked all the empty stalls, even knocking on the back walls to test for hollow places.

Kendall pushed past the other kids, out into the corridor. She ran back over the small bridge, down the winding steps, into the atrium. She stood in the centre, cupped her hands to her mouth, then turned in a circle as she yelled upward, "Britneyyy! Britney!"

The others quickly joined her. Like some pagan circle in a forest, they, too, turned and called out to the spirits of the sky, to the rafters of the great house, to the heavens and anyone who might be listening, adding "Aadab!" and "Isabella!" to the cacophony.

They did it for a full thirty seconds, bellowing out their frustration and fear. Then they fell silent again.

There was no response. The house was empty, silent. Dead.

Then it came alive.

The house began to hum. The sound came from all directions at once.

"What the hell *is* that?" Kendall asked.

One of the girls pointed, "The blinds! Look, it's all of them."

Kendall hadn't registered that the blinds were open in the atrium. They had been closed when she first arrived at the house. Now they were shutting again, drawing a curtain of shade across the marble floor and over the staircases, furniture, pillars, and finally, over the kids' faces. In every adjacent room, motorized blinds did the same.

The house was shuttering down, like a bunker. For a very large space, it now began to feel claustrophobically tight.

At least the lights are still–

All at once, every light in the house went out, plunging them into utter darkness. The girls around Kendall shrilled in panic.

A soft digital *bing* sounded from the elevator right behind them.

✗

They're coming! Kendall thought. *Right there! Someone is right there and they're coming!*

"Hide!" she yelled, but the darkness was disorienting. She dropped to the floor and crawled.

Even as she slid toward what she hoped might be the safe cover of a wall or couch, she thought, *Surely, they can see us, though?*

There were sudden aggressive noises all around her: shuffling and bumping, terrified shrieks from at least three of the girls, the odd sounds of fabric rubbing and shoes thudding betraying rapid human movement.

Kendall's head slammed into the front of a boot. Strong hands grabbed at her shoulders. *Strong* hands. This was no teenager hauling her up.

Without hesitating for a second, Kendall curled the fingers of one hand into a claw and swiped upward, putting everything she had into the motion.

Her aim was good. She felt coarse cheek-skin tearing. She

also felt her fingers bump off against something hard, maybe metallic. The person hissed "Fuck!" and let her go. *Deep voice. Adult. Male.*

From the ground, Kendall kicked hard where she thought the man's shins were, connected again with a scrape, then got up into a crouching position and ran.

There was no natural light whatsoever in the atrium. A miniscule amount leaked through the blinds far off down the corridors, so that she could see the dullest hint of grey, but there were so many obstacles between her and them, a tangle of inky shadows.

All around her, the sounds of scuffling and struggling continued, heightening in intensity, occasionally breaking into shouts. One of the girls squealed, "Let go! Leave me alo-" but her voice was suddenly muffled.

Still crouched, Kendall slowed her run. She was blind as a bat, and could brain herself on a wall or stumble down one of those odd split levels on the floor, twisting ankles, tearing ligaments.

Trying not to make any sound, she waved searching hands before her. Finally, she touched something: a railing. Kendall grabbed hold and turned to face the various noises, like a wild animal in a corner.

She believed she had run slightly right of the water feature. If so, that put her near the staircase and mezzanine level where Timothy had fallen. Or been pushed. Then this was probably the handrail going up the centre of those stairs. She sent one foot out like a probe, found one step, then another. *Good.* That seemed right. Now she tried to picture the rest of the room from that angle.

How hard could it be to remember its layout? She'd been looking at it a scant forty seconds ago.

If she could get to the water feature, Kendall was fairly sure she could find her way from there to a corridor.

There were still sounds of shoving and dragging around the room, though no one spoke. The kids who hadn't been caught were hiding quietly, the kids who had been caught must have been silenced, and the hunters weren't saying a word. So much movement in the dark, but no speech. It was deeply eerie.

Through the tense sounds, Kendall heard water. *That way. It's that way.*

It seemed to be farther away than she might have guessed, though sounds were hollow and deceptive in this strangely proportioned space.

Should she walk calmly and hope not to bump into anyone? Sprint and pray?

The decision was forced upon her when loud footsteps, *the sound of boots*, thudded right at her at what sounded like a running pace. They were a short lunge away from her when she ducked and sprinted.

She dashed in a crouch toward the pool of endless dark where she hoped and believed the water feature would be. She imagined that the man in boots was right behind her and she put on more speed, expecting fingers to clutch her at any second.

Then her fear of being chased began to morph into a fear of running blind into something before her.

She had correctly guessed the location of the water feature. But she had overestimated the distance. Still loping at a crouch, she pummelled headfirst into it. Her skull connected with the corner of the ledge, which was about hip height, and hot white stars tunnelled through her vision.

She tried to tell herself to crumple down and to the side, but all control failed her and dizzy thoughts turned to distant dreams. She bundled face first into the trough of water.

Not dead.

That was her first thought through the intense pain. Through the confusion. *Not dead, I'm alive!*

She was lying down. On the floor. One of her hands spread into a starburst on the floor beneath her. *Tiles. Wet tiles. Am I still in the house?*

She groaned. Instantly, someone clamped a hand over her mouth. "Shhh! Shut up!"

The hand released her mouth. The tone, even in that small admonition, sounded so very frightened. It spiked her adrenaline. That made her head pound.

Kendall realized she was squinting against bright light. She raised bleary eyelids to see where she was, tried to focus her eyes. Her chest and collarbone hurt and badly. And she was sopping wet. On top, anyway.

The lights were back on. The shutters were open. Painful daylight streamed into the house once more.

Who was beside her, hunched down here on the floor?

When she saw the braided hair, Kendall drew a sharp breath. *Britney!*

The girl looked urgently at her and indicated a finger on her lips. Britney's eyes looked red and puffy. She leaned right down beside Kendall and whispered right into her ear, "I think they might be gone. Don't know for sure."

Kendall took stock and realized that her hair was utterly soaked, and her lips were starting to go numb. She wanted to dry herself, but she was too scared to move. And her chest felt like she'd been smashed there with a bat.

Why? She thought she had only hit her head.

The two girls remained there, together on the floor, for another ten minutes. They were in a corner, slightly behind a large flower box. Kendall didn't think that that was where she had fallen. She wondered whether Britney had dragged her there. Now that she looked, there was a trail of water from where Kendall had fallen to where Britney now squatted.

Kendall watched as Britney finally risked peeking out, then standing up.

Slowly, scanning in every direction for movement, Kendall joined her.

Walking almost on their toes, they both stepped out into the open.

On the other side of the atrium, two female faces looked out at them from behind a couch. Kendall thought their names might be Claudette and Tina. Cautiously, they, too, left their hiding place and joined Kendall and Britney. They said nothing. Tina was still crying, and Claudette was not far behind.

That makes four, Kendall thought.

She touched at her hairline. Just at the base of her fringe, a lump that felt like a separate entity swelled from her skull. Just touching it caused flares across her vision.

Britney opened her mouth to speak out, realized that her voice was creaking from the sustained tension, cleared her throat, then tried again, "Guys? Guys, come out. They're gone."

From behind another of the couches, Kweku emerged. If it were possible, his face looked grey.

Oh good! Okay, that's five.

They found Timothy balled up in a corner in the kitchen. He flinched in fright when they touched him …

Six.

… and Ricardo was beyond the kitchen, outside in the amphitheatre garden, having crawled through that high space that was the serving hatch.

Ricky brings us up to seven.

When they waved to Ricardo, he climbed back into the house through the serving hatch headfirst, landing awkwardly on the serving counter of the kitchen within. For the first time, he, too, had nothing to say. He looked rattled.

Is that it? Are we the only ones left? Seven kids?

When Ricardo saw the lump on Kendall's skull, he whispered, "¡Dios mio! Did they hit you with something?" Then, "Why are you wet?"

"No, no one hit me. I accomplished this all by myself. No, don't touch it, it hurts." Ricardo retrieved his hand. "Ran head-first in the dark into the wall by that fountain thing."

"Shit. That is really, *really* going to need some ice. You're lucky you weren't knocked out."

"I was, actually. But wait, are you bleeding?"

Ricardo had blood down one leg.

"Yeah. It's not bad. I hit a corner somewhere in the dark. A counter or something. It cut my leg. Looks worse than it feels."

Britney opened a freezer drawer in the kitchen and broke blocks of ice onto the counter. "I'll tell you everything, mate, but let's get … I don't know … somewhere safe. Or the closest thing we can find to safe. That area clearly wasn't it."

Kweku suggested, "What about the roof?"

Britney wrapped the ice cubes in a cloth and handed them to Kendall. Kendall winced as she pressed the ice against her head. Not only did it hurt, but her hair was still wet and she was freezing.

Ricardo accepted the second piece and held it against the torn part of his pants, then lifted it off and said, "That's only making it bleed faster."

Holding herself together, Kendall said, "The roof. Yes. I can't think of anywhere better. It's as far from the front door and the elevator as we can get. Plus, no one can watch us through mirrors up there."

Kweku said, "Come to think of it, there *are* actually a couple mirrors up there. But we'll smash them all. First order of business."

Kendall wondered whether that would be sufficient. Or did they, whoever *they* might be, have other ways of watching, of listening in?

Britney helped Ricardo tie a kitchen cloth around his leg as a sort of tourniquet. Ricardo said, "Thanks. Okay, good. Let's go do that."

Kendall added, "We should get some blankets on the way up. And a towel for me; I'm so cold and so wet. Maybe some pillows too. I have a feeling we're going to be spending the night up there."

Timothy said, "Okay, but only if we all go together."

*

THE FINAL REMNANT

Night fell over California.

On their way up, they had found one more girl, Himari from Japan.

That brings us to eight. Five girls and three boys.

Something echoed through her mind, dredged up from memory. 'Eight there are here, yet nine there were, set out from Rivendell. Tell me, where is Gandalf?' *Damn fine question*, Kendall thought. *We need a Gandalf, and if lore served, even then they wouldn't stand a chance without a faithful Samwise.*

Through fearful hiccups, Himari recounted how she had fled, stumbling into one of the corridors in the dark, and then, when the lights finally came back on, used a series of staircases to scamper up to her room and hide in there.

"I thought I could lock myself in, but the bedroom doors only close. They don't lock." Himari had looked very shaken – just like the rest of them – but also immensely grateful to see Kendall and her friends when they arrived to retrieve blankets. Cringing in her room, she had thought she was the only one left.

Now they sat in a circle on the roof, all wrapped in their blankets against the chill.

"I'm *so* hungry," said one of the other two girls. Their names were Claudette and Tina. Kendall had never really spoken to either of them. Both had dark hair, but Claudette's was trimmed short like a pixie, and she wore glasses, while Tina had the longest hair Kendall had ever seen. She wrapped it over her shoulder to avoid sitting on it.

"There's plenty of food down there. But, do we want to go get it?" Ricardo asked.

There were mutters of "no".

Ricardo and Kweku had smashed the mirrors they'd found on the roof. The exploded glass lay spewed before their frames, but they bore no cameras.

Kendall turned to Britney, "How did you get away?"

Britney seemed hesitant to talk about it. "I nearly didn't. It was *so* close. Mate, they took Isabella right out of the bathroom, right there! But they didn't see me. They didn't even know I was there ..." She heaved a great sigh. Weariness or guilt, or a combination of the two. "So, you remember Isabella was like, leaning on me, all the way to the loo? She's one of those 'let's go together' girls. We went into the same stall, 'cause we were both freaked out, so, you know, it didn't seem weird. That ... might have saved my life. She was ..."

Britney choked up. She tried to continue but the crying overtook her.

Little Timothy put a hand on her shoulder, stroked her back.

"I'm okay," she sniffed. "Let me just tell it." After a quavering breath, "She was sitting on the toilet when we heard those men walk in. But you could hear straight away there was something wrong, like, just the way they moved and talked in low voices and only a few words, like orders. They were older guys, not exchange kids."

Kendall thought, *They knew someone was in the bathroom. Went straight in after her. So they must be able to see down there. Those cameras are* everywhere.

"They were whispering things to each other, real fast, like they were on a mission or something."

"They just walked right in through the bathroom doors?"

"Well, I was in the stall, but yes, I think so. Straight in. You guys didn't see them go in? From out in the corridor?"

"No, nothing."

"Then I guess they didn't come into the house from that side. They must have come in some other way."

Kendall made a mental note of that.

"They started bashing against the stall door, I think with their shoulders. And the latch is just one of those little metal things, so it was obviously going to break with another bash or two. I was next to Isabella, so I just ducked down and crawled into the next booth along. The door was even open, but they didn't see me. But I ... I heard them ..."

Here Britney choked up again, sobbing hard. "I heard them take her! Right off the toilet! Right next door! I only got away because they only saw one door closed, so I guess they thought it was just one girl! I thought they'd see me 'cause my door was open, but once they had her, they took her the other way. They pulled her right off the toilet!"

The indignity of it somehow rendered kidnapping even uglier.

"I couldn't do anything! I couldn't help her! I couldn't stop them and I just, like, sat there in a ball, up against the wall next to the toilet! I was so scared!"

As she sobbed, Timothy put an arm about her shoulder.

Kendall thought, *The men knew someone was in the bathroom. But they didn't know it was two girls. So ... their information wasn't perfect? Maybe it wasn't a camera down there after all. But what, then? Someone talking to them?*

To her shoes, Britney said, "There was even some of her wee on the floor where they dragged her away. So I ... I cleaned it up with toilet paper. Like that would somehow help her or something. Fuck, I'm useless!"

A coldly calculating part of Kendall thought, *If you're telling the truth.*

Britney wiped at her face and said, "I thought they'd already taken you guys. So I just stayed in the bathroom for a few more minutes. Then I snuck out and ran to a room down the passage. I hid behind a desk."

"Is that where you were when the lights went out?" Kendall asked.

Britney saw the way Kendall was looking at her and frowned. "Yes. I thought I heard you guys coming out the bathrooms. I guess you were looking for us?"

"That's right," Kendall said.

"And then I heard *you*, Kendall, shouting my name. And then everyone was shouting, so I thought maybe the way was clear. I started getting up, but just then, all those shutters started coming down. The lights went out. I couldn't even find my way out of that room. So I just stayed."

Kendall regarded her for a few more seconds. Then she filled in, "I think they could see in the dark. I scratched one of the men across the face when he tried to grab me. I think I felt something on his face."

"On his face? Like what?" Timothy asked.

"I think those see-in-the-dark goggles."

"Night vision, seriously?" Ricardo said. "So, like, they actually saw us? Running and falling around in the dark and trying to hide?"

Kweku added, "Well, that's not half fucking creepy, is it? Bloody hell!"

"Then you pulled me out of that fountain?" Kendall asked.

Britney wiped at her moist nose again. "Yes. When the lights came on, I waited another few minutes. Then I didn't know *where* to go. *Again*. So I snuck along the side of the walls back to the atrium. I couldn't see anyone else, just you, Kendall. You were lying half over that fountain. I thought you'd drowned, or maybe someone had pushed you in. Your face was most of the way in the water. I pulled you out and dragged you behind that flower box thing. That's where you woke up."

Kendall thought about the extraordinary pain across her chest.

"Was I ... *dead*? Did you revive me?"

"I did CPR. Behind the flower box. You came around quickly."

Kweku said, "Holy crap."

Ricardo said, "Chica! She saved your life!"

They spent another half hour comparing notes about where each of them had been, how they had hidden, who was missing. They speculated about the fate of their missing friends, then quickly dropped that topic by mutual, unspoken consent. Kendall couldn't bear to think about pretty Agnieszka with her mermaid-long white-blonde hair, somewhere out in the world right now, being used by someone. By some *complete pig!* Being *used* as his ...

She shook her head, refusing to finish the thought.

Even wrapped into blankets, and with her hair now dry, she said, "I'm so cold."

"Hey, that's one thing we can fix!" said Kweku, pulling a lighter from his pocket. "Bonfire, yeah? Right here on the roof."

Kendall said, "A lighter! You have a lighter!"

"Yeah ..."

"Excellent! I think our next step should be to set a fire. Burn this house down."

Kendall was now familiar with the silent pause that ensued every time she suggested anything bold. This must be what it felt like to be a radical.

Pulling at her long hair, Tina said, "Do we do it ... like ... *tonight*?"

Kendall thought for a second. "The longer we wait, the worse our chances become."

"Right now, then?" Timothy asked, uncertain.

"Yes. Why not?"

Ricardo said, "Well, a fire *would* be visible at night. But what if they turn off the lights again? We'd be stuck down there. Or *worse*, stuck inside a burning house."

185

They were decent points. Yet the source bothered her. Her eyes narrowed as she regarded Ricardo. He sat with one leg crossed over the other, the injured one on top. Once again, he was suggesting a delay.

Clearly time was *not* on their side. The longer they waited, the more the vultures in the shadows picked away at their number. All the same, the thought of being chased once again, of fleeing once again, way down in the bowels of the darkened house, was beyond the limits of her remaining courage.

"Okay, we go as soon as the sun comes up."

The group murmured consent.

"And I think we should take turns on guard duty. Two of us must be awake at any one time, while the others sleep. We take it in shifts and switch every few hours."

Britney said, "Still. A bonfire's good."

It was funny how little it took to change everyone's mind.

✗

They burned the outdoor furniture. They did it with glee. They broke the deck chairs apart and cast them into the fire-pit.

It took a while to get the fire started, but Kweku ultimately coaxed the fabric from one of the deck chairs to catch, and once one caught, in less than five minutes, sparks from healthy flames were flickering off the balcony and off into the night.

Kendall thought of the Statue of Liberty holding aloft her flame, and idly wandered whether they might build a big enough beacon of flame up here to get the neighbors' attention. Trouble was, you couldn't even see neighboring homes from the roof. The curving amphitheatre of rock blocked them from view on both sides – if there were even houses in either direction. She couldn't quite remember from the drive here, when she'd thought this place was a hotel.

Kweku sat on his haunches, admiring the fire he'd built. After a while, he stretched his legs, took a few steps away from the flames, and lowered himself onto one of the seats. "Thank God we're done running about for the day," he said, rubbing at the insides of his legs. "I have the world's most epic case of chub rub."

"Chub rub?" Ricardo said, jolting up with delight.

Kendall got it instantly, and it made her smile. Then it made her giggle.

Kweku clarified for Ricardo's benefit. "Chubby legs rubbing together, mate! Like when a hippo runs. Dooom, dooom, dooom!"

Claudette, who'd been taking an ill-timed sip of a Pepsi from the downstairs kitchen, spurted it out onto the stone tiles. Some of the sweet liquid fizzed out through her nose and she said, "Gack!"

Suddenly, and despite everything that had happened to them, the entire group was in hysterics.

Kendall tried to stop laughing. She tried to tell herself that this was the most inappropriate moment in the history of the universe to descend into fits of stupid hysteria. Yet the spasms of laughter kept coming until tears escaped her eyes. Just as it started to die down, and they began to catch their breaths and yawn, Britney said, "Chub rub!" and the hysteria revved up again.

It was like they were all drunk. They cackled and spluttered into the night air, gasping for breath and hauling in gulps of oxygen. And it felt incredible to be laughing again, despite how it hurt Kendall's chest after the CPR, despite the desperation of their scenario. It was such a stupid form of camaraderie. So undignified. So silly and spluttering and utterly wonderful.

The noise ebbed into coarse breathing, satisfied sighs, and, ultimately, more yawns.

Kendall noticed Kweku's lighter lying on the floor beside her. It was one of those expensive ones with the silver gilding and *Jack Daniel's Old No.7 Brand Tennessee Whiskey* written on the side.

It gave Kendall an idea. She looked around. They were all watching the fire and recovering their composure.

She quietly pocketed the lighter.

⁂

Kendall got the first shift. That decision was actually an act of charity. Timothy suggested it, telling the group, "She was badly hurt today. We ought to let her have a full night's sleep. Otherwise, she might not be able to stay alert if we wake her up some time late into the night." It was a kind suggestion, and Kendall was glad of it; glad that it had come from someone else and not her.

Britney said that *she* still felt okay. "I'm in pretty good condition. Not tired. I'll take one of the later shifts." So Kendall was paired with long-haired Tina.

The sleeping arrangements might have been questionable under any other circumstances, but they were beyond caring. The circle around the fire devolved into some primal human bundle in one of the corners. Everyone pressed up against everyone else like a puppy-dog pile, huddling for warmth and reassurance, and keeping as far from the door back into the house as possible.

Before Kendall and Tina began their shift, Kendall took the lighter out of her pocket. She eased in beside Ricardo and quietly handed it to him.

When he looked at her in puzzlement, she nodded in Kweku's direction and said, "He can be a bit clumsy. Better if we don't lose it. Mind just sticking it on that ledge behind you?"

Ricardo regarded her for a second, seeming to consider. "Sure," he said, and accepted the lighter.

This was taking a risk. Kendall didn't know if there were any other lighters or matches in the house. But she needed an answer, and this was one way to probe for one.

She had additional bait. "You ever miss that girl you met in Puerto Rico? Maria?"

"Who?"

"The girl from that story you told us, about your little brother. During Ghost Stories Evening. Maria?"

"Oh, that was *Mariana*. No, not really. We just kinda made out and hung for a week. Why do you ask?"

"Nothing. Just wondering. I'd better start my shift. You'd better get some sleep."

"Cool. How's the head?"

"Throbbing a little, but okay," she said. "Your leg?"

"Same here."

"Good night, Kendall."

"Night, Ricky."

Hmm. One out of two. Kendall had known that the girl's name was Mariana, and Ric had rightly corrected her. But she'd also said Puerto Rico. On Ghost Stories Night, it had been Colombia. Nevertheless, the conversation felt natural enough, and it had progressed past that point. He'd been thrown specifically by the girl's name, and may just not have noticed the second error. He may even have been to Puerto Rico.

So that part of her experiment had been ... inconclusive.

She wished she could remember the brother's name.

In the night air, as the fire crackled and settled, the group swapped muted good-nights. For a bunch of kids who had been wired moments earlier, the heavy breathing of sleep seemed to come quickly. Although at least one of the kids was making tiny sobbing sounds.

Kendall and Tina sat off to one side, apart from the sleeping group, with a view of the door to the terrace. Tina didn't talk much. She pulled ritually at a section of her long hair and glanced repeatedly at the glass door. Kendall also developed a ritual rubbing habit, focused on the lump on her head. She, too, kept glancing at that exit. If the snatchers came for them up here, there was nowhere to flee to.

Two hours into their three-hour shift, Tina confessed, "I've never been so tired in my life." She kept gulping at air, flexing her eyes, but her head still jerked up every few moments.

"I'm wide awake," Kendall said. It was true, despite her pain, or maybe as a product of it. "I'll make it through the shift okay. You kept me company for two hours. Why don't you head for bed?"

"Really, you sure?"

"Sure. Go for it."

"As long as you really don't mind," she said, but she was already leaving.

Kendall said, "Just put another of those chair legs on the fire, please. Quietly as you can."

The girl agreed and mouthed, "Thank you soooo much!"

Even though Tina hadn't talked much, Kendall now felt as though she finally had her mind to herself. It was always easier to think when she was on her own. It had always been the case for her. That was just an introvert thing.

The fresh wood made pleasant snapping noises on the fire. Kendall watched Tina snuggle into a makeshift bed between two other sleeping forms. The girl was out cold in under a minute.

Kendall's eyes became focused. She twirled her silver cross in her fingers. *Time to think.*

Like the voice of a spirit emerging from the night, Addie was already at her shoulder.

'Right, squido. Start with that mirror. The one that you damn well knew had a camera. And when you went to smash it?'

When we went to smash it, the camera was gone.

'The camera was gone. That's right, Kendall. Only that one. Cameras behind all the others. So, someone knew to remove it. And what does that tell you?'

Kendall completed the thought in her own voice. *There's no way anyone heard our conversation. We were under a blanket. We had the lights off. And we were whispering.*

'Then say it, kiddo.'

Kendall didn't want to. It was too awful a thought, and it changed everything.

'Say it.'

She breathed in, sighed, mouthed the words under her breath. "We have a traitor."

'Yes. Yes, you do.'

Not for the first time this week, the clear realisation, the admission of it, made it feel like ice was running down her neck.

Kendall glanced over the sleeping forms. They all looked so small out here. So vulnerable. What a frightening, awful, terrible thought. Yet it had to be true.

One of them must *be a traitor*. Kweku, Timothy, even Britney. Britney who said she'd climbed under a stall and hidden right next door to an abduction, then magically reappeared.

Or Ricardo. Ricardo of the charm, the magnetism. The only one who'd been able to speak to the chef. Ricardo, oldest of the group, a natural leader, irresistible to all the girls. The least perturbed of them all, the most laid back.

Still, she didn't want to believe that one of these people she now considered a friend, or even a potential boyfriend, could be capable of that. And he'd *touched* her. Right *there. A kid, working with kidnappers?* That was beyond sick. That was ...

'Evil,' whispered Addie over her shoulder. *'Yes, it's evil, Kendall. But if you can't conceive of evil, can't believe in it, then it* will *have the upper hand, and it* will *destroy you. This is not a game, Kendall. You will be sold. You will be sold to strangers and we will never see you again.'*

Kendall breathed in and out for a sober minute. Then she responded in her head, *Thanks, sis, no pressure!*

The voice was silent.

Okay, so if someone had passed on information from under that blanket, *and they must have*, then what had happened next? She thought her way through the timeline.

First they broke the mirror. *Well ... after Ricardo had objected and said they were nuts for destroying anything in a sixty-million-dollar mansion.* Someone had removed the camera, but then Kweku called the bluff by breaking another mirror, and they found a camera there, all right. That seemed to rule out Kweku, by a process of elimination. Didn't it?

Then we tried to go downstairs and break a window. Who suggested which room?

Of course, it had been Ricardo. He even suggested which window to try, and *surprise* – that one didn't break. On the other hand, Kweku then tested the room next door – tested it convincingly – and *that* one didn't break either. So ...?

So that was inconclusive too.

The new wood on the fire splintered again, cracked, and settled lower, releasing a flurry of sparks. Kweku sniffed and adjusted his head on the cushion. Claudette turned over. The rest of the kids were deeply asleep, probably suffering through the nightmares of their lives. Except, *maybe*, for one of them.

Something else was bothering Kendall too.

'*Let's talk about grand entrances,*' Addie suggested, whispering over Kendall's shoulder.

Yes, let's.

'*The men who snatched Isabella out of the bathroom – who nearly got Britney as well – they didn't enter through the front door. Or through the elevator. Did they?*'

No. No way. We know they didn't. We were camped out there, so they couldn't have.

'*Plus, the Indian girl, Aadab. Don't forget her. She went up to her room, Kendall. She went upstairs ...*'

Kendall finished the thought verbally, "And she never came back."

'*She never came back.*'

Soft enough not to wake anyone, Kendall again spoke the words aloud. "There's another way in and out of here."

✗

Kendall's shift as sentry came to an end. She wasn't certain how she would go about this next step, but she was pretty sure she knew where she had to go. She had mentally walked through the house a hundred times now, exploring every possibility, and almost snorted when her mind's eye settled on a room. *It had to be in there.* In retrospect, it actually seemed so obvious. *What a simple, clever way to hide it!*

She lowered some extra wood onto the fire and awakened her replacements, Kweku and the short-haired girl named Claudette. Claudette took up Kendall's vacated seat and rubbed at her eyes. Kweku said, "I just have to go do some ... boy business." He looked around. "Guess I'll go round the corner."

Right, she told herself. *Time to go.*

Claudette said, "Wait. Aren't you going back to sleep?"

Kendall tiptoed back to the girl and said, "No. I'm going to—"

'Lie to her.'

"... I'm going to the upstairs bathrooms. They're just through that door."

'Good. You need space away from everyone. Your friends included. Whoever is in on this, your traitor, you've been taking them with you.'

Claudette looked almost panic-stricken. "But we're all sticking together. That's the plan!" She looked around for Kweku, clearly hoping for backup.

Kendall said, "Just five minutes. Ten maximum."

"I'll come with you. In case."

"No. Look, I don't think those men will come now, but when they do come, we know that they can take two kids just as easily as one. So it's better if it's just me."

"How is that *better*?"

"Just ... I'll be right back, okay?"

*

DOWN INTO THE HOUSE

Midnight. Wednesday.

Kendall said a prayer, touched at the cross around her neck, plunged right in before she could overthink it. Her heartbeat pounded against her sore chest.

The lights were still on, from the top of the mansion to the bottom. Viewed from down in the valley, this house must look like a glowing beacon on the hillside.

Was she being watched? Kendall hoped not. *How could she know?* Hopefully, the mirrors with the lenses were only secreted in the private spaces. She guessed that most of them were located where girls took off their clothes.

And if not?

If not, then they were watching her right now. That's all there was to it.

Kendall's only hope was that no one was paying attention at this time of night. If the watchers knew that their quarry was up on the roof, which seemed likely, they would probably believe they were all asleep by now.

The house was worse at night.

Walking through the cavernous spaces, it was all glaringly bright. Marble columns cast shadows in multiple directions from the ever-present, multi-angled lighting as she progressed. Echoing. Empty. Kendall had never been more conscious of the noise made by her shoes and softened her footsteps.

There was the only room that made her feel a little less scared: the smell of leather and wood, the vaulted ceiling with its lovely Renaissance painting. She *loved* libraries.

It was time to test her theory.

The wooden floor was so well varnished in the sections without carpeting that she could make out reflections in it. Just off the centre of the floor, there was a romantic spiral staircase leading up to a higher level of books. Here and there, tasteful sculptures and busts of old writers added dignity. Everything was pristine, everything was orderly, calm, quiet, tastefully considered and arranged just so ... with one exception.

Opposite the sliding ladder was the one place in this entire house that wasn't perfect. Its only blemish. It could only be what it was.

And yet.

Why didn't the varnish and its stink bother us? We didn't even see it – not really. It was the only thing in the whole house not noticeable by being so utterly ordinary. They'd all been so busy ogling the unknown that they'd ignored what was known.

Kendall stepped up to the recently varnished wood panel. It was wider than her body and went from above her head down to the baseboard, and perfectly matched the other panels. It was ever-so-slightly tacky when she touched it.

Kendall thought for a second. If someone leaned against it, nothing should happen. She bumped her shoulder against the wood. Sticky. But it stayed solid.

She stood on her tiptoes and pressed along the top edge. Again, solid. Then down the side, pressing. In the utter silence of the night, she heard the slightest squeak. That made her gasp. Faster now, she felt all around, further down, prodding and nudging. Still, nothing at all. She went back up to the squeak and pressed. In fear and frustration she banged on it twice.

The panel clicked open. Quietly. Smoothly. Like a well-oiled machine.

For an instant, she stood there in disbelief.

She cast one quick look back into the library, then turned

and stepped tentatively through the gap, disappearing right into what should have been the wall of the house.

⚹

It was a passage. Right through the wall. A secret tunnel.

As Kendall peered into this surprising hole, she immediately thought of that ramp Kweku had described, by which the sheep went to their slaughter. *Had her Polish roommate, Agnieszka, been dragged down here? Had all the others?*

It turned off at an immediate right angle and led into a long corridor wide enough to stand in, two or three abreast. Certainly wide enough to drag a kid along.

Kendall was operating on the assumption that they – whoever they were – would be asleep at this late hour. Indeed, she was betting her very life on it.

If the rest of the house was a study in opulence, this undecorated tunnel was pure utilitarian functionality. The lighting in here, just about adequate, was not gently recessed or ambient, like everywhere else. Instead, it pounded directly out of long, bare, buzzing strips on the ceiling: ugly yellow puss from a cut. It even made the walls look green.

She stepped inside.

Rough stone surrounded her on both sides. Kendall was almost afraid to touch the walls – they appeared wet. A hundred feet ahead both walls and floor dropped down out of sight, perhaps into a slope or staircase. The lights ticked and flickered. There was a bug stuck in one of them, knocking against the glass, and it was creepy to think that this ugly space had been here all along.

Kendall took another step or two, padding from heel to toe. She listened hard for movement. She was desperate to turn back. Get the others and get out quickly.

'No, Kendall. You can't do that. And you know why.'

Yes, Kendall admitted. *I do. I can't do it that way because*

*there's a traitor among us. What Kweku's Dad called a Judas Goat.
A snitch.*

She considered the enormity of the problem. *Anything whatsoever that I tell the group, the snitch will spoil. And this could be a way out; maybe the* only *way out. I have to think this through. I need to know more.*

She was here now. May as well keep creeping forward.

Silently, she arrived at the end of the passage. It terminated in a metal staircase like a fire escape, plunging down at a steep angle.

Kendall hunched down, but couldn't see the bottom for the sloping roof. There was nothing for it. She would have to risk going down. Again, the lights above buzzed, perhaps consuming another incautious insect.

She inched onto the first step, then winced as it creaked appallingly. She came to a dead stop, breathing only at the top of her chest, like a hunted rabbit. Her heartbeat made her clavicle and chest hurt where Britney had punched her doing CPR.

Kendall stared down the staircase for what felt like a lifetime. No sound, no movement from below. No one came. So she lowered her weight fully onto the offending step and tried to make her next footfall quieter.

There was simply no way to do it. The problem wasn't her shoes. It was the metal itself. And there was no handrail here that she might use to lessen her weight.

She tried something. *What if I only step right at the sides?*

That was better, though not perfect.

Another step. Another outlandish metal squawk.

Well, if they haven't heard all that!

Kendall thundered down the rest of the staircase at a full trot. At the bottom, she darted off to the side and made herself as small as she could, until she knew whether or not she was alone.

It was certainly quiet. Chances were, she was alone.

But she was no longer in a dank, claustrophobic tunnel. Nothing of the sort.

Kendall rose to her feet, her pupils dilating as she looked around in astonishment.

It wasn't the banks of screens displaying rooms in the house to a series of empty chairs in the dark, like some sort of abandoned mission control, that immediately captured her attention. It wasn't the row of expensive cars, each sitting on its own turntable in the shadows. It wasn't even the round, red, hobbit-shaped garage doors, which Kendall recognized from the day she had arrived here. It was the fact that one of those doors was *open*. Kendall could see starlight.

The winter sky softly illuminated the outside driveway, a mere short sprint from where she crouched. That was where she wanted to go.

The floor space in the garage was nearly as long across as the house above, but it all appeared to be unoccupied, at least at this hour. Kendall took a couple of ginger steps forward.

The screens – there were several of them in a long bank – showed CCTV of the rooms. Each screen was divided into five or six smaller quadrants. One of them sure looked like the rooftop. Squinting at the small box, she thought she could just make out a pile of blankets and sleeping kids in one deep grey, low-resolution quadrant.

Right now, nothing moved on the various monitors. Every view of the house showed dormant scenes of empty corridors, semi-dark bathrooms, luxury lounge spaces. She could learn a great deal by studying those boxes and discovering where the cameras were positioned.

There was movement outside.

Kendall froze.

Through the open door, out in the driveway, she caught the clear silhouette of a man. Certainly not a kid. That was a fully grown man, and a big one by her estimation.

Could he see her? Was he looking right at her? If so, he wasn't moving, so neither did she.

Then his arm came up in a casual movement. Kendall saw the cherry-burst glow of a cigarette. Then the arm dropped back down.

Shit! Okay.

Kendall knew she had only moments available.

She looked at the cars. She tried to judge distances and the time it might take to cover them. It wasn't a long way from the end of the staircase to the open garage door.

If he's the only one here, she thought, *I could hide between one of those cars and a garage door. When he comes back in, I could just slip out. Easiest thing in the world.*

She took a step. She braced herself, like a sprinter on a road race.

Addie's voice, clear and dry, stopped her in her tracks. *'No, Kendall!'*

I could get out! Right now!

She was almost tempted to shout at that other voice, which was bizarre because ultimately it was really her own. The other Addie was entirely animated by her own thoughts.

Instead, she calmed her breathing and asked the Addie in her head, *Why not?*

'What's that around your neck?'

It's a cross.

'But so what, right? You're just going to save yourself?'

Kendall let out air. The rancour drained out of her.

… no.

'Good. You're going to get them out too, yes?'

Yes. Yes, I am. All of them. I'm going to get them out too. But I can't just run upstairs and call them, because I have a problem. One of them is a traitor. The traitor will ruin it.

'Good, Kendall. Good. Now, what's the next thought? Keep going.'

So … I think I have to …

She wrestled with the tangle of her own psychology for a moment, rubbed her face in frustration, glanced at those creepy screens. Then an idea came to her. She thought she knew what she had to do. She looked at that wide open garage door – the unfettered freedom of it, right there.

The silhouette outside popped the cigarette shape into its mouth, then placed both hands on its lower back and stretched against them. It remained stationary.

Kendall sprinted for the control centre with the bank of screens. Soft as she could, she pulled out drawers in the desks. *Nothing.* There were papers on the counters. She lifted them, looking beneath. *Not there either.*

Outside, the silhouette dropped something to the floor and ground it with a toe.

Shit, shit!

She had only seconds remaining.

Where?!

She rattled her hands through the contents of a small basket filled with odds and ends sitting on a desk. *Not here, either.* However, there *was* a pair of scissors; the sharp kind, like her mother used when trying to sew. Those might come in handy.

She looked around again.

As she did so, she glanced over the monitors. Her eye fell on one in particular. There was a monitor dedicated to the backyard. One of the squares showed a view that Kendall recognized instantly, because one of the most intense moments of her life had taken place there. A wonderful, private, scary, and exciting moment. An *almost*-moment. It was the inside of the painted changing room. It was precisely where Ricky had manoeuvred her for his attempts at fondling. Right in front of an unseen camera. *Ricky.*

Kendall shook her head to erase the image, then saw what she'd been searching for.

There! On the wall!

A wall-mounted key holder. Suspended from it like an Olympic champion's medallions were several sets of high-end car keys, tantalising to behold.

Just take a bunch!

Kendall scooped three of them into her hand. Then she thought about it. If she took so many, they might quickly notice. *Just one, then. Pick one. But which?*

She had no idea, and the man was coming back.

Any one, Kendall, just take one and go!

She chose one with a shiny black Darth Vader curve and a tiny 'T', stuffed it into her pocket beside the scissors, then crouch-ran back to the stairs.

Just in time. The silhouette's footsteps padded audibly on the floor. He was inside the garage now.

Kendall waited until he looked away, then darted around the corner to the stairs, where she ground to a halt, catching herself just before leaping onto them.

The noise! How do I get back up?!

She was cornered. Creaking steps on one side. A large man who was clearly part of this child-smuggling syndicate on the other.

And down by her feet, a bundled set of wires leading from the wall to the control centre.

Kendall considered the scissors in her pocket.

She pulled the scissors out, split them open, and held one blade like a knife, positioned over the wires. It would be easy enough to saw through them.

What if it killed her, though? She thought of the boy who'd been electrocuted right off the cliff face outside. This could actually be worse.

No, not worth it. She was gambling her life against merely damaging the equipment slightly. *Not smart.* She folded the scissors and put them back in her pocket.

She heard the creak of a chair, alarmingly nearby, as the man leaned back.

The car keys would have to do. Fine. But how could she get back up?

She could think of only one thing. She tried leaning far enough forward that her hands reached the fifth step. That way, she might distribute the weight over both her hands and feet.

Remember: the middle creaks – the edges aren't as bad.

This was going to take some acrobatics.

She leaned her weight onto her hands, wincing against the pain that this semi-upright push-up placed on her aching chest muscles. But she got away with it. She risked putting a foot on the bottom step and another sprawled widely to the opposite side. It worked, after a fashion. She began to crawl forward and up, her arms and legs as wide out as she could get them.

The scissors in her pocket poked her leg slightly, might actually be gouging her, but she would have to endure that. She looked like some bizarre crab clawing its way out of a hole.

She was almost at the top – so very close – when one of the stairs creaked, loudly, then made what sounded like a cracking noise.

Go! Just go! Kendall launched herself the rest of the way. She sprinted along the passageway, then jolted to a halt. The panel had closed, and there was no door handle on this side. She scuffed at it, but nothing happened. She tried to get her fingernails into the cervices, but couldn't.

For a paralysed moment, she stared at the unyielding rectangle.

There has to be a principle to this. A button or a release.

She looked down the passage. *Noises, coming.* She looked back. Kicked at the door. It yielded.

She whipped through, hurled the panel shut, sprinted out into the light of the library, then dashed behind a desk, crouching. The scissors in her pocket had been stabbing at roughly the same spot as her burn. That bit of leg skin just seemed fated for injury.

Mere moments later, the silhouetted man emerged, swiftly but quietly pushing aside the fabric. From where Kendall squatted balled behind a desk, she could see him reflected in the glass over a wall-mounted painting. He hadn't seen her.

He made no sound whatsoever as he entered the library and paced across the floor, looking all around.

Silhouette-man reached the library door, glanced out into the corridor beyond, then seemed to change his mind. He jogged quickly back to the panel, pushed it open, disappeared.

Oh crap! He's going back to check the cameras!

If she didn't want to blow her own cover, Kendall had to make it all the way back to the roof before he made it down the corridor and to the monitors.

Run!!!

"Oh good, you're back!" said Claudette. "I was getting real worried."

The innocence of it, and her young face, somehow seemed bizarre after what Kendall had just seen. Claudette didn't even notice that Kendall was panting. The girl looked so young, so silly and helpless, juxtaposed against the slaughterhouse ramp and high-tech equipment looming in semi-darkness below them all. And, of course, that one camera somewhere on the roof looking down at them right now.

We really are the sheep, aren't we?

Kweku looked up from some sketching he was doing on his lap. He sounded irritated at her. "Don't you do that again! Not even for the loo. That is not funny. You *know* we stick togevuh." He looked back down and continued sketching. Kweku put a hand in front of his eye to block out one of the lights where Kendall was backlit. "Hey, you all good? You look out of breath."

She fought to regain control of her breathing. Her heartbeat began to slow. "All good. I think I'm still ... just having ... little panic attacks."

Claudette said, "I know what you mean!"

Kendall took a few final calming breaths, then tried to decide how she could gain a little clarity on the problem of the Judas Goat.

Buying time, she wandered over to see what Kweku was drawing.

In spite of everything she'd just gone through, or perhaps because of it, she found the drawing delightful.

"It's Timothy!"

On Kweku's lap was one of the tiles from the roof. Atop of it was a small spiral artist's pad, on which he was adding the finishing touches to a caricature, a tiny Timothy with thin neck and ears sticking way out, hair combed straight to the side in an iron parting, and the soft outlines of that modest sweater he wore so often. Although it was a pencil drawing, the sweater even managed to look sky blue.

"That's really good!" Kendall was happy to indulge a few moments of normality. She needed a little time to calm herself, and then to think about the next few steps. "How many have you done?"

"I'm having a go at doing all of us – our whole remaining group. Here's yours, by the way."

Kweku flipped back past Himari, with accentuated eyes and teeth, then arrived at Kendall's page.

"No refunds if you fink it blows. But I will be gutted."

Kweku looked up to see Kendall's reaction, betraying that he cared about her opinion. She smiled as she studied the drawing. It had a bandage around an exaggerated bump on her forehead, and her eyes were squint, as though she had just this moment run into a wall, while stars circled her hair. The effect was cutesy rather than mocking. Other than the cartoonish expression, it was quite flattering.

"Wish my boobs were genuinely that big. Where'd you get the paper?"

"Had it in me little fanny pack, along wif a couple o' pencils. Had me back-up phone in there as well, didn't I? Until we went through that metal detector. Dianne was properly cross I hadn't given it to her along with the first one. Now we know why. Oh, hey! You haven't seen my lighter, have you?"

"Yes. I actually have."

That reminded her. She had set a little trap for Ricky. The results might come in useful.

Kendall manoeuvred around the sleeping kids. Despite the night air, they all looked warm and cosy.

Let's see …

She stared for a second. Well, Ricardo had passed *that* test. The lighter was exactly where she had asked him to set it down, on the ledge. She handed it to Kweku.

If Ricardo was the Judas Goat, he hadn't availed himself of the opportunity to prevent them from setting fire to the house. Did that imply points in his favour? *If so, damn it!*

It wasn't that she wanted Ricardo to be the traitor. It was just that knowing for sure would have simplified everything. She knew a way out. She could tell the others. But she simply could not do so until she knew beyond doubt which one of them was a pariah.

Kendall settled into her own pile of blankets. Ricardo had made sure it was right next to his, though much good it did him now, unconscious and snoring.

Kendall lay on her pillow, looking over the contours of his sleeping face.

Geez, he's nice to look at, even asleep.

Of course, traps were supposed to be attractive, that was how they worked. The nature of a trap was to be compelling, or you would have no incentive to fall for it. *The sweeter the bait, the better the trap.*

Kendall dearly did not want to believe that this beautiful young man, warmly at peace and breathing so calmly on the floor beside her, looking idyllic in the flow of dying firelight, could harbour such malice toward them. Not even malice. *Indifference*.

She was very, very nearly in love with him. And if it came to it, she might have to trap, harm, or disable him, in order to save all of their lives. If it came to that, she would have to do it without hesitation. The cruelty of it broke her heart.

THE GOAT AND THE RAMP

Dawn arrived, bright and harsh, creeping over the balcony like a silent molester. Kendall took stock. It was Thursday morning. They were all still there.

The early sunlight was frigid, with not a cloud in the sky to retain warmth overnight.

Himari was so startled when they awakened her that they had to spend two minutes calming her sobs. The whole group remained wrapped in their blankets as they compared notes about their shifts during the previous night.

Britney inspected Kendall's face, then told her that her lump had turned into a spectacular bruise and was beginning to go purple down the side of her eye. Kendall didn't doubt it. Kweku would have to add some dark shading to his pencil sketch of her.

Claudette said, "It's totally freezing. Should we start another fire?" and Kweku answered, "No."

"Why not?"

"Because the next fire we start is the one that burns down this house." He looked resolute. "Come on. Let's go."

It felt to Kendall like she had passed through a magic portal, or been gifted with a revelation. She viewed the whole situation differently now. She was in a post-Copernican Revolution world. She had accepted that this house was a con, she had worked out that one of their number was like the unfaithful disciple of Christ, she had actually seen the monitoring equipment with her own eyes, and, most importantly, she knew a way out.

The universe had turned on its axis and spun the other way. She could see it end to end.

Her fear was still there, in no small measure. But now she was working a strategy that had a purpose, rather than running blind through corridors set up to confound her.

Besides, she, too, wanted to see this awful kingdom on the hillside burn to the ground.

They walked down into the house together, five girls and three boys, wary that at any moment the blinds might shut again or strangers grab at them from unexpected quarters. Kendall fell into step with Timothy. He leaned against her.

"I'm glad you got away yesterday," he said quietly. "I'm glad we all did. I'm really sorry for what happened to you." He looked up, pointed to her head. "How's it feel?"

"Not too bad today, although it does kind of throb every time I take a step."

Timothy hugged her, the way a little brother might hug a big sister. "If Britney hadn't saved you ... You're my favourite. I mean, I want us all to survive, but ..."

"We're going to get out of this, Timothy," she said. "You'll see. Don't give up yet."

"How?" he cried. "*How* are we going to get out of this? There's just a few of us left. And they keep coming for us, from all sides!" The boy was able to walk, though he still had a slight limp. "And we don't even know where they take us, and we don't even know what happens next, and I can't even run if they come! So how, Kendall?"

He sniffed, then wiped a hand at his nose. "I don't want to be sold. I don't want to be raped. I want to go home."

Kendall leaned right up into his ear. "It's not going to happen. I'll tell you how. I've found a way out."

Timothy looked up at her through disbelieving eyes. It took him a second to muster the word, "Really?"

"Really. I'll explain later. But Timothy, there's a ... well, there's a problem we have to solve first. One of the kids is working *with* the people running this thing, telling them stuff. I think it's Ricardo."

Timothy looked shocked. "Why?" he asked. "Why would he ... why would *anyone* do that?"

"Don't know. But I've been trying to catch him out. Running little tests. I think we're going to have to ..."

She stopped speaking. Three members of the group, Tina, Claudette, and Himari, were walking a little too close. As they all rounded a statue on a plinth and started down another staircase, Kendall nudged him to slow down and allow the girls to get a ways ahead.

Timothy leaned close again and whispered, "What, Kendall? What are you going to do to him?"

"I was thinking we might have to try to lock him up or something. Once he's out of the way, I can get us all out of here."

"Okay ..." Timothy said, with reviving hope. He sounded like a frightened child after Mommy had promised there were no ghosts in the closet. He was silent for a few steps. "Just remember, he's quite strong. The way he pushed me ..." Timothy shook his head. "It just seems so unbelievable."

Kendall nodded. "Sometimes life is full of surprises. And sometimes, not all of them are good."

Timothy concurred. "Yeah, I guess that's true. Scary but true. I guess sometimes life is piles of crap on toast."

✗

Ricardo wanted to choose the room again.

Timothy made meaningful eye contact with Kendall, then asked, "Why don't I choose one?"

"Why?" Ricardo asked, taken aback. "What's wrong with this one? What difference does it make?"

"Just let him," Kendall said, and Timothy pointed across

the hall to the smallest of the downstairs offices.

Good, Kendall thought. *One less decision by Ricardo. Let's see if this time it actually works.*

As they filed into the room, Kweku flicking and playing with his lighter, Ricardo gave Kendall a strange look. Himari remained out in the passage as sentry.

Timothy gestured toward the windows. "This one's on the driveway side of the house. It's a small room, so hopefully it will catch fire quickly. And if it works, we'll have a blaze showing on the street side."

"Makes sense to me," Kweku said. "Aim me at sumfing flammable."

Although this was the smallest of the downstairs office suites, the room was nevertheless big enough to include more than one writing desk. There was also a recessed wooden wall panel with ambient lighting in biscuit colours and several half-sized bookcases, all packed with hardcover anthologies, probably merely for decoration.

Britney said, "We need paper to get the blaze started." She headed for the bookshelf, pulled out the largest, oldest-looking tome she saw, and began to rip. Kendall winced but said nothing. Burning books seemed an especial sacrilege.

The kids held their breaths as Britney and Kweku applied the flame from a wad of pages to the bottom of a gauze curtain.

The curtain curled slightly, repulsed by the insult, but the fire didn't take. Kweku wafted the burning ball back and forth beneath the curtain. Still it didn't ignite.

"Look at that! Bugger all!" he said.

Tina volunteered, "Maybe it's been soaked with fire retardant?"

"Let's try that rug," Timothy suggested. He walked to the far side of the office, where a white rug disappeared beneath a writing desk. Kweku joined him, and Kendall handed over several more balled pages.

"Use a few together," Timothy suggested. Kweku lifted a corner of the rug and placed three crumpled sacrifices in a pyre beneath it. He flicked his Zippo, cupping his hand against an imaginary breeze.

The fire took, and the rug showed every sign of being flammable. Tiny crests of flame spread out over the tips of the wool. It smelled pungent.

They stepped back to watch.

Tina started to shout, 'Yay!' when a soft beeping emitted above their heads, and a fine but thorough indoor rain turned their hopes into foul steam and sent them coughing for the exit.

Out in the corridor, they waved at the air about them and brushed beads of water from their clothes. Tina, who had quickly tucked her long hair into her shirt the instant the sprinklers initiated, now pulled it back out and inspected it.

"Barely even got it started," Kweku said.

Ricardo said, "I'm guessing every room in the house is set up to do that. Seems like *fire* is out."

Timothy sidled up to Kendall. Discreetly he asked, "Does that tell you what you need to know?"

Kendall kept her eyes on Ricardo as she replied, "I think it does."

⚹

As the group made its way to the kitchens, Tina said, "What could we even do if they just walked in here, plain as day, and carried us out now? We've only got three boys." She searched for a way to say it tactfully, then just forged ahead, "Timothy is small, and no offense, Kweku, but you don't look like you're built for a cage fight."

She was right.

Tina added, "We didn't even take knives the last time we ate. Why didn't we take some *knives*?"

They arrived at the dining area and stopped in their tracks.

Timothy was the first to speak. "Where's all the ... Who packed away all the food?"

The heating lamps at every station were turned off. The counters were baron and gleaming. The refrigerators that had dispensed free sodas and energy drinks were empty.

Claudette rushed to one of the buffet sections and lifted an iron lid. She lifted the next one and the next, slamming each down with a clatter.

Even the fruit had been removed.

Timothy repeated himself, "Who took it? And when?"

"Who cares when?! It's gone! It's all just gone. Just *gone*, and that's it!" said Tina, beginning to sob.

This had been one nasty development too many for the girl. Tina slid down the wall and buried her head between her knees. Kendall rubbed her upper back.

"Give her a moment," said Ricardo.

Ever the performance artist, Kendall mused. *So very concerned about the ladies.*

"Try the fridges?" Kweku suggested.

He and Ricardo slipped behind the station where the chef had prepared their meals and into the long kitchen/pantry area. Kendall heard the opening and slamming of wooden cabinets, and the '*shunk*' and '*chuuk*' of the better insulated refrigerator doors.

Kweku reappeared. "Not a damn thing."

A second later, Ricardo popped out. "No, nothing, it's all gone!"

Right, that's it, Kendall thought. *We have to get out of here now. That means we have to separate Ricardo from the group, and maybe* – she tried to think of that military word, a euphemism for causing ambiguous levels of harm, right up to and including death – '*immobilize*' him.

Could she kill him if she had to?

Ricardo helped Tina up from the floor. He gave her a gentle

hug and whispered something reassuring to her.

Kendall pursed her lips in disbelief. *Gigantic asshole.*

Without discussion, the group began ambling back out of the dining area. They wandered into the corridor, and then Kweku walked over to the little faux bridge above the fake indoor stream. He slumped down and hung his feet over the trickling river.

Ricardo helped Tina to a couch. He sat down beside her. She was still crying. Claudette sat with them, looking out at nothing, blank and empty.

Britney sagged down against the wall outside the kitchen, mirroring the way Tina had sat on the other side. She didn't cry, though. Her face just looked void. Himari stood near her, not knowing what to do, who to go to.

"Psst. Would you come with me?" Kendall said. "Let's just take a slow walk that way. Alone."

Timothy gave Kendall the subtlest nod. They meandered off together, trying not draw attention, trying to look as purposeless as the others.

✗

"Right *here*? This is where you almost drowned?"

The two of them were in the atrium, just beyond view of the others. Kendall looked closely at the corner of the ledge by the water feature. A scuff mark was evident where her head had connected.

"I must have hit just here. Then, I guess, I collapsed facedown in the water."

Kendall tried to picture herself lying in the trough. *Elegant.*

Timothy hauled his weight up onto the ledge. He indicated for her to sit. She glanced uneasily at the bubbling lake just behind him. Technically, she *had* drowned right there. Of all the places she didn't want to hang out. Nevertheless, she lifted herself up, dangled her feet like him.

"So you know a way out?" Timothy asked.

"Last night, after my shift, I snuck back down into the house."

"You did? What, all by yourself?"

"Claudette wanted to stop me. I told her I was just going to the loo. But I remembered something I saw in the library."

Timothy gave her a thoughtful look.

"Didn't they see you? What if they had?"

"No. There was one guy, but he was outside in the driveway, smoking. Timothy, listen. You can get to the *driveway* from those garage doors."

"You got right to the driveway? You could *see* it?"

"Uh-huh. And that leads right down to the front gate. And out."

Timothy thought for a second, then chuckled. "Well ... allowing for a half-mile trek."

Kendall chuckled too. "True. The drive to my local Spar is shorter."

"*Spar?*"

"Uh, it's a grocery store in South Africa. Point is, we can get *out* that way. We can get away!"

"Kendall, that's truly amazing. Have you told anyone?"

"Just you."

"You haven't told Britney? Or Ric?"

"No."

"You sure?"

"Yeah, absolutely!"

"Good."

They listened to the bubbling of the fountain behind them.

"Whoever is ... *telling on* us," Timothy said, "you say it's probably Ric. If he found out, he could just let those guys know. And there are only, what? Eight of us left now?"

"That's right," Kendall said. "So now we have a couple of tricky problems to solve."

Timothy looked about them. No one else was in view.

"First, we have to find a way to contain Ricardo," Kendall said. "Maybe lock him in a room."

Timothy rolled up one of his sleeves, pushing it well past his elbow.

"I guess that wouldn't be too very hard," Kendall said. "You and me could do it together. We just need a room with a key. Shove him in, lock it, then explain it to the others."

Timothy rolled up his other sleeve.

"And then we'll need to be clever about getting past the guys in the garage. There was only one guy there last night, but I don't think we can wait until night again. I don't think we have that much time, not even close. And I'm guessing there might be more than one during the day. There almost certainly is. With the food gone, we'll have to act soon. *Very* soon. Like, we need to make a call and get going now."

Timothy looked back in the direction of the others. He leaned slightly, the angle allowing him to see further along the corridor, then he sat back upright.

To Kendall's surprise, he put his hand to the bruised lump on her forehead. That was quite bold for him. It was also a surprisingly alpha-male thing to do, much more like Ricardo than himself.

Gently, tenderly, but with apparent self-assurance, he ran his fingers over the lump, examining its contours. She let him do it, and he looked in her eyes. Then his hand strayed to the back of her head, cupping and rubbing her hair.

Kendall didn't pull away, but she wasn't quite sure what to do. Was he going to try to kiss her? She didn't feel that way about him, had never given him any such sign. *And of all the times.* She studied his face, trying to read the boy's intentions. He had a slight smile but Kendall didn't know what it meant. He was inscrutable. The strange moment dragged on.

Then Timothy looked directly into her eyes again, and his

own eyes registered something strange, something she had never seen there before. She frowned.

He tensed. Then, with all his might, he plunged her head beneath the water, pinning her down and holding her there.

*

For a half-second, Kendall didn't think it was real. A part of her thought it was some outrageously stupid joke.

She was shocked by the cold of the water, irritated by the weirdness of the act, but completely believed she'd be back up in a moment, sputtering and telling Timothy off as he apologized and tried to explain. She believed she could easily push his hand away.

Then she discovered that she couldn't. Then it dawned on her that the small boy genuinely had every intention of holding her head down until she drowned and died. And that it really wouldn't take very long at all.

Judas!

Kendall thrashed, harder and harder, her cheek scraping painfully against the tiles beneath the surface, the water mere millimetres above her nose and eyes. But the boy, *the traitor*, the Judas Goat, had his full weight pressed down on top of her, and she was forced to push up against him. And she simply could not buck him.

In an appallingly short span of time, her vision began to swim, her head to throb and pulse and hammer with pain.

This was worse – *infinitely worse* – than the last time. Here was a boy she'd thought was a friend, murdering her. Murdering her with his own hands, his little white fingers so intimately pressed on the side of her face.

Kendall thrashed for all she was worth. Swinging flailing arms at Timothy was futile. The angle was so bad that even when her fists connected, it wasn't hurting him. Stars swam before her eyes. Her attempts to punch grew ever lamer.

Any second now, she would be forced to draw breath. That would be the end of her. Terror at the thought of gulping water and drowning made her heart race to exploding, and that only increased her desperation for oxygen.

Then it came to her. With her left hand, she gripped firmly onto one of the arms that held her down, holding him in turn. With her right hand, she searched for her pocket. Her fingertips first missed their goal, running past the opening. Then they split the lips of denim in the right place, slid in, clamped around the handle of the scissors. She grappled until she caught a firm hold, yanked them out, swung the scissors up and over in a mighty stabbing arc.

She nearly dislocated her shoulder. But the point found its target. She landed a solid shot. Even beneath the water, with the foam of the fight in her ears, she heard him cry out. She even felt the metal dig cleanly through muscle and gristle, lodging deep and solid and with a disturbing sense of meaty texture.

Timothy let go, jumped back. She came up gasping.

She knew she should scream, but for a few seconds, it was beyond her. Through a sheet of water pouring down her face, through the racking coughs that convulsed her, she caught sight of him. His small face radiated hatred. The demonic malice surprised her even more than the attempted drowning had. This was like a whole new person, a stranger. *The puppet master behind the soft blue jersey.*

Glaring at her, the small boy took two steps back, away from the ledge, even as she wheezed for breath. It felt like she would never get enough air into her lungs. She tried not to, but collapsed to her knees on the floor, one hand desperately gripping the ledge beside her, her lungs making alarming rasping sounds. She looked up, not daring to lose sight of him for an instant.

The scissors were embedded into the boy's upper chest. They must be inches from his heart. *Had they punctured a lung?*

A safe distance back, Timothy turned his glare from her and examined his wound, as though irritated by an inconvenience. He grabbed at the scissors, felt how deeply embedded they were – and *tugged*.

For a bizarre moment, Kendall wanted to shout, "Don't! You'll bleed to death."

All things considered, she held her peace.

Another yank, and the tip came free of his chest. He dropped the scissors, clattering to the floor, then studied the blood on his own fingers, as if surprised.

Get up, Kendall. Two steps and he could kick your face from there. Then *it's all over.*

It looked for all the world like he was about to do just that. She spasmed up to her feet in time. Then faced him. She was still coughing, though less now. She tried to make herself stand tall, like she'd regained control. Rising up, she was also slightly taller than him.

Timothy betrayed a moment of indecision. *An open fight or swift retreat?* Kendall watched him weigh her up with those brand new eyes, an entirely different person, and it was chilling.

Blood ran in runnels down his shirt, and he cupped the wound. He gave her one final look, poisonous and twisted, as she hauled in air and opened her mouth to scream.

He broke and sprinted for the elevator.

✗

Even as the fading notes of her scream echoed around the atrium, Kendall tried to go after him. She scooped up the scissors. Sticky blood gave the metal a repulsive, tacky feel.

She was still coughing too hard to run at full speed. Besides, what would she do if she caught up with him?

'Stop him from warning the keepers, Kendall! The people in the basement. That's what!'

She wasn't confident she could win a physical fight with him just now. He was injured but mobile, while she was in bad condition.

The others came running, Kweku and Ricardo in fight mode. "What?! What is it?"

Britney said, "Are you *bleeding*?! What happened?"

A second ago, Kendall had mustered a full-blooded scream. Now, she could barely talk as the droplets of water in her throat and lungs plagued her once more. She pointed with the scissors. The elevator doors closed.

"Timothy ... tried to ... drown me! He's with them."

Staggered, they all turned to look at the elevator.

Britney said, "You *stabbed* him?"

Kendall wanted to know whether the elevator might dip down. If so, it would mean Timothy knew how to get to the basement that way. *And if he got there first*, she thought, *they were screwed. If he got there first, they would each live lives of rape and torture.* But the carriage didn't dip down. They all watched as it started up instead.

So, he doesn't have some special tag or something.

The elevator gathered speed.

He'll make his way to the library ...

Addie's voice. *'Best you get there first. Before he can warn them.'*

"Come!" she said to the others. "I know how to get out. Through the library. But we have to get there first, before he warns them."

"*Who* warns *who*?" Britney said.

"*Timothy!* Warns the guys running this house!" Kendall shouted. Brooking no argument, she spread her arms wide and gathered them like a mother hen. "Go, go, go! The way out is through the library." She coughed again. "It leads to a control room. That's where they watch us, on TVs. But he's going to warn them, right now. So run!"

⚹

"*Listen.* Quick. *They know about the library. They're heading to the corridor. Now.* Right now. *Be ready if you want to stop them.*"

"Shit. Okay, I'll call them."

"*Wait! You also need to send someone in to help me. I'm hurt. I've been stabbed.*"

A click. And the radio fell dead.

⚹

"Ricardo, answer me quickly. Do you have it in you to stab someone?"

"I ... uh ..."

"No, for real!" she said, handing him the scissors even as they ran. "I need you to be ready to do it, and *really* do it. Ric, you're the biggest guy here. Kweku? Could you hit an adult with ... I don't know, maybe a chair or a lamp or something? But seriously do it, *full on*, without hesitating?"

Kweku didn't answer either.

"Because we're going to get one chance at this, and our best hope is *not* to hesitate. If you can't do it, we're dead. We're all dead."

Kendall briefed them as they jogged from level to level, making their way to the library.

"There's a passage," she said. "A tunnel. It leads along to a staircase. The staircase goes down ... down to ... wait ... I gotta catch my breath."

Kendall stopped in the corridor, hands on her knees.

Britney said, "Take your time."

"No!" Kendall said, straightening up and filling her lungs with one big breath. "No, we *have* to get there before he can warn them. It's our only chance. Walk fast and talk ... okay ... staircase goes down to the garage ... with the cars. There's a bunch of screens and chairs ... down there. Screens where they watch us. Past the chairs is the garage door. There's a whole row of garage doors."

"A way out?"

"I've got the keys for one of the cars ... *here*. Guys, the only way we're going to get out of here is if you rush at anyone we find down there. Take them out. Hurt them bad enough that they can't stop us. I really mean it. You *cannot* hesitate."

They arrived at the entrance to the library. Cavernous and quiet.

Kendall put her hands on Ricardo and Kweku's chests. She stood right up close to them. "Guys, if you don't do that, it's over. *We're* over. We're dead. Do you understand that? You have to hurt them, badly, even kill them, and you have to do it brutal and fast."

Claudette said, "Aren't you supposed to be some big Christian?"

Kendall looked at her, then replied, "Luke seventeen two."

"Huh?"

"Let's go."

They made their way across the library floor. Kweku grabbed a hefty glass vase from a stand. It had a red core with twisting glass spirals running down its length. He touched a finger to one of the spiral lines, feeling its rough edges, then swung the vase once, testing its weight and heft. Satisfied, he marched on, arriving at the wall first. Kendall was just behind him. She reached up and pressed hard twice on an edge. The door swung noiselessly. Kweku peered through and said a muffled and echoey, "Bloody hell!" to the dark gap. "I thought it was just a wall."

"Quickly!" Kendall urged. One by one, they all stepped through.

Ricardo and Kendall were last. Ricardo put a hand on Kendall's shoulder, holding her back for a second.

"What?"

"Timothy was a traitor?" he said.

"Yes. He tried to kill me."

"All this time you knew there was a traitor. But ... you thought the traitor was *me*?"

He searched her eyes, examining her with a seriousness she hadn't seen in him before. Ricky the sex pot. Ricky the raconteur. Ricky the perennial comedian and laid-back life of the party.

Her lips fell apart as she fumbled for a justification. She settled on the simple truth: "Yes."

Ricardo held her eyes a second longer, then gave a sober nod. He looked down at the scissors in his hand. He disappeared under the canvas. Kendall breathed out, then followed.

✗

They gathered in the gloomy corridor, beneath the buzz of the sputtering strip-light. Kendall had never seen their eyes so large. It occurred to her once again that they really were just a bunch of scared kids. Scared kids lost in a sophisticated trap. Sheep on that final ramp to the slaughterhouse.

"Straight down there." She chopped at the air with one hand as she whispered. "Then straight down the steps. The steps are metal and very, very loud. Don't even try to be quiet. Fast as you can down them, then rush at anyone down there. I'll go straight to the car – whichever one *this* opens. I'll get it started."

Britney asked, "Can you drive?"

"Kind of."

Ricardo nodded again, then took over, easily resuming his charismatic leadership role. "All right, Kweku, listen. I'll go in the lead. I'm gonna shove this directly into the first guy I meet. I should have an easy enough time of that. If there's a second guy, I reckon that's where my trouble begins. I want you directly behind me. Bro, *seriously*, not more than *one* step behind. The first time you see me struggling – someone getting the better of me –"

"I beat the living shit out of them. Wif zero hesitation. I got your back, mate."

Kendall had never seen Ricardo look nervous before. He chewed at his lip, took two deep breaths like a bodybuilder about to attempt a terrific lift, then said, perhaps to himself, "Don't think. Just go!"

Their sprint down the grimy concrete passage made no sound. *The steps*, Kendall knew, *would be another story*.

Ricardo didn't hesitate when he hit the staircase. It clanged and echoed as though a poltergeist were smashing chains down its length. Led by Ricardo, the group plunged down into the bowels of the house.

⚔

Kendall ran at the rear of the group. She held the key fob firmly in her hand, gripped it so hard that her thumb hurt.

It seemed cowardly to her to go last, but it was also necessary. She needed her friends to buy enough time so she could locate and start the right car. Himari's pitch-black hair bobbed as it descended before her, second to last of the group.

Once they were all down and off the staircase, Kendall jumped the last few steps, landing hard at the bottom.

Four. There were *four* figures at the screens. All were looking in the direction of the noise. One was already standing behind his monitor, his chair pushed back, a radio to his ear. *The warning call.*

The man slammed the radio down and yelled, "Stop them!"

Ricardo just kept walking, full stride, straight toward them at the monitors. Chairs slid backward, voices rose in a babble. The man closest rose to his full height. He was a big man, easily double Ricardo's bulk, with jowls and really bad skin. *No, not bad skin*, Kendall saw. *Deep scratch marks.*

The man from the darkness. Those were *her* scratch marks.

He held his arms out and braced himself like a rugby player about to tackle.

Ricardo kept the scissors hidden by his side until the last instant, stepped right up into that bear-embrace, and drove his concealed hand straight into the man's abdomen, pushing upward with all his strength. The sound the man made was a sort of "Hooof!"

Ricardo held tightly to the scissors, then ripped them clear back out of the man's abdomen. The blade made a squelching '*shhlick!*' as it slid out. The jowl-bear gasped long and hard, then doubled over in collapse, pulling down a screen that trailed wires.

Ricardo didn't pause. He continued directly past the fallen figure on the floor, toward the second of the watchers.

It had all happened so quickly that the second man didn't appear to understand what he was seeing.

With no hesitation, Ricardo stabbed him too, hard. And then repeatedly.

Two down.

By now there were shouts echoing around the room – from both adults and teenagers – overlapping, shrill and indiscernible.

As he went down, the second man grabbed Ricardo's arms and pulled the boy to the floor with him. A third man – scrawny, clad in shorts, with knotted calves and muscular, tattooed arms – leaped over a chair, landing on top of them both. He started beating at Ricardo with hammered fists. Tina and Claudette screamed.

In an instant, Kweku was on him. The crunching sound from the vase as it struck the top of the broiling pile of conflict sounded like a caved-in skull. The pile collapsed, and after a moment, Ricardo wriggled out from beneath it.

Now Kweku kept going, scything relentlessly forward along the path Ricardo had just about cleared. Kweku stormed the last person in the control centre, the vase raised again and brandished for a blow. But Kweku hesitated. The last person was a woman – *a young woman* – perhaps in her early twenties.

She remained in her chair, holding an arm above herself to protect her face, her headphones, and the many piercings around her nose, lips, and eyebrows. She winced, anticipating the blow, but she said nothing. Unsure of what to do, Kweku started lowering the vase.

Kendall knew she should already be pressing the buttons on the car fob, but it seemed this thing was just about over. *They had won.* Then she noticed the woman's other hand behind her, reaching into a drawer. From his angle, Kweku couldn't see it.

"She's reaching for something!" Kendall yelled, pointing.

The three men were on the floor, two of them clutching at deep wounds and making moaning sounds, one very still after Kweku's almighty blow with the vase. That one at least would never get up.

Britney skipped over them all, snatched the vase from Kweku's hand, and swung it sideways at the woman's face, just as her other hand emerged, holding a toy-sized pistol with a light-blue handgrip.

The vase had proved itself an even deadlier weapon than the scissors. The sound it made against the side of the woman's face was awful, a combination of a crunch and a wet splatter, shooting a sprayed debris of blood, spittle, and teeth.

The woman slumped in her seat, convulsed twice, then slid by slow degrees to the floor, blood from one crushed ear trickling rapidly over her face and piercings. Her mouth and jaw were completely caved in. She would have fallen all the way to the floor, had her headphones not arrested and suspended her ruined head like a grim noose.

"Stay down," Ricardo ordered one of the stabbed men, putting a foot squarely on his back. The man had been trying to leopard crawl. Now he collapsed. A dark pool of blood seeped out beneath him. He wheezed, "I'm dying!"

Ricardo answered, "And wouldn't that be a shame. Kendall, *go!*"

Kendall studied the glossy key fob. It didn't seem to have any buttons – the whole thing was just a mini spaceship, floating in her palm. She pressed repeatedly on one side. That part of the fob seemed to yield and click with a little haptic feedback.

Somewhere down the row, she heard a *clunk*. Claudette pointed. "*There*. It's the red one. Not the Ferrari, the closer one."

Kendall headed in that direction.

Three cars down, the opened bonnet of a red car was gawping slightly at the garage door. The car was the same sleek spaceship design as the key fob. Kendall ran to slam the bonnet closed, and as she passed by the car, its door handles read her presence and popped out, of their own accord.

Whoa.

That was her first surprise. The second came when, as she lifted the bonnet slightly to slam it shut, she didn't see an engine. *Maybe it's in the back.* She called out, "Find the button for the doors, the garage doors!"

Ricardo remained near the men on the ground, monitoring them for movement. Kweku and the girls fanned out, searching for buttons.

"Here! I think this is it!" Himari called.

Click. Spotlights came on at various points down the line of cars and Kendall said, "No, those are lights. Keep going."

"This one?"

There was a sound like a dull vacuum cleaner. One of the other cars, a big Bentley, began to rotate on its turntable. Each car had its own display lighting, built into a floating square above it, with a starlight effect shining down on the metalwork. The Bentley was polished to such a sheen that each individual star was crystal clear, moving over the vast oceanic space of its turning bonnet and roof.

"No, sorry. Not it!" They kept searching.

Kendall grabbed at the driver-side door handle of the

gleaming spaceship car. She plopped into the seat, then took a second to process what was wrong with this picture.

American. The steering wheel's on the other side.

She shuffled her hips over the centre console and plopped herself down in the left-hand seat. It still looked wrong. There were not enough ... *controls!*

Tina yelled, "Here! I think this is it! A whole row of switches."

There was a deep *'whoomp'*, then Tina yelled "Yes!", and the hobbit-red door in front of the car began to rise, beautiful daylight climbing the bonnet then spilling over into the cabin, like a wash of golden Californian freedom.

Kendall searched for where to insert the key.

Shit. Where is it? Where's the ignition?

All she saw was a steering wheel. In fact, not even an entire steering wheel. It was just a sort of two-sided grip, like a yoke. *What the hell sort of car was this?*

Her hands patted and scuffed and slid all around the sides and underside of the dash and all over that weird yoke.

Come on! Where does it go?!

Nothing.

She heard the back doors of the car open behind her. Himari piled in on one side. Britney, Tina, and Claudette, on the other.

"Go!" one of them shouted over her shoulder.

"I don't know how to start it!" Kendall yelped. "I can't find the ignition!"

Himari said, "It's a Tesla. You don't have to *start* it."

Oh.

For her next surprise, Kendall looked down at her feet.

Right ...

Two pedals. *Where was the third? For that matter, where was the handbrake? Or the gear shift?* Could she have chosen a more confusing means of escape?

Kweku opened the front door and hurled himself into the passenger seat beside her. Kendall asked him, "Can *you* drive? I don't recognize anything in here."

Kweku shook his head. "Don't fink so. I know less than you do," he said. "Proper confusing."

"The whole thing is just ... *screens*. I don't even know how to switch it on."

Himari said again, "You don't switch it on. You've got the key so you just drive. Try."

Like an ice fisher testing tension on dangerous ground, Kendall put a foot onto what she hoped was the accelerator. She pressed forward. The car remained silent and planted.

Ricardo arrived at the window beside them. He looked around for a seat.

From the back, Britney leaned over. "We can make room. Get in!"

Ricardo indicated to Kendall to roll down her window.

She searched for a button. That seemed to work ... *thank goodness*.

Ricardo pointed over his shoulder and said, "Everyone back there's out cold. I think two of them are dead. The other two might be on their way out." For a young guy who had possibly just killed two men, he seemed to have himself under control, though Kendall noticed a slight shivering around his hands. "Kendall, pull the car out into the drive. Go far enough so you can see the gate."

"Okay. And you?"

"I'll press at buttons here and see if I can open that front gate. We still have to get through it to get out. Someone get out of the car and wave back to me if that front gate opens. Go, go, go!" He thumped the top of the car.

"What's wrong?"

Kendall pressed the accelerator again. She made a frustrated gesture above the steering yolk. She placed a foot on the other pedal, which she hoped and prayed was the break.

"Put it in gear," Ricardo said, leaning in. "That lever on the right. Pull it down to D for Drive."

Kendall pulled the stalk down.

This time, when she gave the accelerator a shove, an atomic bomb blasted the car forward and slammed their heads back into the headrests.

Ricardo sprang back onto his toes like a toreador with a bull, as the sleek red paint warped by. The girls shrieked and Kweku doled out several colourful British curses.

Kendall stomped on the break. Instantly, the almighty beast fell still again, whiplashing their heads forward. They had only gone a few feet, weren't even completely out of the garage door, but the experience silenced them all.

"Yussus!" Kendall said.

There was no stuttering, no stalling from the car. Just the resumption of perfect masterful quiet. The car seemed to calmly await her next command.

"Okay. Sorry everyone. Let's try this again."

"Gently, please," Britney said.

Perhaps it was the tension, but everyone in the car tittered at that.

Tina piped up, "Was it as good for you as it was for me?"

The chortling grew.

Then Kweku asked, "You know what happens if we go that fast, don't you?"

"What?"

"We all get chub rub."

The laughter was explosive. Even shy Himari held a hand over her mouth and convulsed.

Ricardo waved them out and said, "All right, you bunch of weirdos. Let's get a move on and get out of here."

From out in the driveway, Dianne stepped through the door, holding a dull black Glock 9mm outstretched before her. She shot Ricardo twice where he stood, at point-blank range. Fine blood spray from the exit peppered the side window of the car.

Right beside Kendall, the boy slumped out of sight to the floor.

⚔

The shriek of the car's tires on the garage floor merged with the screaming from the backseat. Nevertheless, it all sounded dulled and distant in the wake of those deafening gunshots.

As Ricardo fell, as the Tesla shot out into the light, as Kendall's knuckles whitened around the steering wheel and she tried to ignore the ringing in her ears and just *go!*, Dianne dropped down to one knee, turned, and pivoted, tracking in line with the accelerating car.

Kendall expected the next shot any second, wondered why she wasn't yet dead, looked up, and saw Dianne in the rearview mirror, over the heads of her wildly panicked friends. The calm precision in the woman's movements as she tracked their movement over the handgun's sights was chilling.

Then the shots came. Dianne put two into the back of the car. They landed with dull thuds that Kendall could feel reverberating through the steering yoke. The impacts didn't seem to slow them.

Dianne stood, drawing herself up to her full height. She walked out into the driveway, but the Tesla moved so fast that they were already well out of range of her handgun.

"Quiet, quiet!" Kendall yelled over the babbling and crying from the back. She slowed the car in the driveway.

"What the fuck are you doing?! She's coming!" Tina yelled.

"We can't leave Ric. And I don't know if we can get through those gates. We need them open."

"Bash them. *Bash* right through. Just drive."

"No, those things weigh a ton or more. It'd be like crashing straight into a wall, we'd die. And even if we dislodge them, imagine if they fall on us."

"She's walking this way! She's coming! She's gonna shoot us!"

Kendall grappled with a moment of indecision. She glanced back over the seat in the direction of the threat. In the back, Himari quietly showed her something.

Dianne was advancing down the driveway toward them, her walk still eerily upright, dignified. Now she broke into a run. Even her run was machinelike, as though she had long shed the last vestiges of her humanity in some pursuit of mechanical precision.

"Right," Kendall said. "I'm gonna run her over."

Kweku warned, "That woman will shoot you straight frew this glass." He added in a small voice, "And me."

"I'll get as close as I can. You just duck. When I see her aim, I will too. I'll keep the pedal down."

"Kendall ..." Kweku said.

"No time!" Kendall did a U-turn that took them slightly onto the bumping surface of the grass.

The power of this car was ludicrous.

She slowed a little, lined the bonnet up facing the great house and the determined figure of the advancing woman. Floored the accelerator.

"Freakin' shitballs!" Kweku said, trying to grab at anything as his head slammed back into the headrest yet again.

From the back, Britney said, "At least veer. Don't give her an easy target."

"I will. When I'm closer."

Ahead, Dianne stopped running. She slowed, then took up her place in the middle of the driveway, the gun hanging insolently by her side. The enormous mansion framed her behind.

"Look at her!" Kweku said. "It's like she finks authority will make her car-proof."

"You know what?" Britney said from the back. "I hate her. I fucking *hate* her, and I hate that house, and I hate what she did to us. Kendall, you mow that bitch down!"

"No, turn around, get us out!" Tina countered.

With just a few hundred feet between them now, Dianne lifted the gun. She supported it with her left hand and took careful aim, right at Kendall's head. There was something astonishing, revelatory, about a grown-up standing openly in the sunlight, so brazenly focused on harming you.

Copernican Revolutions. Of the grimmest kind.

Kendall held the accelerator flat.

As the distance rapidly closed, and the relentless Tesla hauled the house closer, Tina and Claudette shrieked from the back of the car and hunched down as best they could, leaning over one another in a pile. Kweku slumped down too, leaning his body as far as he could over the place where the gearshift should have been. Kendall began to weave. She went side to side across the driveway in erratic swoops, a drunken pirate captaining the world's fastest sloop through a storm. The wheels threw up grass on either side.

The weird little yoke-style steering wheel actually worked. Once you got used to it, the control was excellent.

From within the well-insulated car, the gunshots speeding their way sounded like little pops – so undramatic for something so lethal. The girls shrieked at every pop. The weaving seemed to work though. Only one round hit the car, on the bonnet.

They were close. The terrible woman appeared more focused on her aim than on getting out of the way. *This might work.* Kendall pointed the nose of the car right at her, right at the gun barrel aimed squarely at her face, and at the last instant ducked down with her head on top of Kweku, hammering her foot down hard.

Something strange happened.

Instead of a thump from the bonnet, or even a double bump

from the front and back wheels, the car became a sentient thing – and betrayed her. The accelerator pedal pushed itself back up, the ghost in the machine grabbed and hauled its own steering yoke to the right, and the car swerved with astonishing force, traitorously missing Kendall's prey, refusing to allow her to murder a pedestrian, its electronics beeping and shrieking all the while.

Surprised, Kendall stopped. The car stopped. Kendall sat up, and discovered the looming figure of Dianne, standing comfortably right beside her, just outside the window, the beginnings of a smile spreading across her face.

Kendall had one clear, cold final thought as the woman pointed the gun right at her: *I'm going to die now.*

There was an almighty bang, the crash and shimmy of falling glass, and when Kendall opened her eyes, a black spot appeared and blossomed in Dianne's neck. It spread into a bleeding hole, and the surprised woman crumpled out of sight, just as Ricardo had done moments prior.

In the backseat, hands shivering, Himari dropped the pistol with the light-blue handgrip. Looking more like a toy than a weapon, it tumbled, smoking and stinking, into her lap.

✴

Kendall felt utterly numb. The sight of Ricardo's body rocked her sense of stability even worse than Timothy's betrayal had. She kneeled beside the beautiful boy with the too-long black hair, placed one hand on his shoulder.

The energy went out of her.

She stroked his hair. Touched his face. The skin was cool.

The others finally found a switch that opened the front gate. The car stood in the driveway, right where they'd abandoned it, all four doors open. Dianne's body lay at an angle on the driveway beside it, one arm trailing out as if pointing at something far away.

Kweku crouched beside her. "We got to go ... find help."

Kendall breathed in. And out. "Okay ..."

Kweku looked at Ricardo's body, put a hand on Kendall's shoulder. "He's coming too."

✗

Everyone in the vehicle was silent. In the backseat, they held Ricardo's body across them. Kendall looked in wonder at the open road curving away down the hill, not a hindrance, not an obstacle in sight.

"I'll see if I can close it by hand," she said.

She got out, pulled at the gate, braced herself, then attempted a second, harder pull. It was no good. The gates would have to stay open. If there was any way of containing him, she couldn't think of it. *The Judas Goat would be able to flee.*

She glanced back up the long drive at the house.

In a top window, she saw the unmoving outline of the Goat, looking right back at her, watching them go.

DOWN BY THE SIDE RAMP

Kendall inched the Tesla onto the switchback road. One back tyre missed the gradient, and thudded down from the pavement to the tarmac, and everyone in the car gasped.

"Sorry."

In a moment, they were on the tarmac, aiming downhill. Despite the fact that their freedom from the house was now assured, nobody said a thing. They seemed shocked, spent, each needing a moment to process all that had just happened. They didn't even seem uncomfortable holding Ricardo's body across their laps – merely numb.

A mere fifteen minutes had elapsed from the time Kendall had told them to run to the library – *the Goat was about to rat on them!* – to now. In that short span of time, their small group had killed and been killed. Kendall's hair was still wet from the attempted murder back in the house.

Now they were *free*. It was dizzying.

Kendall tried not to overthink the prospect of driving on public roads. She gently encouraged the Tesla to follow the switchbacks, cruising even slower than she had during her lessons with Addie. The speedometer barely registered fifteen.

Something slowly expanded within Kendall's mind, blooming within her as they took in the giant vistas. She suspected the others felt it too. After days couped up in the same place, she now profoundly experienced the wonder of basic autonomy, how good it felt to move freely in any direction at will, beyond roofs and corridors and containment, unhampered beneath an immense American sky. Right now, and quite suddenly, no corridors hemmed them in. No traitor manipulated their path. No cameras watched their every move. Just pick a direction and go – you were at liberty to do so. *Freedom.*

Kendall eased them around another bend, descending ever further.

They were out. They were out, and no longer awaiting a fate determined by someone lurking out of sight, beyond knowledge. They could go wherever they aimed the front wheels. For that awesome privilege, they had paid a dear price.

The Tesla bore them in silken silence all the way down into the valley.

"Does anyone know ...?" Kendall thought for a second, trying to configure an end to that sentence. "Uh ... which way we should go to find the police?"

Ten seconds of silence elapsed. Kweku said, "Just drive 'til you spot a copper. None of us really know where we are."

The suggestion was oddly pleasing. *Just drive.* No one was chasing them. They were out. Eventually, they would find someone. They would hand over Ricardo's body to a grown-up, who would know what to do. The weighty burden of their decisions would be taken from them. Kendall couldn't wait.

For now, just drive.

The mountain route gave way to a flat, multi-lane road. It ran on and on through the wonderfully ordinary world of strip malls, car dealerships with balloons outside, and real human beings walking, *just walking*, along open pavements, bags in their hands, children by their side, some jogging, some with dogs or pushing prams, flags flapping in the breeze here and there. There was even a McDonald's up ahead, universally recognizable and comforting in its mundanity.

Occasionally another set of traffic lights stopped her. At other times, Kendall could simply drive right through. She kept going straight, unsure of how to stay in what felt like the wrong lane while turning a corner.

Still, no one spoke.

The aimless stop-and-go stretched on. Despite everything, Kendall was finding this drive, if not exactly *enjoyable,* at least *comforting.*

"There," Kweku pointed. "That black and white cruiser up ahead. I fink that's police."

Kendall could imagine how it would go. She would just pull over and, surrendering to the grown-ups, let the authorities run the show from that point onward. She'd been the adult long enough.

But then the rear lights of the police cruiser lit up and, suddenly, it pulled out into traffic. As Kendall slowed, it accelerated.

A shout from the back, "They're getting away."

Anger flashed through Kendall, altering something behind her eyes. Salvation was running away from her. What should have been the blessed end of a difficult journey receded hopelessly toward the horizon.

"No! That's enough! This needs to end. *Now.*"

She floored the Tesla.

In mere seconds, they vacuumed up the distance between the two vehicles. This was the fastest she had ever driven. Kendall wasn't sure if they had seen her yet, but she pulled right up alongside the cruiser, reading the word 'Police' on the side.

"Everybody hold on tight!" she called. No objections from the back, though hands reached out and braced against doors. In a flash of courage that surprised even her, Kendall nudged the front of the Tesla at the side of the police vehicle, with every intention of bashing into it.

Yet again, the car took control, preventing collision. Its circuits emitted a series of electronic beeps and corrected away. They got close enough, though, that the police car veered and blared its horn. Kendall planted her foot on the accelerator, blasted past the police, then slammed on the brakes right in front of it.

Britney shouted, "Holy crap, Kendall!"

In the rear-view mirror she saw the driver, a man wearing dark glasses, throw his wheel to the side. The black-and-white cruiser shuddered sideways to a halt, both doors opening with impressive immediacy, two figures bolting out, weapons aimed.

Apparently, that'll do it.

All around them, traffic shuddered and halted and horns blared. People on the sidewalks stared, and a kid about their age pulled out a phone to film them, stepping right out into the street.

At first, Kendall couldn't tell where the booming voice of the wrathful god was coming from. Then she realized it was the policeman, speaking through some form of loudspeaker. His partner, gun trained on them, was already most of the way to the Tesla, running in a semi-crouch and yelling about raising their hands where he could see them.

The noise and anger were short-lived. Whatever the policeman had been expecting, this was not it: frightened teenagers, tear-stained, quietly sitting with their eyes wide and their hands up. And across the laps of the kids in the back, the unmoving body of a young man with slick black hair.

The policeman lowered his gun, trying to understand what he was looking at. His partner joined him, still barking into a radio.

"Ma'am, what's going on here?"

"Sir, my name is Kendall Mayor. I'm from South Africa. We're all from different countries. We just escaped. Some people were keeping us in a house, up that hill over there."

Britney said, "We were being held hostage. My name is Britney."

"I'm Kweku." Voices chimed one after another, taking it in turn to identify themselves.

The policeman looked from them to his partner and back again. Something changed in his face, and he said, "Oh my god, it's them." He leaned right in. "You're *them*. You're the exchange students?"

"Yes!" they all said.

Kendall continued, pointing, "We were in a huge house. It's a few miles back, up that way. We were told it was an exchange program, but it wasn't."

"Yes, we know." Straight to business, the cop rattled out, "Where are the rest of you? Can you take us to them? Do they need help?"

Kendall felt the full weight of this man's hopeful anxiety, this officer's genuine desire to do his duty, and it broke her heart. This was just like her mother managing her hopes when they found Dobby dead, the second time.

Her lips began to quiver. Then tears overwhelmed her and blocked her throat, and she could speak no further. She sank her head down, folding in on herself. Someone else could say the ugly words, speak the awful truth. Someone else could be in charge now. She was done.

Kweku leaned forward, "They're all gone, sir." Then he looked down at the body across their laps. Quietly, he said, "This is Ricardo Alverez."

The policeman said, "Your parents have been ... *all* your parents, for *days* now, they've been ..." But though his face remained stoic, the man couldn't complete his sentence either. He took off his sunglasses, looked away for a second as he touched at his eyes. "My god," he said again, and began opening their doors to help them out. "It's really you."

*

WHERE HAVE YOU BEEN ALL THIS TIME?

Kendall was beyond exhausted. Past the cup of tea on the desk before her, she no longer registered information. The interview room was a blur, faces and ranks and offices were a blur. She couldn't even recall whether she'd answered questions for three or four different individuals.

The current voice – male – grew quiet for a moment, possibly having asked an unanswered question – *she wasn't sure, didn't care* – then said, "Look, I can see this has been tough. You've done so very well." There was a hand on her arm, to show sincerity, but Kendall flinched. The hand quickly retracted. "Would you like another sandwich? Some tea or coffee, or maybe juice? Perhaps just a bottle of water?"

"Maybe a charger for my phone?"

Male Blur smiled kindly. It was good to see open concern in an adult face. It made a nice counterpoint to undisguised malice.

A Female Blur arrived. Removed one cord from an outlet in the wall and replaced it with a charger. Handed the end of the line to Male Blur, who handed it to Kendall.

Kendall slotted the end into the base of her phone. There were a few seconds of inaction, then the screen lit up. It asked for a passcode. Kendall stared blankly at the screen without even the beginnings of numbers presenting themselves in her memory.

There was simply nothing.

Instead she watched the battery blink on and off as it charged. Blur One and Two were speaking to her but the words were gibberish.

Then, wading through the fatigue, came the passcode. Half her birthday and half Addie's. She keyed the numbers in and there was a soft bleep.

Once her phone's launch sequence concluded, a cascade began.

Bing. A message from her service provider, welcoming her to roaming in the United States. Bitter laughter almost choked her.

A deluge of texts via SMS flooded behind it, each *bing* merging into the next, vibrating in her palm. Her phone, dancing in her hand.

She read the first one. Her Mom:

'Hi there, Munchkin. Have you landed in California yet? Hope it's nice and sunny. Love you!'

The simplicity of this caused a sudden heat to rise. The next one was from her Dad:

'Greetings, Hooligan. Did you get your Mom's message? If we're calculating times right, you should be out of the airport now. How's the weather? How's crazy California?'

Pretty darn crazy, Dad.
Then another from her Dad:

'Kendall? Was your plane delayed? Talk to your two nervous parents, pls. We haven't heard from you, so we're assuming we can rent out your room to a biker gang, yes? Love you. Pls answer.'

Then again from her Dad:

'Kendall, pls answer! Are u getting these messages? Is something wrong? Pls, we're genuinely worried now.

It must be late night for you there by now. Did they pick you up, get you to the house, etc? What's happening?'

The next one was from Addie:

'Hey, Knock Knees! You're thoroughly freaking out Mom and Dad. What the actual hell? Also, meet any delicious gentlemenfolk yet? Sordid details, immediately!'

And another from Addie:

'Kendall? Please, love, Mom and Dad are in tears. They've been trying to make calls to the agency but getting nowhere. This isn't funny. Are you okay?'

Then her Dad again:

'Kendall, we're assuming an emergency. We've called the police in the county and town where yr supposed to be. They are investigating. If yr getting any of these messages, you MUST tell us.'

And a part two:

'... meanwhile, me, Mom, and Addie, are all praying for you. Nonstop. We love you. I hope you're safe, angel. Be strong. I love you.'

It got worse from there.

Kendall scrolled down through the long, long list of messages. Several hundred at least. Interspersed with the constant attempts by her parents and by Addie. Messages from Kendall's cousins, from her school friends, and even from a large number of teachers and kids from her school that she barely knew.

Saying essentially the same thing:

'Hi Kendall, we're all praying for your safe return. You're not alone ...'

'... saw you on the news. We've been praying for you and your family. I hope you're safe.'

'Our youth group has been praying for you. We want you to know everyone is looking for you. You're loved, you're missed, and we have every faith you will be found ...'.

'Be strong, and know that your family and friends love you. Everyone is praying for your safe return. Everyone is looking for you.'

Blur Two, the female one, sounded excited: "Miss Mayor? Great news! Your parents are on the line! This way."

Kendall followed Blur Two out of the door and left down a corridor.

Three doors along, Blur Two paused and flung a door open and flourished the way in. Kendall couldn't stop herself. She hesitated, double checked what was in the room before entering. She was looking for what exactly? *The sucker punch. The universe to spin in a different direction. A friend to become a traitor.*

It was a simple office. Papers tacked to a wall, a computer, a chair behind a desk. On the desk, a black corded phone, the receiver a lifeline to another world, stretching from California to the southern tip of Africa, all the way home to Johannesburg.

Kendall lifted the phone. Her nose started to run as fast as her eyes. She used her hand to wipe at them both.

She placed the receiver to her ear. "Mom? Dad?"

✳

The reunion was organized for July.

The escape had made global headlines. It remained lead news for nearly a week, the reporting growing in enthusiasm as ever juicier details emerged from the excavation of the now-infamous house. 'What if you sent your child overseas, straight into the hands of child traffickers? The story making international headlines: California's House of Horrors. A ring of paedophile brokers posing as a harmless exchange program, the teenagers who singlehandedly overcame and killed them, plus the mystery of the missing kids – were they sold as sex slaves? Where are they now? Don't go away, that's up next!' It was a potent mix that enraptured the popular imagination, and the footage of the house was vivid, generally shot at low angles to emphasize its foreboding height. One reality show even etched in a stormy background, complete with melodramatic lightning, and told the tale in the first person, 'Stolen! I was a child victim!'

The funding for their return visit came from Washington as a sort of PR do-over. The editorials and talk shows were right: most of the kids *were* still missing.

In an effort to make the event look positive, only the families of those who had made it out of the house were invited. The families of the missing kids – nearly thirty of them – had received different phone calls and were being updated by different agencies, though not with tones of hope.

✳

Kendall's family arrived early. It was a perfect California day, crystalline and fresh. She'd wanted to curl up in a ball and hide, not walk through the lobby of a Best Western. Just to get through the day seemed to require the courage of a hero. Since Kendall disappeared, Addie had taken leave from her PhD. First to help find her. And then to help put her back together. Even so, Kendall felt as if she'd been stuck together with bits of blue tack. It wouldn't take much for her to fall apart again.

Twice now she had spoken on the phone with Ricardo's parents. Today, she would meet them. She wondered how they would handle this event as the only invited parents of a dead child. They were here because, technically speaking, their boy had gotten out too.

Like a small child, Kendall walked in the sunshine between her mother and father, carrying the tribute in her arms. Kendall discovered that her palms were sweating. Addie followed behind, looking up and down the massive lanes and taking in the scale of it all. She looked movie-star glamorous in her new Californian sunglasses, though she did mutter, "Yea, though I walk through the valley of the unhinged ..."

Past the foyer they arrived at the double doors to the conference hall. An awkward, smiling man in a suit greeted them like VIPs. He gave the impression that he would like nothing better than to help you across the road or feed your dog while you were away. He even called Kendall "Miss Mayor", very nearly bowing a little as though she were royalty, before he waved them through.

The room was perfectly, wonderfully, reassuringly bland. Windows let in that golden sunlight on both sides of a large rectangular space. You could see everything in a glance. No angles, no curved terraces or artistic recesses casting strange shadows. No spirals or levels or threatening water features where traitors might drown you. These days, Kendall spent a lot more time outside in the open. Or up on the roof.

The main feature were tables combined at the front. Kendall bore her burden there, where she found photos of all thirty-two kids. The missing ones were in the back row; Kendall and the other survivors made up a smaller row up in front.

It was chilling to see how few of the total number had

made it out. There were small candles beside the pictures of each of the missing children. *Alive? Dead? Suffering? No one knew.* And there was one small candle beside Ricardo's portrait in the front row.

Kendall lowered her bundle of frames, spilling them into a pile on a blank spot on the table, then wiped her sweaty hands against her sides. Each frame bore a cartoon caricature by Kweku. She placed each drawing beside the larger photos of the survivors, marvelling at how closely Kweku had caught their personalities with so few strokes.

Here were Tina and Claudette. Kweku depicted them with extra-long hair and extra-short. Mermaid and pixie. Kendall leaned in. Next was Britney. She looked like an Octoberfest fräulein with her braided hair. Kendall's own photo showed her with lumps and bumps and stars, like an injured coyote from the old cartoon, and she smiled at it as she set it beside a genuine school photo of her.

Kendall's gaze drifted farther off, to the back row of faces. She stared for a long while at the picture of Agnieszka. The photo must have been a year or two younger than when Kendall knew her. It was clearly a school picture, and the friendly student stared hopefully outward, sporting braces and acne on her cheeks. Her white-blonde hair looked the same, though here it was tied back with pink and blue ribbons.

"Is that her?" Addie asked, sidling up next to Kendall.

"That's her."

"She's lovely."

"She really was."

Addie leaned in and studied the photo. Kendall had spoken about her often. Addie repeated a line in a Polish accent, "I shower tomorrow. For now, I dream about Ricky!"

Kendall chuckled, then ran a finger over the girl's face. "That's exactly how she said it."

"*Who* dreamed about Ricky?"

The accent was Latina, and the voice was female. Kendall turned and met Ricardo's parents.

She knew who they were in an instant. She was horrified they might take offence at the overhead conversation. Yet Ricky's mother was smiling with the openness of an auntie you've known forever, even though her eyes were red and looked like they'd been rubbed many times that morning.

"Hi Mrs Alverez. Hello Mr Alverez. I'm Kendall."

The father had a sterner face, but on closer inspection, seemed more nervous than angry. With his olive skin and straight black hair, Kendall could see the blueprint of the beautiful boy from the house. *Oh yes, this was Ricardo's father, all right!* He seemed not to have his son's natural gregariousness, but held himself tall and still, with great dignity.

Mrs Alverez engulfed Kendall in a hug that was all plump curves and flowers. "We know. Oh, but we've wanted to meet you for so long now, *chica!*"

Kendall tried to breathe above the floral embrace and the pleasant smell of her perfume. The woman pulled back and looked into Kendall's eyes, still holding her very close.

"To answer your question, Mrs Alverez, *everyone* dreamed of Ricky. Your son was so full of life, so popular. Right from the first day in the house. I don't think there was a girl in there who didn't have a great big crush on him."

Kendall worried about her phrase 'full of life'. Not to mention the word 'was'.

But Ric's mother cocked her chin with pride. It seemed that this had been exactly the right thing to say about her boy. Even the father broke the straight line of his moustache, smiling in an aching way with tight lips. Kendall noted that his smile also went slightly to the side, like Ricardo's.

Kendall's parents joined the conversation and introductions were made all around. Kendall's father shook hands with Ricardo's father and said, "I'm so terribly sorry for your loss, Mr

Alverez. Kendall says your boy was outstandingly brave. They wouldn't have got out without him and what he did. We owe our child's life to your son's bravery. Thank you seems insufficient."

The two men held their handshake for a very long while. Kendall had never seen her father look so vulnerable. Ricardo's father, who managed to speak volumes with very little movement, placed his other hand tightly atop their handshake and whispered, "*Gracias*, Mr Mayor."

They all separated, handed tissues around, and Addie observed with a puff, "Well, that cleared out the sinuses!" She was leaking tears too.

Ricardo's mother took something from her purse and placed it before the small memorial to Ricardo. It was the pair of sunglasses Ricky had worn on Songs Evening.

"Well, now! Vat looks like someone I recognize, right off the bat!"

Kendall turned in delight. "Kweku!" She barrelled into his arms, then said, "Holy crap, dude! You're wearing a suit!"

"Yeah, nice, innit? Hides the chub. Vese are me mum and dad. As you can see, they're also woefully overdressed. I kept telling them it's California, not London, but you know, *old people!* Oh hey, you framed my drawings."

"Yeah!"

"Well, now. I should fink I'm honoured."

A deep base voice, with a Ghanaian accent tinged with London formality, said, "It is a great pleasure to meet you, Miss Kendall. Kweku has told us everything you did to get him and the others out. We owe you a deep debt of gratitude. This is my wife, Akuba."

Kweku's father was greying at the temples, just as Kweku had described him on Ghost Story Night. He wore a suit but Kweku's mother wore the traditional Kaba and Slit, a combination of blouse and tunic in explosively patterned diamonds. Her headdress, like a bundled scarf, was a lively orange and yellow.

"Kweku tells me that he related the story of our farm in Ghana," the tall man said with a dignified smile. "It seems a strange fate to me that the son, like the father, should be destined to meet his own Judas Goat. Everything is patterns."

Kendall caught how this comment made Addie smile.

Kweku said, "That bloody little sod fooled us all. Nearly did you in, Kendall."

His father continued, "I am grateful every day that you led them to safety. You saved my boy."

"Your boy's a fighter, sir. Without him and Ricardo, we'd have had no chance. I couldn't have got out at all. None of us would have."

"You are kind."

From behind came a new voice. "Kia ora, mate."

"Britney!!!"

Britney looked like she wanted to say something upbeat and witty, but then simply burst into tears. Kendall vacuumed her up into a hug and said, "I know, mate! I know!" Kweku joined in, and the tears morphed into laughter.

Britney said, "Mate, no references to chub rub or we'll just never stop."

And somehow they were both laughing and crying at the same time.

"Folks, may I have your attention for a moment please? May I have your attention?"

Gradually, the chatter died.

The official in the suit, trying his best to look relaxed and friendly, and failing spectacularly, explained which department he was from and told them he didn't want to take up too much of their time.

"This is a reunion, and the day belongs to you. We've been in contact with each of you separately, but we did want to take the opportunity to let you know that there have been some new developments."

Some of the audience now turned, interest growing.

"Our forensics teams have been working backward from the computers and equipment recovered in the garage of the house. It's an ongoing investigation, and sensitive, but we wanted to assure you, we have leads. *Strong* leads. We are investigating what we believe is a promising channel into the network. We have every confidence that justice will be served."

Here he seemed to grow a little awkward.

"Though ... we have no way of knowing if this means we may be able to recover some of the children, I must stress that. Of course, our hearts are in it and every effort is being made. And, uh ... there are elements of this investigation that pertain to some of you individually. Please, may we ask that you not leave today before we've had a chance to speak."

Some of the audience murmured to one another.

The agent was saying, "... the young man we know only as 'Timothy' remains a priority in our investigation."

That turned the mood.

Under her breath, Britney said to Kendall, "After you stuck those scissors in his chest, we know he won't be doing it again."

Kendall thought about those scissors for a long moment. He had certainly been bleeding like a stuck pig when she'd last seen him. Then again, he'd fled quite capably. *If he survived, was there a chance that the whole thing might have, as it were, 'scared him straight'? Would he change the course of his life, go honest?*

The thought made her chuckle sardonically. This was a young man who had conned a houseful of kids into accepting their own trafficking by various subtle devices, including friendship. Timothy was a great many things. But he was not weak. He may have been small, may have appeared timid, but the reality behind those blue eyes was stone-strong. Though his veins were undeniably twisted, they were harder than granite.

Kendall estimated that this was an artform for him, a performance piece at which he excelled, and therefore took pride in. Looking back on his feigned tears, the whispered conversations, the subtle misdirects, the spectacular vomiting, the weaving of a trusting friendship, if anything, Kendall believed he'd enjoyed it.

"Once again, the United States of America and the State of California thank you for the opportunity to make the very beginnings of amends."

From the front, the man then walked directly up to Kendall's group.

"Miss Mayor, may we speak for a moment?" He looked pointedly at her family. "In private?"

⚹

They sat in a tiny room. There were two agents present. The man held an iPad, queued to play something.

"I realize this might be hard for you, Miss Mayor," the man said. "But could you help us make a positive identification here? Perhaps provide us with a few pointers as well? Of course, we can do this at a more appropriate time if you'd like. It's just that *time* may be of the essence."

"Just go ahead and play it," Kendall snapped. All this delicacy was beginning to grate.

Without another word, the man tapped the iPad screen.

It was audio only. The voice, chillingly familiar. The only difference was that in this incarnation, it made no attempt at warmth, bore no trace of childish need. *No, this was him ... as he really was.*

THE HOUSE AND THE GOAT

"So you're the one? The kid they call the Goat?"

"I am indeed."

"I heard what happened in California. Whole world did. Fucking disaster. That entire crew, stabbed, shot, beaten to death, including the madam."

(Silence) Then the first voice continued.

"The stock turned on them. And then got away. Feds spent the next two weeks tearing the place apart. That one cell alone could easily expose the whole network."

"That's why you need me."

(A pause) *"Yeah? And why is that?"*

"Because I know what they did wrong."

"What they did wrong." The voice repeated sardonically. *"And what was that exactly?"*

"Hire me and you'll find out."

"You got nerve. A lot of fucking nerve given that you're the one who blew it up."

"I didn't. They did. And you know it. That's why you're talking to me. And by the way, we moved most of the stock first, so don't go pretending it was a failure. So we lost a madam and some staff. So what? I know the margins as well as you do."

"Margins. You don't talk like a kid."

"Imagine that."

"Give me something then."

"Alright. They based the monitoring crew onsite. You don't do that, it's dumb. The only onsite crew should be security and removal. Take me onboard and I'll also tell you what they did wrong with the exits."

"If we use you, and I'm only saying if, what would you do differently?"

"I want to be part of set up. Preparing the house. I know how the stock behave, what they look for, how they think. Get me in from the start. Do that, you'll have a perfect operation. No losses. And no leftovers."

"Mmm ... Tell me about your role. Why does it work? What's the key?"

"Spider and fly. No one comes to a confident spider."

"Huh. And you don't lose sleep? Knowing what comes next in their lives?"

"Their lives! Life isn't real. Life is piles of crap on toast."

"Is that right?"

"It is."

"You think you're very smart, don't you?"

"I think this conversation is getting boring."

(Another pause). *"All right, look. We have a house in Rio."*

"I'm listening."

∗

Then silence. The agents both looked at Kendall. The female agent said, "Are you going to faint? We can get you some water."

"No, I'm fine."

In reality, Kendall was perilously close to passing out. Her head felt cold, as though she had an ice-cream headache, and she fought to stop herself from swaying. A few deep gulps of air as she leaned forward, her head near her knees. The sensation passed.

"Clearly that's him, then."

Kendall nodded. And swallowed. She tasted bile in her mouth.

"Right. Kendall, this is Jane. That's not her real name."

'Jane' stepped forward and Kendall wearily lifted her head to examine her.

"Jane is going into that house in Rio."

"Into the house? With *him*?"

"With him."

Kendall's jaw fell open as she stared at the young woman. "Holy shit!" The woman's mouth ticked up – almost a smile.

"Aren't you scared?"

Jane walked over and pulled a chair from behind a desk. She sat, facing Kendall directly. *She could easily pass for a teen*, Kendall realized. Kendall didn't know how old she really was, and didn't even want to hazard a guess. *Twenty five?*

"Kendall, I'll be honest with you. I'm terrified. But it's important work, and at least I know exactly what this is and I've been trained to deal with it. We've intercepted their outgoing communication and they've accepted me onto their program. So it's happening."

"But if you know where it's going to be, why let it happen at all? Why let the kids go there? There will be other kids, right?"

"Yes, there will. And they will all be perfectly safe. We'll work with the authorities there, and we'll have a circle of law enforcement around that house that popes and presidents couldn't expect."

Kendall found herself starting to shake. *This seemed monstrous.*

The man said, "But there are several things we can achieve by allowing it to play out ... for a day or two."

Jane said, "I will know in advance who the Goat is. That means I can create a relationship with him. And that means I can determine where he is at any given time, so that our team can investigate other aspects of the house. I will also know to look for cameras. And I'll be smuggling in our own camera equipment, which will be so tiny and cleverly concealed that it won't even register on scans. I will be recording everything, and I will be able to take him – Timothy, that is – alive."

Kendall marvelled at the bravery of going through all that

again on purpose, stepping into another such house, when you could choose not to.

The man added, "Finally, the links from their cameras are traceable. And that's why we're going to all this trouble. We can work backward from there. That means we can go after buyers from all around the world. Get the big fish."

Jane added, "We're also hoping to catch that crew on-site, although as you heard in the conversation, Timothy is going to recommend they don't set up base within the house. Nevertheless, we believe that over the course of several days, many of their operatives will visit the place, in one guise or another. They'll likely have their own 'madam', who can be followed. We'll deface a camera or two to compel them to come. Then we'll trail them."

"You want to catch them *all*?"

"We want as many of them as we can get," the man said. "And as much information as we can generate, yes. That's why it's worth allowing it to play out. But Kendall, I reiterate, those kids will be in no danger whatsoever."

Kendall wasn't so sure. The Goat *saw* things. He turned tables. He was subtle.

"Then what do you need from me?"

Jane grew animated. "Tell me how he ticks! How do I befriend him, what do I need to know?"

The answer to that one was easy. "You need to need help. You need to be in trouble."

"How so?"

"Don't even try to befriend him. Seriously, don't. He'll smell a rat in a second. If you're really going to do this, then what you need to do is to be in a group and get yourself into an embarrassing situation. Spill a drink on yourself or something. Let him rescue you. He looks for that." She thought for a moment. "I think he gets off on that."

Jane made notes.

"And he plays on guilt and emotions too. After he's rescued

you, show interest in another boy. He'll start ... I don't know how to put this ... he'll start acting like he's jealous, so that *you* try harder to be nice to *him*. I think that's what he does. He creates emotional bonds with this weird mix of thoughtfulness and neediness. But he doesn't, like, push. At all. *He reacts.* That way you think it's all you. One second he's rescuing you, the next second he needs to be rescued."

"Sounds like quite the mind fuck."

"Jane, or whatever your name is, listen to me. You will not believe how real it is. Make no mistake. If he needs to, that kid will murder you with his own hands." Jane's pen stopped above the page. "And you will not see it coming."

"Thank you. I tell myself I'm ready for this operation. And I have a healthy fear. But you've reminded me never to underestimate the enemy. I won't forget, Kendall. I promise."

"He also has an injury. About here," Kendall touched her chest. "Where I stabbed him with scissors."

"Got it."

"And Jane?"

"Yes?"

"If you need to, *you* stab him with scissors too. If he figures you out, you do it immediately. Because he's dangerous. Will you?"

"Oh ... okay ..." The woman hesitated for a split second. "Thank you. If I need to, I will."

Kendall stared at her for a long time, evaluating that momentary hesitation. She came to a conclusion. She turned to the man. "You're going to need a plan to get her out. Within, like, thirty seconds or less, if her cover gets blown."

He shuffled slightly at Kendall's assertiveness. But he placed the iPad aside and asked her frankly, "Why?"

Kendall nodded toward Jane. "Because she hesitates."

She turned back to Jane. "No offence, you seem nice. And smart. And I think what you're doing is really brave."

She faced the man again. "But if he figures out what's happening – and I think he will –"

Jane prompted, "Yes?"

"Then my money's on *him*."

ABOUT THE AUTHOR

DOUGLAS KRUGER is a multiple award-winning international speaker and the author of eight business books with Penguin Random House. Douglas's thought-leadership ideas have been featured on CNBC Africa and he has been published in Forbes and Entrepreneur magazines.

House of the Judas Goat is his first horror/thriller.
It is published by Claret Press and is available in paperback and ebook.

CLARET PRESS

GREAT STORYTELLING DOESN'T JUST ENTERTAIN,
IT ENERGISES

Claret Press' mission is simple: we publish engrossing books which engage with the issues of the day. From award-winning page-turners to eye-opening travelogues, from captivating historical fiction to insightful memoirs, there's a Claret Press book for you.

To keep up to date about the going-ons at Claret Press, including sales, special events, zoom talks and book clubs, sign up to our newsletter and social media:

www.claretpress.com
Instagram @claretpress
BlueSky @claretpress.bsky.social
YouTube @claretpress

Thank you for purchasing an authorised edition of this book and for respecting intellectual property laws by not reproducing, scanning or distributing any part of it by any means without permission. You are supporting authors and enabling Claret Press to continue to publish diverse voices and foster a dynamic culture. No part of this book may be used or reproduced in any manner for the purpose of training artificial intelligence technologies or systems. Claret Press expressly reserves this work in its entirety including its design from the text and data mining exception.